RANDOM
HOUSE
LARGE
PRINT

BURNTOWN

BURNTOWN

A NOVEL

Jennifer McMahon

RANDOM HOUSE
LARGE PRINT

Copyright © 2017 by Jennifer McMahon

Published in the United States of America by Random House Large Print in association with Doubleday, a division of Penguin Random House LLC, New York, and distributed in Canada by Random House of Canada, a division of Penguin Random House Canada Limited, Toronto.

Cover design by Michael J. Windsor
Cover images: tent © mashabuba/E+/Getty Iamges; rocks © Carlos G. López/Moment/Getty Images; bridge © ChengRainie/Moment Open/Getty Images; river © Cultural/Adam Pass Photography/Getty Images; shack © Nicolas Economou/NurPhoto/Getty Images; clouds © MSPT/Shutterstock; pallets © ultramansk/Shutterstock

The Library of Congress has established a Cataloging-in-Publication record for this title.

ISBN: 978-1-5247-8026-5

www.randomhouse.com/largeprint

FIRST LARGE PRINT EDITION

Printed in the United States of America

10 9 8 7 6 5 4 3 2 1

This Large Print edition published in accord with the standards of the N.A.V.H.

In memory of my father,
Donald Eugene McMahon,
whose stories live on

BEFORE

Miles

〰〰〰

His mother glides across the flagstone patio slowly, hips and long legs working in time with the music, a kind of undulating dance that reminds Miles of the way tall grass moves just before a thunderstorm. She clutches a drink in her hand—a mint julep in a sweating glass with daisies painted on the side. Captain and Tennille sing from the tinny portable radio that rests on the table: **Love, love will keep us together.**

She hums as she dances her way to the aluminum-framed lounge chair. The brass elephant charm on her beaded bracelet swings, sniffing the air with its trunk. Miles loves the elephant bracelet. She won't say where she got it, but she's been wearing it for almost a month now.

In her white cotton dress and gold sandals, she looks like one of the goddesses from the book of Greek mythology Miles has been reading. Aphrodite maybe. Her toenails are painted a rich velvety plum, her skin is a summery bronze, and her light brown hair is highlighted with gold and feathered back from her face. She sits down in the chair, resting her glass on the little metal table beside it. She picks up the pack of Pall Malls and shakes out a cigarette.

Miles holds his breath and shifts uneasily in his hiding spot. He's on his belly behind the rock garden, stretched out like a snake as he watches his mother across the yard.

She'd promised to quit. But she keeps cigarettes hidden in the bookcase, behind the huge, leather-bound classics no one in their house ever reads: **Moby-Dick, David Copperfield.**

Miles has told his mother about the movie they watched in health class—the images of the healthy, pink lungs and the dark, mottled smokers' lungs. He hates to imagine that his mother's lungs might look like the sooty inside of a chimney; worse still, he hates to think of her dying, which is what his health teacher, Mrs. Molette, says will happen if you smoke. Your lungs will become blackened. Diseased. They will not work anymore. They will not bring oxygen to your body. Without oxygen, you die.

"And I might get hit by a bus, too," his mother

had said when he repeated this. "Or struck by lightning. Or the brakes could go out on my car and I could go over a cliff."

Miles has to admit that this last scenario seems possible, too. His mother drives an old MG convertible coupe that was a wedding present from her parents. It's spotted with rust, and spends more time in the shop than out. Miles's dad wants to trade it in for something more practical—a nice station wagon maybe, like all the other moms drive. Miles tries to imagine his mom behind the wheel of a station wagon, like Mrs. Brady on **The Brady Bunch,** but his mom is no Mrs. Brady. And his mom loves her old MG. She's even named it. Isabella, she calls it, the name sounding musical. And sometimes, she'll say she's running to the store for milk and Frosted Flakes but then be gone for hours. Miles asks her where she goes and she says, "Just driving. Just me and Isabella and the open road."

It seems like every week some new, impossibly expensive imported part breaks: a valve, a pump, a drum . . . things that, to Miles, sound more like body parts than car parts. But when a car part breaks, you take the car in to Chance's garage and they order a new part and replace it. You can't do that with blackened, cancer-filled lungs.

He has to find a way to stop her.

That's why, earlier today when she was out at

the market, Miles stole his mother's hidden pack of cigarettes. It was half-empty, with only ten cigarettes remaining. He took out two, and carefully worked half the tobacco out of the paper. Then, just as carefully, he replaced it with the two paper packets he'd made, each filled with black powder from his toy gun caps along with a pinch of sulfur from his chemistry set. Once the tobacco was placed back on top, they looked just like the other cigarettes. He wanted her to get a few good drags in before a small, stinking explosion would turn her off of smoking forever.

Ten cigarettes, two of which will explode. The chances she's chosen one just now are one in five. Miles likes numbers, understands odds. Hunkering down, he watches as she lights up.

He's wearing his Robin Hood costume: green corduroy pants that are a little too tight, tall cowboy boots, and one of his father's brown work shirts with a tag that makes Miles's neck itch, but he forces himself to be still, not to scratch. The shirt is cinched at the waist with a thick leather belt that holds his wooden sword. A quiver of arrows is on his back, and he holds his homemade bow in his hands. His father had helped him make the bow and arrows, had even made sharp metal arrowheads for them, reminding Miles that these were not toys and he needed to be careful. His mother wasn't impressed: "Wonderful, Martin. And I suppose you'll deal with it when he kills one of the neighborhood cats by accident?"

They argued, but in the end, Miles got to keep them.

His father loves the old Robin Hood movies, and he and Miles sometimes watch them together on the little TV in his dad's workshop. But lately, his father's been too busy. He's an appliance repairman, and drives a white van with his name on the side: MARTIN SANDESKI, APPLIANCE REPAIR AND SERVICE. His father also uses the van for hauling equipment for the jazz quartet he plays in, Three Bags Full. His dad likes to tell the story of how he once played the trumpet onstage down in New Orleans with Count Basie. Miles's father is full of great stories. Stories of jazz legends he's rubbed elbows with, or a producer he met at a little club in Albany, New York, who's working on pulling some strings to get Three Bags Full a recording deal. And the best story of all: that his grandfather had worked for Thomas Edison, the guy who invented the lightbulb and movies and records. "He gave me some of Edison's original plans," Miles's dad claimed. "Plans for a secret invention he was working on just before he died. They're worth a fortune. A million dollars, easy."

"What are the plans for?" Miles had asked once, when his dad had polished off a six-pack of Narragansett.

"A special sort of telephone. A telephone that

does things no one would believe, impossible things."

Miles's mother had laughed. "Stop teasing the boy with your stories, Marty." They were sitting in the living room with the TV on, but no one was paying attention.

His father had drained the rest of his can of Narragansett. "I'm not teasing, one day you'll see."

Miles's mother had told him she didn't believe the Edison plans existed (she'd certainly never set eyes on them), and even if they did, no way were they actually from the real Thomas Edison. "Honest to God, you can't believe half of what your father tells you," she'd said, blowing out a stream of smoke, crushing a cigarette butt into the heavy glass ashtray on the coffee table with a little too much force.

Now, Miles peers anxiously through a clump of tiger lilies, waiting for the bang from his mother's cigarette.

He feels an odd combination of anticipation and guilt; though he knows he's doing this for her own good, it seems like a cruel trick to play. His mother is so easily frightened; Miles and his father tease her with rubber snakes in the bathtub, plastic spiders in the butter dish— practical jokes that always make her scream. Then, when she realizes it's a joke, she laughs so hard she becomes breathless. His mother is beautiful when she laughs, and there is some-thing truly stunning about catching her in the moment her fear turns to blissful, almost hysteri-cal, relief. It almost embarrasses him to catch her in these moments, like he's seeing something he shouldn't; it's almost like walking into the bath-room without knocking and seeing her just get-ting out of the tub.

Suddenly, a shadow moves over the grass, crossing the yard and moving stealthily toward the patio.

Could his father be home early?

He's supposed to be repairing a washing machine for Old Lady Mercier all the way across town. Then he was going to stop by the shop and work on an air conditioner a guy had dropped off.

No. This is not his father, nor is it a child from the neighborhood, or anyone else he recognizes.

It's a man.

A shorter, slighter man than his father. And **this** man wears yellow socks and black dress shoes that are too large for his feet, making an awkward flip-flop sound as he walks. His trou-sers are also too long, but have been rolled up. With each step, there is an absurdly bright flash of yellow from each ankle. But the oddest thing about this man is not his too-large shoes and yel-low socks, or his quick determined walk toward Miles's mother reclining on the patio.

Covering his face, his whole head in fact, is a rubber chicken mask. The mask is white, the beak yellow, the comb and wattles red.

Miles feels as if he's somehow slipped into one of his Saturday morning cartoons. He watches as the Chicken Man approaches his mother from behind. She's lying on the lawn chair, eyes closed, sunning herself; oblivious.

Up until now, Miles hadn't noticed the man's hands. He's been keeping them tight to his sides, but now, in the right, Miles sees the bright glint of a blade.

Miles rises slightly and tucks one of his sharp arrows in the bow—his lucky arrow, the shaft painted black, the feathers red. He pulls back the string. The Chicken Man is directly behind her chair now, and he leans down to whisper something in her ear. Keeping her eyes closed, she laughs.

Then, in one swift motion, the Chicken Man draws the blade across her throat.

His mother's eyes dart open, frantic and disbelieving. The blood pumps from her throat, soaking the chest of her white dress and dripping through the yellow nylon webbing of the chair and onto the flagstone patio. Instead of a scream, all Miles hears is one final resigned sigh.

The arrow flies from Miles's bow, hitting the Chicken Man on the left side of his lower back, making him bellow. As Miles stands up on wobbly legs, the Chicken Man swivels his head and pulls the arrow out with a roaring cry. Then he looks right at Miles. Holding the knife in one hand, and the arrow in the other, he takes a step in Miles's direction.

Miles is trying to get his legs to run when there's a bright, explosive, sulfur-scented **POP-POP!** from the ashtray. The Chicken Man freezes, then takes off running back across the yard, rubber mask quivering, shoes flapping, socks glowing brighter than the sun.

TIMES UNION, JUNE 17, 1975

MURDER-SUICIDE RATTLES THE TINY VILLAGE OF BRAXTON

BRAXTON, VERMONT

At approximately three o'clock Monday afternoon, thirty-six-year-old Elizabeth Sandeski was slain in the backyard of her family home. Her son, ten-year-old Miles Sandeski, witnessed the crime. Police were called by a neighbor, Kelly Richardson, also of Cold Hollow Lane.

"Miles came to our house covered in blood, hysterical. He said a man in a chicken mask had killed his mother," Mrs. Richardson told reporters.

The police searched the Sandeski home and garage, where, neighborhood witnesses say, they discovered bloodstained clothing, a rubber chicken mask, and a kitchen knife in the trunk of the family car. Chief Francis Bonnaire, of the Broom Hollow police, declined to confirm or comment, reporting only that what they found led to a warrant for Mr. Sandeski's arrest.

Martin Sandeski, who runs Sandeski Appliance Repair and Service and plays trumpet in the local jazz band Three Bags Full, was taken into custody. Neighbors stated that the couple had been fighting a great deal lately and that Martin told several friends that he believed his wife was having an affair.

Martin Sandeski took his own life hours after his arrest. Chief Bonnaire confirmed that Mr. Sandeski hanged himself while in police custody and that attempts to revive him failed. Chief Bonnaire offered this statement: "We have never had an incident like this before. A full investigation will be completed, as well as a thorough review of our policies and procedures for handling those in our custody."

Martin Sandeski's sister, Holly Whitney, of Ashford, declined to comment on her brother's state of mental health or the rumors of his wife having an affair. "We'll never know what really happened. All we can do is move forward and do the best we can to heal. We've got to do all we can for Miles, now. The poor boy has suffered a horrific loss."

Dear Miles,

I am hoping that you never read this, because if you do, it means I am gone. I have entrusted your aunt Holly with making sure you get this letter should anything happen to me. I'm hoping to live a long, happy life, to see you grow up and get married, to hold a grandchild in my arms. But if you're reading this, I guess it means I ran out of luck.

This letter, and what I'm about to tell you, is not to be shared with anyone. Not your aunt Holly. Not even your mother. No one. This is for you and you alone.

I own only one thing of true value. One thing that could change lives. And I am passing it down to you as my own father once passed it down to me.

Over the years I have told you about how my father worked for Thomas Edison at his factory in New Jersey. I have also mentioned the plans my father gave to me.

What I might not have told you is that my father was not exactly given these plans by Edison. They were stolen.

But that is another story altogether. What matters is that (despite your mother's very vocal opinions to the contrary) they are real. Authentic. And worth a fortune, though it isn't the monetary value alone that makes them such a treasure—it's far more than something anyone could put a price on.

You will find the plans in the garage. There is an old empty metal gas can way up on the top back shelf. Open the can by twisting off the spout. The plans are tucked inside, rolled up in a plastic bag.

Hold tight to them. Tell no one you have them.

One day, I promise you, those papers and the machine shown on them will change not only your life, but quite possibly the entire world.

I love you, Miles. Forever and ever. No matter what.

—Dad

Miles

~~~~~~~~

1975–1997

Miles carries his mother's little brass elephant in his pocket the way other boys carry a rabbit's foot or a good luck stone or the way the old ladies at church carry rosaries. The elephant charm is his talisman; he rubs its back, worries over it, so much so that sometimes it feels almost alive. There are moments when he swears he can feel it move, can feel its tiny heart beating.

He reaches in so often that he wears holes in the right pockets of all his pants; Aunt Holly gives them patches, stitching silently and never scolding him. She understands loss. She understands longing.

The elephant is with him when Aunt Holly

takes Miles back to his house in Broom Hollow one last time to pack up his things. He goes straight for the garage, finds the gas can, and pulls out a Ziploc baggie with the rolled-up plans. Then, he goes into the house, pulls his mother's copy of **David Copperfield** from the shelf (the one she used to hide her cigarettes behind), and stuffs that into his knapsack. He grabs his dad's trumpet in its case.

Back at his aunt and uncle's, he follows the instructions in his spy book that teach you how to turn a book into a hiding place and tucks the plans inside **David Copperfield.** It goes onto his shelves, blending in with **The Adventures of Robin Hood, Treasure Island, The Borrowers, The Lion, the Witch and the Wardrobe, A Wrinkle in Time,** and a full set of **Encyclopaedia Britannica.** He shoves his dad's trumpet under his bed. He gets down on his knees to peek at it each night before going to sleep, the way some kids pray.

The little brass pachyderm is in his pocket on his first day at Ashford Middle School. Ashford's an old mill town that's now a dirty little city with a lot of people out of work, struggling to make ends meet. Even though it's only twenty minutes away from Broom Hollow, it feels like another universe. He doesn't mind, though. Aunt Holly and Uncle Howie have a nice little ranch house on the outskirts of town, and they painted their spare room blue for Miles, covered it with glow-in-the-dark stars. They watch over him as he begins to work on his inventions: little clockwork animals made from scraps of wood and metal that wind up, turn their heads, move their paws. He loves connecting the gears, making the inanimate come to life. Working with tools reminds him of his father, of all the hours he spent in his dad's workshop handing him hoses and washers and screwdrivers.

Sometimes, he opens up the book he's hidden the Edison plans in, lays the papers out on the floor of his room. The schematics look almost alien to him, full of bulbs, wires, tubes, little words and numbers scrawled all over them. He wishes his father were here to explain it to him. His father could build this machine.

He's looking at the plans the day he hears Lily crash her bike on the street outside while trying to do some Evel Knievel jump. Miles takes in her old football helmet, the crazy red hair sticking out underneath, before running to get a first aid kit for her torn open knee. They talk while she cleans off the blood, then he helps her put Band-Aids on.

"So why do you live with your aunt and uncle anyway?" she asks. And he tells her, which is weird. He hasn't talked to anyone about it, but with Lily, the words just come. Lily says her own mother died, and her dad drinks and is rarely around. Her brother, Lloyd, is raising her. He drives a tow truck and can fix just about anything.

"He's gifted," she tells him. "I'm gifted, too." She digs around in the pocket of her cutoff shorts and pulls out a clear blue marble. "It's my miniature crystal ball," she tells him.

"What do you do with it?" he asks.

She holds it to her eye and looks through. "I see things with it. Things other people can't." She turns toward him, still looking through the marble.

"What do you see?" he asks.

"Sometimes good things, sometimes bad," she says, tucking the marble back into her pocket and squinting at him in a funny way, like she knows something she isn't saying.

Miles pulls the elephant out of his pocket and shows it to her. "It was my mother's," he tells her. "She had it on the day she died."

He tells her the story of the elephant, the same story his mother told him just days before she died. He'd noticed her new bracelet and asked her about it. His mother had smiled and said there was a story that went with it.

"Once upon a time," he tells Lily, recalling each detail of his mother's story, "in far-off India, lived a beautiful golden elephant. But see, the elephant wasn't really an elephant: she was a princess who had been turned into an elephant by a sorcerer who had this big fight with the girl's father, the king."

Lily's eyes widen. "So what happened to the princess? Did she stay an elephant or did she find a way to break the spell?"

"My mother said that she's out there still. Waiting for someone to break the curse. And you know the worst part?" Miles asks. "The worst of it is that the princess is the only one who can break the spell. She carries the secret inside her but doesn't know it."

Lily smiles. "That part doesn't seem sad to me. It's like . . . like Dorothy in **The Wizard of Oz,** you know? She had the power to go back home the whole time, but then she wouldn't have gone on the journey; she wasn't ready to go home, right? The princess, she'll figure out how to break the spell when the time is right. And then, think of it, what an amazing story she'll have to tell people. All about being an elephant."

She asks him if they caught the man who killed his mother, and he says no, but he's going to find the killer himself one day.

Lily pulls out her marble again, looks through it. "You will," she says, "I can see it."

"What else do you see?" he asks, and she only smiles, puts her little crystal ball away.

He has his first kiss with Lily, two years later, and when he starts going over to her house every day after school. Lily's brother, Lloyd, turns out to be about the coolest person Miles has ever met, and the three of them eat dinner together all the time. Lily cooks—Kraft macaroni and cheese, tuna casserole, hot dogs and beans.

"Lil told me about what happened to your parents," Lloyd says one night. "I'm real sorry." Miles isn't sure what to say, so he only nods, looks down at his empty plate, at the ketchup smeared across it like blood.

Lloyd shows Miles how to solder and build an AM radio receiver; how to take an engine apart and to ride a motorbike. Also, it's Lloyd who gives Miles his first beer, a Narragansett, and shows him how to crush the can when he's done, like Quint did in **Jaws**. Lloyd teaches him to drive a stick shift out on the old roads by the river.

The day Miles gets down on his knee and asks Lily to marry him, he pulls out the ring from his pocket, where it's been riding around next to the elephant for days. They're out at dinner at an Italian place Miles can barely afford. He's just finished grad school. They've been living together in a tiny hole-in-the-wall apartment near the paper mill. When Lily says yes, he kisses her, puts the ring on her finger, then touches the elephant to say **thank you.**

It's there, in the pocket of his good khakis the day he's teaching his Sociology 101 class at the college and Lily calls to say she's in labor—

"The baby's coming!" His car is out of commission—needs a new alternator that they just can't afford—but Lloyd picks him up in the tow truck from the garage he now owns. They run all the lights on the way to Mercy Hospital. Miles gets there just in time to welcome his first-born into the world.

The elephant is there, listening, as Miles and Lloyd stand on the slushy sidewalk outside the hospital smoking cigars that are a little crushed from riding around in Lloyd's pocket. Miles thinks of the exploding cigarettes he once made, how back then, he'd thought smoking was the most evil thing in the world. He knows better now, as he stands, happily puffing his cigar; knows there are far worse things. Miles has pulled the elephant out, and is holding it in his hand, giving it a thank-you rub.

"What's that?" Lloyd asks, exhaling a puff of smoke.

"My good luck charm," Miles says.

Lloyd stares at it for a minute, then says, "Do you have any idea how lucky you actually are, Miles?"

And Miles says, "Yes."

Yes, yes, yes.

And all along, each day, from the time he is ten until he is a grown man, a husband and a father—in spite of how lucky he feels; how he knows in his logical mind that he has everything he's ever dreamed of—Miles wishes the elephant could speak. Could tell him where it came from. Who had given it to his mother. And what the killer had said that last day that had made her smile.

He knows he should let it go, but he can't. And sometimes, after his wife and newborn baby are fast asleep, he slips into his office, pulls the book down from the shelf, takes out the Edison plans, and thinks, What if he built the machine and it actually worked? What if the dead could speak? What if he could finally have the answers he's been looking for all these years?

Miles

〰〰

Halloween. A day for spooks and the spooky. And the day, he's heard Lily say, when the veil between the worlds is thin. "Ghosts walk on Halloween," his wife told him once with such surety that of course he believed. Which makes today the perfect day for turning on the invention.

Lily made little Eva a ladybug costume: a red fleece suit with wings and black felt dots sewn on. She's taken her to the children's Halloween parade downtown. Afterward, there's a party at the library with games, a magician, apple bobbing.

So Lily and little three-year-old Ladybug Eva are off to see the world of parades full of Barneys, princesses, and pirates. They'll bob for apples with vampires and ghosts. And it gives Miles the whole afternoon and evening to test the machine.

About six months ago, Miles and Lily bought an old farmhouse out at the end of Birchwood Lane, a winding, dead-end dirt road that runs along the east side of the river. It's a thirty-five-minute commute to the college, but Lily could no longer stand to stay in downtown Ashford, where you could smell the sulfur smoke from the paper mill and see the poisoned film on the two rivers, which people said you shouldn't swim in either unless you wanted to grow extra fingers. They're full of toxic sludge, ruined from the decades of chemicals and dyes and dioxins that have been dumped by the mills. The Jensen Mill, machine shop, and foundry have been closed forever—Two Rivers College, where Miles has studied and now teaches, is housed in the old foundry building—but there's a paper company that still runs, still stinks. The EPA has cracked down, so they're not dumping as many chemicals into the river these days. They're putting their waste in barrels that are carted away and become some other town's problem. Lily said she didn't care—Ashford was filthy and full of poisons. She wanted to be out in the country in a house with a yard and gardens and space for little Eva to play. Miles built Eva a sandbox. Put up a swing set. His little girl could spend hours swinging.

Miles is in his workshop now, a little

aluminum-walled garden shed in the backyard, puffing on his pipe (a joke gift from Lily in honor of his first teaching position). He looks at the brass elephant, which he's given a new home by a favorite photo of his mother. In it, she's on the couch holding a book, and the photographer (his father) has caught her by surprise. She's smiling, but slightly startled, her mouth open.

Miles is writing his PhD dissertation about the little brass elephant; not the elephant exactly, but the ideas inspired by the elephant and the story his mother once told him. **The Princess and the Elephant: A Sociological Study of How Personal and Cultural Stories and Myths Shape Individuals and Society.**

Miles lets himself believe, at times, that some piece of his mother is trapped inside the charm, as with the princess trapped inside the body of the elephant in the story. He strokes its tiny brass back, the curve of its trunk, remembering how many times he'd stared at it wishing that it would tell him what he wanted to hear.

But now maybe, just maybe, he's found something that might. It's Halloween, after all. What better day for a conversation with the dead?

He looks down at the machine laid out on his table: tubes and wires, coils and capacitors, pieces scavenged from old radios or bought from eBay. He has spent the past four months building Thomas Edison's secret machine. He has worked in his shed with the door locked and the plans spread out before him, telling no one what he was doing. When Lily asks, he tells her he's just tinkering: building more mechanical animals like the windup metal raccoon she loves so much. He's thought of telling Lloyd, of showing him the plans and asking for help, but this is something he needs to do on his own.

He knows what his friends and colleagues at the college would think if they could see him now. He'd be out of a job, probably. "You can't be serious, Miles," they would say. "You can't possibly think such a thing would work."

But he would argue. Say, "If you had plans believed to truly be from a secret machine of Thomas Edison's, wouldn't you build them? Wouldn't you want to see for yourself?"

Now, he's just making adjustments, fine-tuning things. But really, there's nothing left to fine-tune. The machine is a near-perfect replication of the one drawn in the plans. It has taken months of trial and error to get to this point, but now, at last, everything looks perfect. So what he's really doing as he tightens tubes, rechecks connections, is stalling. He's not sure what he's more afraid of—that it won't work (which is, his rational mind tells him, the most probable result)? Or that it will?

And what if it does work and actually gets through to her?

He's gone over it a million times in his mind. How he'll finally say what he's waited all these years to tell her:

I'm sorry.

I'm so sorry I couldn't save you.

He closes his eyes and he's a ten-year-old boy again, dressed up as Robin Hood, feeling the arrow leave the bow, the red feathers brushing against his right cheek, watching it go right into the back of the Chicken Man.

He touches the elephant one more time for luck, flips the on switch, watches the machine glow. He adjusts knobs, turns the volume all the way up. He hears the dull crackle of static, the way you do when you're between radio stations. Then, he takes the handheld receiver and speaks into it.

"Hello," he says tentatively.

The crackling changes, he thinks he hears something behind it: voices, people talking, calling, laughing from far away, as if at a distant party.

"Hello," he says, louder this time. "Anybody there? Can you hear me?"

It feels idiotic, pathetic, even: a grown man talking into a cobbled-together radio, hoping for a response.

"Elizabeth Sandeski?" he says, voice tentative. "Are you there?"

All he hears is his own heartbeat. Then, a crackling from the speaker.

She's here, a male voice says, clearly. **We're all here.**

Miles flinches back, nearly drops the receiver. Then, from the machine, he hears someone saying his name.

"Mother?" he says, fearful. "Are you there?"

Yes, a voice comes back, louder and female, swimming through waves of electrical interference. It's a voice he recognizes. A voice he's heard in his dreams.

His heart jolts, and what he says next isn't what he's planned for and rehearsed, but it's what he most needs to know.

"Who is he, Mother?" Miles says into the machine. "Who murdered you?"

A dull roar of static.

"Please," he says.

And then, in a crackling whisper, she tells him.

"No," he says, voice trembling, stomach churning. "That's not possible."

She repeats the name, and then, she's gone. He fiddles with the knobs, calls for her again and again, but there's only static.

And he knows what he must do.

He turns off the machine, covers it up with a tarp, and, hands and legs shaking, goes to find the man who killed his mother.

Miles

⌁

APRIL 12, 2011

"Miles, I'm worried about the rain. The radio says the worst is yet to come. Flood warnings for the whole county. And if the dam goes . . . we'll be underwater in minutes. There won't be any warning."

Lily's wrapped in one of her chunky, hand-knit sweaters, and her hair is held back in an untidy ponytail. She still looks lovely, but there's a certain light in her green eyes that comes on only when trouble is brewing. There are dark circles under them now; she hasn't been sleeping well these last few days, not since the rain began.

He takes her hand, kisses her knuckles, which smell of turpentine. She's been working in her studio, doing a new series of paintings of the moon on huge canvases. She's showing the moon in all its phases in a series she's calling Birth, Marriage, Death, Rebirth. She's taken to referring to the moon in her painting as **She.** Miles got her a telescope for Christmas and Lily spends hours looking through it, studying the moon and all her craters and shadows, trying to bring the far-off stars into focus. Miles has suggested that she take an astronomy class at the college, but Lily prefers exploring on her own, giving her own names to things.

"The dam will hold," he promises her now. "That dam has seen far worse storms than this."

Their house is miles and miles downstream, on the east side of the river. Right in the flood-plain—as the mortgage company was quick to point out whenever they demanded proof of his flood insurance. But it's never flooded. The dam, originally built by William Jensen to harness the power of the water for his mill back in 1836, has always held. The river has never crested more than a few feet above the banks, even in the years they've had heavy spring melts and ice dams.

He sops up the last of his soup with a hunk of Lily's homemade bread. The kids are in the living room with the TV on, some police drama turned up loud, the whole house echoing with sirens and gunshots. Errol and Eva are on the floor below it playing cribbage on the oval rag rug. Eva is ahead and is teasing Errol mercilessly about it.

"You're going to get skunked," she says.

"Am not," he says.

"Smell that, Er? That's the smell of a big old skunk coming your way."

He gives her a playful shove. "It ain't over till it's over, Little E," he says.

She pretends that she hates the juvenile nickname, but Miles knows she secretly likes it. He's always amazed at the bond these two have, at how unconditionally they love each other. At how much Eva worships her older brother. At how she never seems to remember a time when he wasn't there, when he wasn't one of the centers of her universe.

It's their break time. After this, they'll get back to their studies. The kids are home-schooled, their studies supervised by both parents: he tackles math and science, and Lily teaches them art, English, and occasionally, more esoteric subjects like astrology and divination. But these two kids have little interest in trying to see beyond; they are rooted in the real world, in the here and now, and go along with the lessons only to placate their mother. Both kids are excelling, doing work far beyond their ages. Errol's been accepted to Two Rivers, starting in the fall.

Lily looks down into her own half-eaten soup. "It's just . . . I've had a feeling all day." She rubs

at the back of her neck. "A feeling that something terrible is about to happen."

Miles sets down his spoon and looks hard at
his wife. Lily believes in premonitions; she's sure
that she is hard-wired to predict the future, to
have visions about things to come. And Miles
has known her long enough to realize that she's
often right.

"Okay, then. I'll go check the river. I've already
sandbagged around the workshop, but we can
build a barrier around the house."

He goes into the living room, looks down at
the kids playing cards. There's candy on the rug
next to each of them: root beer barrels for Errol
and a roll of Necco wafers for Eva. There's a fire
in the fireplace, its birch log crackling and popping. Above it, on the mantel, rests a collection
of photographs. There's a shot of Miles, Lily, and
three-year-old Eva standing in front of a giant
snowman they'd all built. Then one taken a little over a year later—all of them camping in the
White Mountains, eight-year-old Errol holding
a trout he'd just caught. Next to it is Lily and
Miles's wedding portrait. Lloyd is to Miles's left,
his arm draped around him, the best man.

Miles can sometimes hear Lloyd's voice in his
ears, asking if he has any idea how lucky he is.
He looks at the kids on the rug, then the bookshelf in the corner, which holds a copy of the
book that changed his life: the book he'd writ-

ten based on his PhD dissertation: **The Princess and the Elephant: How We Are All Trapped Inside Our Own Mythology and How We Can Break Free.** Lily had talked him into expanding his dissertation, simplifying parts, and publishing it as a pop-psychology, self-help book, something she has always been into, especially if they have a New Age slant. The shelves in her painting studio are full of books on meditation, dreamwork, and using creativity to get in touch with your spiritual side. With Lily's help, Miles found a small publisher in New Hampshire, and to everyone's surprise, Miles's book took off.

It wasn't a bestseller by any means, but it developed a small cult following. People started showing up at the college to hear his lectures and sign up for his sociology classes. Enrollment was up. The college even asked Miles to develop a course based on his book. The book made him the star professor of Two Rivers College.

"Errol," Miles says now, taking his eye off the bookshelf and looking down at the kids again.

"Yeah?" The boy looks up. At seventeen, he's tall and gangly, ropy with muscle, his hair dark and too long. He needs a trim. But he likes it long to cover the scar on his forehead above his left eye. They don't ever talk about the scar and where it came from, but they both remember all too well.

"Get your slicker on," Miles tells him. "We're

going to sandbag around the front of the house. And we need to see how close the water's coming to the road down by the bend."

Errol's eyes get huge. "If the road washes out by the bend—"

"I know. We'll be stuck here. But we've got a cellar full of food and supplies. And there's always the boat if we need to evacuate."

"Cool—we'll have our own island!" Errol says. "Totally cut off from the rest of the world."

Lily has come into the living room. She pulls her sweater tight around her shoulders and shivers. "I don't think that sounds one bit cool," she says. Miles puts his arm around her, kisses her cheek.

"Can I help, too?" Eva asks, shoving a chalky pink candy into her mouth. "I want to go with you to see if the river has washed out the road."

"You can come help me check the workshop," he says. "Make sure that hole in the roof we patched up isn't leaking and that the sandbags are all in place."

She jumps up and clomps across the floor in her new purple cowboy boots. She'd wanted them so bad, these crazy boots, enough that Lily got them for her for her birthday a couple of weeks ago. Miles had given her a special gift, too: the elephant charm on a long gold chain. She'd always loved it so much, and Miles decided it was time for him to let go of the past, to let Eva turn the necklace into something positive. She's been wearing it every day since, the little brass elephant gracing each carefully planned outfit. His little girl, who used to run around in messy pigtails and dirty overalls, is now fourteen and has all of a sudden developed a fashion sense: she wears tapered jeans tucked into boots, and she borrows long flowing scarves and dangly earrings from Lily. Miles has even noticed her wearing makeup every now and then, a hint of Lily's eye shadow and lip gloss. Gone is the girl who had her bed piled high with stuffed animals and dolls; now she's painted her pink room a deep purple, tacked up posters of bands, and the only doll she keeps out is the one Miles made for her: Mina the talking doll, who used to sing Eva a lullaby each night when she pulled the string on the back of her neck. "Rock-a-Bye Baby," recorded in his own voice, singing in a high, doll-like pitch.

"Maybe we should just go," Lily suggests, with a slight hint of panic. "Get in the car and go wait out the storm somewhere."

Miles thinks of his workshop, of what he has tucked under a tarp on his bench. The Edison invention has been sitting there, wrapped up for years. Every now and then, he uncovers it, looks at it. But he's never turned it on. Not since that one Halloween eleven years ago.

He's never told Lily a word about it. She knows about the machine in his workshop, but he's never told her what happened the one time he turned it on. "It doesn't do anything except hum and crackle," he told her when she asked. He thinks, sometimes, that he should destroy it, but he's never been able to bring himself to pick up a hammer.

"No," he says now. "We stay. At least for now."

He kisses Lily again, this time on the forehead, as if his kiss could drive all her dark thoughts and predictions away. "Don't worry, Mrs. Sandeski," he says. "We'll be fine."

But her look tells him she's not buying it.

He pulls on his raincoat and boots and pushes open the front door, Errol and Eva right behind him. The rain pounds on the hood of Miles's coat and blows against his face, little droplets covering his glasses, which have already started to fog. Although it's only two in the afternoon, the sky is so dark it almost looks like nightfall. Across the yard, the river roars like a great beast longing to be set free.

"Errol," he says, shouting to be heard over the rain's percussive din. "I want you to walk down the road to the bend. See how high the water is and if it's covering the road yet. Eva and I are going to check the workshop. Then we'll all start sandbagging the house."

"Yes, sir," Errol says, taking off down the driveway, pleased to have a mission.

Eva runs to the workshop, gets there before

him, and goes in. Two seconds later, she sticks her head out the door. "Dad!" she calls, her voice panicked. "Come quick!"

He runs the rest of the way across the yard, his feet slipping on the waterlogged grass.

He gets to the workshop, and Eva looks flushed and frightened. He glances around, doesn't see anything out of place.

"What is it?" he asks her. Eva. His clever daughter, who loves his inventions and mechanical things. She comes into the workshop and winds up the animals, delights in finding the secret compartments he's hidden in some, like the raccoon with a tiny door in his chest that pops open when you twist one of its ears just so. Miles sometimes hides pieces of candy or other treasures in these, knowing Eva will find them. She's been helping him in the workshop since she could walk, handing him wrenches, fueling the fire for the forge. Eva always asks to hear the stories about what came before, paying close attention and nodding her head as he fills in each detail: **Tell me about how you met Mama, tell me about what happened to Grandma and Grandpa.**

"They died," Miles tells her. "They were killed in an accident." It's the only lie he's ever told his daughter, but he just can't bring himself to tell the truth.

Eva loves the picture of her grandmother that sits above Miles's workbench.

"Do you think I look like her?" she asked once.

"Maybe a little," he said. "Mostly, you look like your mother, which is a lucky thing because she's the most beautiful woman in the world."

Eva wrinkled her nose. "Mama's pretty, but Grandma, she looked like a movie star."

Now, she points to the machine sitting on the corner of the workbench, still covered with a tarp. "I heard a voice."

Two clumps of red hair stick out from under her yellow slicker. Rain is dripping down her face. Her green eyes are enormous. She's always been fascinated by the machine, but lately she seems afraid of it. And right now, downright terrified.

"But what does it do, Daddy?" she'd asked once, when she was younger.

"Well," he told her, "Edison believed it was a special sort of telephone. One that would let you speak with the dead."

"That's impossible," she'd said.

"Maybe," he'd told her. "But remember, people thought the electric lightbulb was impossible, too, once upon a time. And movies. And the telegraph."

He goes to the workbench now, pulls back the tarp, and Eva lets out a little muffled cry.

The machine is on, the tubes glowing.

It hums as its needles jump; static crackles through the speaker. And then a voice emerges—not a random radio signal, some female DJ in New York, but one he recognizes at once.

Danger, his mother says. **You're in danger.**

Miles turns and looks at Eva, who has her back pressed against the door, mouth open and panting, frantic with fear.

Then, Elizabeth speaks again, louder this time, more urgent: **He's here!**

The signal fades, and there is nothing but a faint hum.

"Who's here, Daddy?" Eva asks him, her voice strangely dull and quiet.

"I don't know," Miles says, fiddling with the dials, grabbing the receiver, and speaking into it. "Hello? Hello? Mom? Are you still there?"

Receiver in hand, he glances out the window above his workbench, toward the driveway, where Errol is standing by the car looking at the windshield. There, stuck under the wiper blade, is something that looks like a piece of trash blown in by the storm; something bright and colorful, yellow and red, almost glowing in the washed-out gray landscape. Errol picks it up, and Miles knows what it is in an instant.

"Impossible," Miles says, as he drops the receiver. The empty hum of static washes over him.

Through the window, Errol lifts the rubber chicken mask, turns it in his hands.

The Chicken Man is dead. Miles knows that for a fact. He knows it because he's the one who killed him.

"What is it, Daddy?" Eva asks.

He turns to her. "Sweetie, I need you to run back to the house and lock all the doors. Do it quickly, but quietly. Don't alarm your mother. And don't open the door for anyone but me or Errol."

"But who—"

"Go now!" he orders. "Hurry."

She runs out of the workshop toward the house, passing Errol, who is hurrying to the workshop, chicken mask in hand. When he bursts through the door, he's soaking wet and panting.

"Dad—"

Miles gives a sharp nod. "I know."

"And the river's covered the road," Errol says. "It's not too deep yet, but it's rising fast. The right shoulder is all washed away."

Miles takes the rubber mask in his hands and stares down into the two empty eyeholes.

"This is all my fault," Errol says. He's crying, his shoulders shaking as he tries to hold back sobs.

"No, it's not," Miles tells him.

Miles looks through the open door at the house, then down toward the river. He lays the mask down on the workbench, then goes to the forge in the corner, grabs his heaviest iron hammer.

"Errol, I want you to destroy everything in this workshop."

"But you can't mean—"

"Smash it to pieces."

"But your machine!"

"I can build it again. I've got the plans someplace safe."

"Where?" Errol asks.

"Your sister will know how to find them."

Errol looks at him, puzzled, frightened. Despite his height and build, he suddenly looks like a boy rather than a young man.

"Destroy it all," Miles repeats. "Quickly. Then, I want you to get the rowboat ready. Grab the life jackets and paddles from the garage. Make sure there's gas in the outboard motor. We'll meet you by the dock in fifteen minutes. If we don't come, get in the boat and go down to the Millers'. Use their phone to call the police."

"But I—"

"Do as I say," Miles orders, taking one last look around the workshop. He opens the door just in time to hear the sound of a house window being smashed, followed by Lily screaming.

Hammer in his hand, Miles starts to run.

AFTER

Necco

~~~~~

The Catholic schoolboys from across the street come looking for her, trolling the waters, sniffing around like skittish dogs in navy-blue blazers and red ties. They believe in Jesus and the Heavenly Father. They believe that Christ's body lives in those tasteless paper-thin wafers, his blood is watered-down wine you buy by the gallon. Glory. Hallelujah.

Necco likes wine. Sometimes they bring some for her. Wild Irish Rose. Thunderbird. Sweet as Kool-Aid. Sometimes it's beer they bring. Warm beer in dented cans that have been riding around in some boy's pocket all day. When she opens them, they spray, spurting like geysers, getting all over her and the boys, making them laugh.

"Hey, Fire Girl," they cry. "You home?"

How long they've been coming, she doesn't know. She's not even sure how long she's lived in the Palace. Four months? Six months even? She moved in just after Mama died, just after she and Hermes got together. She asks Promise to tell her, but the doll is no good at keeping time. She used to sing, back when Daddy first made her, but at some point she lost her ability to speak; Necco can still recall the funny, too-high voice singing "Rock-a-Bye Baby."

Promise had another name back then, too. But just like Necco's old name, that name was left behind. She's tried her best to forget it all.

The Palace is a rusted-out Pontiac without tires, parked and abandoned in a vacant lot. There was once a brick building here, a print shop with an old press, but all that remains are the crumbled lengths of wall, no more than six feet high, and covered in ivy. The lot is full of sumac bushes, bittersweet, chicory, yarrow, milkweed: nature trying to reclaim what was taken. It's been a dumping ground over the years, and in addition to the piles of bricks and old rotten timbers, there's a washer and dryer, a heating-oil tank full of bullet holes, a crumpled shopping cart, piles of old tires, and rusted bedsprings. All of this provides excellent cover and makes the Pontiac blend in, look like just another dumped and ruined thing.

Necco has found things in the lot's rubble:

little metal letters, gears from large machines. She keeps these things, stashes them away. They remind her of her father, of his workshop full of gadgets and gears. She used to visit him there, sit for hours on a stool, watching while he worked on his inventions, passing him tools with lovely names like crescent wrench and needle-nose pliers. She'd wind up his creatures, watch them walk and soar, carefully checking them all for secret compartments, which might hold a surprise: Bazooka bubble gum, Fireballs, starlight mints. She stoked the fire in his forge, watched him bend and shape hot metal like it was river clay. Daddy wore a leather apron, and would whistle while he worked. Old jazz songs, mostly.

"Fire Girl, Fire Girl, Fire Girl?" the boys cry now, their own improvised song as they come around the brick wall, wind their way through the rubble. They stick their heads through her front door, which is actually a smashed-out windshield covered in an old curtain. The curtain has covered wagons with little cowboys and lassos. Giddyup and go.

Resting along the dashboard is part of her ever-growing collection of treasures: a tiny bird skull, the gears and letters from the printing press, the bottom of a bottle she sometimes uses as a magnifying glass to start a fire, and the motorcycle goggles Hermes gave her.

"Show us, Fire Girl," one of the boys orders.

They bring new boys all the time, and she waits in the Pontiac like a queen on her throne. But she doesn't show them for nothing, no. The boys know to come bearing gifts: silver coins, crumpled dollars, jewelry with broken clasps, silk scarves stolen from their mothers, and sweets. Hermes says she should just take cash, but she enjoys these other tributes. She loves candy the most: saltwater taffy, chocolate bars with light and fluffy nougat, red and white peppermints that melt on her tongue and taste like Christmas morning. She rarely speaks to them, so they don't know her favorite candy. Necco wafers. They were her favorites when she was growing up, in the time Before the Flood. Afterward, when she came to soaked in river water and coughing it out of her lungs like a fish-girl just learning to breathe air, her mama asked if she wanted anything, anything at all, and this was what she wanted. And Mama laughed then, loud and relieved, and started calling her Necco.

Today, the boys have brought a girl, which is strange and changes the feeling of the whole afternoon. The girls don't usually come, too scared to walk across the street; too frightened of getting burned or sliced, or of being caught by the nuns with their cruel faces.

This new girl is something of an oddity in and of herself—very tall and thin with dirty-blond hair and red lipstick. She looks older than the bright-eyed boys who crowd around her, more knowing. Tucked around her neck, over the drab school uniform of white shirt, navy blazer, and red tie, she's got a purple knitted scarf, even though it's too warm for such a thing and the purple clashes with the school colors. Instead of the black patent-leather Mary Janes the other girls wear, she's got on a battered pair of Doc Martens, with fuzzy, striped leg warmers in earth-tone colors. Her long fingers are stained with paint and ink, their nails short and ragged. They're the hands of an artist, hands that remind Necco of her own mother when she'd come out of her painting studio. This new girl rests her hands on the Pontiac's hood, drums her fingers like maybe she's got better things to do, other places to go. The boys gather round, give her instructions since it's her first time.

"Hand her a gift and she'll show you," says the boy closest to her—an older one whose cocky sureness Necco despises. He's called Luke.

"Just don't let her touch you," teases a tall boy covered in freckles. "'Cause she can shoot fire from her fingertips."

Necco smiles at this and stretches out her hands, cracking her knuckles just for show.

"She likes candy best," another calls. "Anything sweet."

"I don't know what I have," the girl says as she takes off her school satchel—an army-green canvas bag covered in pins that say things like QUESTION AUTHORITY and NORMAL PEOPLE SCARE ME and I'M WAITING FOR THE ZOMBIE APOCALYPSE. She starts to dig around, laying the bag on the hood of the car so she can use both hands to paw through it.

Finally, she pulls out a tattered box of Good & Plentys, the candy pink and white, rattling around in the box like medicine. "There's not much left, but you can have it," she says, thrusting the box in Necco's direction. "Wait," she says. "Here." And she digs in her bag again before pulling out two pink metal knitting needles and a small ball of purple yarn—the color that matches the scarf around her neck. She seems to hesitate a second before handing them over. "It's the best thing I've got," the girl says.

Necco takes the needles and yarn, delighted. They remind her of something, something from her life Before the Flood—her mother sitting in a corner by the fireplace knitting a long, knobby scarf. The comforting **click-click** of the needles. Her mother's hair was neatly combed and pulled back in a braid, not the scraggly, barely containable tangle of red it turned into After the Flood.

Errol was there, sitting by her feet, shuffling a deck of cards, smiling up at Mama, teasing her, tugging at the end of the yarn like a playful kitten. "I want a scarf, too," he said. "I want one just like Little E's. Or maybe, maybe you could just make it extra long, and she and I can wrap it around both our necks. We'd be like those twins who are born attached."

"Conjoined," said Daddy. He was hunched over his notebook, scribbling, smoking a pipe stuffed with cherry tobacco. Necco had smiled then, liking the idea of being tethered to her big brother, an excuse to never leave his side.

Now she blinks, and the memory is gone; unraveled like a bit of yarn. She's trained herself to do this: to stop the memories before they get to be too much to bear. **It's dangerous to think about the past,** that's what Mama always said. So she lets them all go, locks them away before they can do any harm.

Heart thumping, nervous in some new, unexpected way, she pulls up the right leg of her pants, showing the blade and lighter strapped in the custom sheath Hermes made.

The new girl leans in; she looks excited, expectant, but one of the boys pulls her back.

"Careful, she's dangerous," the boy named Luke warns. "I hear she once cut a boy's spleen out for looking at her the wrong way."

Necco smiles, doesn't disagree as she untucks the lighter from the sheath.

The girl smiles back; it's a conspiratorial sort of smile, an us-against-them smile.

The kids form a rough circle around her; most of them have done this plenty and know the routine. But it's a trick of which they never tire. Reaching into the car, Necco grabs a candle and a small cotton ball from the dash. She lights the candle, palms the cotton ball, then makes a show of tucking the lighter back in the sheath as everyone eyes the blade, wondering if this might be the time she pulls it. She's dangerous, this Fire Girl they've come to see.

The trick works best in the dark, but she's learned to do it quickly in the light, the way her mother taught her. Necco isn't a true Fire Eater, not in the sense that mother was, but she's learned a few parlor tricks. Enough to earn a little spending money.

She stares at the candle flame, passes her right hand over it, making a grabbing, pulling motion at the flame. Then, cotton ignited, she's got a flame of her own between her thumb and index finger.

The new girl watches, eyes wide. There is sweat on her upper lip.

Necco moves the little ball of flame quickly in a ceremonial circle through the air before opening her mouth and shoving it in. She closes her mouth, exhales smoke through her nose.

Everyone applauds, hoots and hollers. Necco gives them a little bow. The boys shuffle their feet, know it's time to go, but don't want it to end.

Then, the girl does what none of them have

ever done before: she reaches out and touches Necco's shoulder, says, "Thank you. That was amazing."

The boys laugh, loud and hard. "Fire Girl's amazing!" they call, faces flushed.

"Marry me, Fire Girl," one boy begs, his hands stuffed into the pockets of his neatly ironed school pants. "Have you ever slept in a real bed, Fire Girl? Huh? Have you?"

Necco laughs. He can't be more than fifteen, this boy.

She doesn't tell him that once, she slept in a canopy bed covered in brightly colored hand-made quilts. Her room was purple and she had a lamp with a stained-glass shade on her bedside table. Her father had made a circle of dragonflies with paper bodies and tiny lights inside that sur-rounded her bed, their wings flapping gently in the slightest breeze.

Promise the doll sat perched on top of the bed, her face new and clean, her pink gingham dress crisp. If you pulled a cord on her back, she'd sing a song.

"Marry me," the boy insists, eyes glistening.

Sometimes, the boys ask Necco to do other things. Dirty things. The cocky boy, Luke, has done this before. "Twenty bucks if you blow me, Fire Girl. I'll throw in an extra five if you're any good at it. I bet that mouth of yours can eat more than just fire." They offer money, promise to get her anything she wants. But she always shakes her head. She rarely speaks to them. This is part of her power.

If they get too insistent, too rude, she shows them the blade. One time, a boy got too close, put his hand on her chest, and she hit him in the gut so hard he doubled over.

"Theo loves Fire Girl," hollers the tall boy with freckles, and the new girl turns and stomps hard on his foot, making him scream. The other boys laugh harder, and Necco actually joins them. And just like that, for about thirty seconds, she's a normal girl.

"Show's over!" a voice booms, shattering the moment.

Hermes is upon them, his shadow long and lean as he whips his backpack around like a heavy weapon. "Go on! Get! Unless you all want to pay again," he yells like they're a pack of stray dogs begging for scraps.

The kids scatter like bugs. The girl is last to leave, and gives Necco a little smile and a wave, then turns and runs to join the others, flipping one end of the purple scarf up over her shoulder as she makes her way around the old bedsprings and back through a gap in the wall to the street.

"Why do you let them stick around so long after the trick?" Hermes asks, tossing his backpack into the Pontiac. His dark hair falls into his eyes and he pushes it back. His face is tense, frustrated. "It's not like they're your friends or anything. They just come to see you do that fire trick over and over like a circus freak. I hate that that's what you have to do to get stuff."

"I like to do the trick. And I don't mind them sticking around. They amuse me," she confesses.

"I don't like you doing it when I'm not here," Hermes says, laying his backpack down and starting to rummage. "I don't like the way some of those boys look at you." He gives a look, part jealousy, part worry.

"I can take care of myself," she says. "And it wasn't just boys today. There was a girl with them."

She looks down at the knitting needles in her hands; then something catches her eye on the hood of the Pontiac. The girl has left her bag. Necco looks for the girl, thinking she should call her back, but it's too late—she's out of sight.

Hermes looks up from his backpack at her and frowns hard. "What have you got there? Another one of their gifts?"

"Nothing special," she tells him, pulling the satchel to her chest.

He shrugs, goes back to looking in his own backpack.

When Necco peers into the bag, she finds the usual things—a school ID card, pens, notebook, chemistry textbook, a couple of paperbacks, including one she recognizes immediately: **The**

Princess and the Elephant by Dr. Miles Sandeski. Heart hammering, holding her breath, she nearly pulls the book out, shouts to Hermes, says, "Look! It's my father's book!"—but it's too much. They're not supposed to talk about their lives before. Fingers shaking, she tucks the book down at the bottom of the bag, turning it over so that she sees Daddy's photo on the back: he's wearing glasses and his favorite corduroy jacket, smiling into the camera, at her mother, who took the photo. She's never read her father's book. She'll take it out later, maybe, sometime Hermes isn't around.

At the very bottom of the bag, next to where she's tucked her father's book, is a thick envelope held together with a rubber band—she can see it's stuffed with cash. And next to that, a clear plastic bag full of pills and capsules bright as candy. She can't tell how much money is there—it looks like a lot. She almost pulls it out to show Hermes, but something stops her. She thinks of the girl's smile, the way her fingers felt on Necco's shoulder; of how she's the first one who hasn't been afraid to touch the Fire Girl.

Amazing.

Necco stashes the girl's bag under the front seat.

Then she turns to Hermes, raises a hand, strokes his hair. When he faces her, she kisses him.

He has a scar over his lip in the place where most people have a slight groove—a faint reminder of the animals we once were. She knows about evolution: her father taught her, showed her textbooks with pictures of early man, told her that all mammals shared a single, common ancestor.

Hermes's scar makes it look like his lip is split right down the middle like a rabbit or a squirrel—something small, soft, and vulnerable. She likes to kiss him there, feel the raised skin, the place where there's no stubble.

She does it now, touching her lips to his skin as delicately as a moth landing.

"Tell me," she says, not needing to finish the sentence. He knows what she wants, can read her mind. Necco believes they were destined for each other. That if things were different, if they'd met in their lives before rather than out here on the street, they might even have gotten married one day. Had a whole herd of little babies with beautiful faces. Maybe send them to Catholic school where they'd learn about the Holy Ghost.

"You know," he says. "I've told it a thousand times."

"Tell it again," she asks, voice cooing. "Make it a thousand and one."

"I fell off a horse," he tells her, irritated, bored.

She pictures him riding a wild stallion through the desert, just like the cowboys on the curtain. They don't talk much about their lives before.

Hermes always says, "There is no before. There is only us. That's all that matters."

Hermes is older than the schoolboys in their pretty blazers. He's all done with high school. He went to college last fall to study computer science, but he says college is just part of the zombie machine, and his father was on his ass all the time, full of expectations, and so he bailed after his first week of classes. He packed a few things in a backpack and came to live on the streets. "Screw college. Screw my dad. I'm not gonna be one of the sheeple, walking around just doing what everyone else expects."

He wears combat boots, green fatigue pants, and a long waxed canvas coat. He keeps a huge hunting knife strapped to his belt in a leather sheath, and he carries a flashlight, screwdriver, pry bar, rolls of duct tape, and paracord everywhere he goes. He believes in being prepared.

"Hermes was the messenger of the gods. He's also the god of thieves," he once explained with a wink. And that's how her Hermes survives now—he goes into crowded places at lunchtime and comes back with a backpack full of wallets, cell phones, laptops, and hundred-dollar fountain pens with ink as blue as the ocean in a kid's painting. Sometimes, he gets whole briefcases. He dissects the electronics, wipes them clean, and sells them. He's got a guy across town who will pay cash, no questions asked.

"This is where it's happening, Necco," he tells her. "The real world. All the stuff that matters."

She knows Hermes is not his real name. He whispered it to her once, just a few days after they met, the day they found the Palace and moved in. They were lying curled up together in the back, his fingers wrapped around hers. "What was your real name?" he asked. "Your name before?"

Her body tensed. "If I tell you mine, you have to tell me yours."

"Okay. But you gotta promise you won't ever call me by it. I'm not that guy anymore. And I promise I'll never call you by your other name either. You're Necco to me, now and forever."

So she told him her name. And he kissed her ear, whispered his own into it, **Matthew,** and it sounded so lovely when he said it, a glittery golden ball sliding over his tongue, through his lips and teeth.

Matthew.

He's never told her his last name. All she knows is that his daddy is someone important. Someone with **more money and power than God,** if you go by what Hermes always says. But Hermes doesn't want any of Dad's money. He's turned his back on the whole thing, and his dad has actually hired a private detective to track Hermes down and bring him home.

"Can you believe it?" he asks sometimes. "My

dad actually paying someone to trail my ass around town?"

And Necco doesn't answer. The truth is, she **can** believe it. If she lost him, she'd pay anything she had to have someone bring him back.

————

Necco's story of how she ended up on the street isn't like Hermes's. It wasn't a conscious choice. It was just what they had to do. That's what Mama always said, anyway. And even though Necco questioned about half the things Mama said After the Flood, what choice did she have but to go along with it all? Mama was all she had left and she was all Mama had left—they had to stick together no matter what.

What bothers Necco the most is that she has no memories of the flood itself: the very event that brought them to live the way they did.

Necco is sure it was the bump on the head that did it. It knocked all the memories of that day out of her. When her mother found her the morning after the Great Flood, she had a big swollen gash on the back of her head.

"Some things are for the best," Mama always said when Necco complained about her loss of memory. Necco would ask Mama, pester her for details about what actually happened on the day of the flood, but Mama always shook her head, told her their own past was not important.

Miss Abigail and the other Fire Eaters found Necco and her mother a few days after the flood. She and Mama were trying to start a fire down by the river to heat a can of soup Necco had shop-lifted. They were cold and hungry, and Necco wanted, more than anything, to go home.

"Please, Mama," Necco begged. "Can't we go back to the house just one more time?" She wanted to go back and get more of her things, her own clothes, her books, her favorite purple boots.

"No," Mama told her in a stern voice. "We can never go back. There's nothing there for us. The flood took everything. The house is gone. Your father and Errol are dead. And it's not safe."

"But, Mama—"

"Listen to me, Necco. There is a bad man looking for us. A very bad man. And he'll be watching that spot, hoping we'll come back to see if anything's left. Promise me you will never return," she said.

A thousand questions filled Necco's head. About the flood, who the bad man was; about how her father and Errol had died. "But I just—"

"Promise," Mama said, digging her fingers into Necco's arms, her eyes frantic.

"I promise," Necco said, and Mama released her. Necco struck another match, setting it to the crumpled, soggy newspaper, trying desperately to get it to light.

Half an hour later, Necco looked up from the still unlit fire to see four women coming toward them. The oldest had long, unkempt gray hair knotted with colorful rags, and was in the lead.

"I'm Miss Abigail," she said. "My friends and I—Miss F, Miss Coral, and Miss Stella—have a camp about a quarter mile downstream, under the Blachly Bridge. We've got a warm fire, shelter, and plenty of food. Will you come join us?"

Mama shook her head. "We're fine on our own."

Miss Abigail looked around. "This spot you're in, it's not safe for you. We can keep you protected. You and the girl."

"What makes you think we need protecting?" Mama asked, looking the old woman straight in the eye.

"The Great Mother told us. She told us you were coming. To expect you and help you. She said there were dark forces working against you."

The women were all dressed in ragged clothing. Clearly homeless and crazy, they were the sort of people Mama would have pulled Necco away from back in their other lives, the kind they would have crossed the street to avoid.

"Great Mother?" Mama said.

Miss Abigail smiled, held out her hand. "Come with us. We'll explain everything. Just stay one night. Get warmed up and fed and listen to what

we have to say. If you want to leave in the morning, you're free to do so."

Mama and Necco followed the women to their
camp, settled in a circle around a blazing fire. The
women lived in shacks cobbled together from
shipping pallets, scrap wood, driftwood from the
river, and tarps. They ladled vegetable stew from
a cast-iron pot into carved wooden bowls.

Necco ate three bowls, studying these strange
women in the flickering firelight. Miss Stella was
young, twenty at the most, and Asian Ameri-
can. Her hair was buzzed on one side, but long
enough to wear in a ponytail on the other. She
wore black leggings and a wool poncho, and from
what Necco could see of her body, she was decorated, head to toe, with piercings and tattoos. She
took a particular interest in Necco, making sure
her bowl was full and draping a blanket around
her shoulders so she'd be warmer.

Miss Coral wore thick, black-framed cat-eye
glasses and had her dark hair pulled back in a
tight bun. She reminded Necco of a librarian.
Miss F was a tiny woman with dirty-blond hair
and fierce eyes. She looked half-wild, like she
was ready to tear your face apart with her teeth
and fingers.

"It was fate that brought you to us," Miss Abigail said once they had finished with dinner. She
was dressed like a strange cartoon character, with

colorful shirts layered one on top of another, and three skirts with striped leggings underneath. "And fate will decide whether or not you stay."

Mama's eyes were fixed on the black water behind the fire. "I've always hated this place. Ashford. I can't believe fate would call on me to stay in such a vile, dirty city."

Miss Abigail smiled. "Everyone sees things through their own set of filters," she said. "I look around this city and I see life, I see the past and present, I see tiny miracles every day. This stew we're eating is made from wild plants gathered around the city. This place takes care of us, nurtures us, gives us all we need."

She pulled a small leather pouch from around her neck, opened it, sprinkled some red powder into her palm, and snorted it up her nose. She held out her hand to the other three women, and they all inhaled a small bit of the powder up their noses. In the firelight, Necco could see the red stains under their noses, the way their pupils expanded, and their eyes got glassy like dolls' eyes. Miss Stella smiled at Necco.

Then, Miss Abigail came forward, held the pouch over Mama's head, watched it swing in a slow, steady circle. "The snuff has chosen you," Miss Abigail said.

"Chosen me?" Mama said.

Miss Abigail opened the pouch again, sprinkled more out.

"What is it?" Mama asked.

"The Devil's Snuff," Miss Abigail said.

Necco got a chill. Even though they had never been churchgoers or read anything from the Bible, Necco knew to stay away from anything with the Devil in its name.

"What does it do?" Mama asked.

"It takes the filters away. It shows you what you need to know."

"My past?" Mama asked, looking both worried and hopeful.

"Your past, your future, your true purpose. The snuff shows you that it's all connected."

"Will it show me what to do next?"

Miss Abigail nodded. "It will show you everything you need to know."

Mama looked into the fire. Necco watched, thinking there was no way Mama would do it. She had only a glass or two of wine a year, never smoked—there was no way she was going to take some weird hallucinogen, even if it had **chosen** her.

Mama's eyes stayed fixed on the fire. At last, she smiled and nodded, leaned forward, covered one nostril, and bowed her head so that her face was over the old woman's hand.

"Mama, no!" Necco cried.

"It's okay," Miss Stella said, putting a tattooed hand on Necco's arm.

"Child," Miss Abigail said, smiling at Necco.

"It won't hurt her. What she's about to do—this is her destiny."

With that, Mama snorted the bright red powder up her nose. And, whether she realized it or not, that one action sealed their fates.

Mama closed her eyes for a long time and sat rigid, like her body had turned to smooth, pale stone. Necco watched, stomach tight, heart pounding, waiting to see what might happen. What if Mama never opened her eyes again— what if it killed her or made her go crazy?

"Mama?" Necco called. She stood up, started to walk to where her mother sat, but Miss Abigail stopped her, dropping her arm down like a railroad crossing gate.

"Wait, child," Miss Abigail ordered.

Mama's eyes popped open, and she took in a deep, gasping breath, like a drowning woman desperate for air. She gazed into the fire, pupils dilated, transfixed, like she was watching a movie no one else could see.

"In the beginning," Mama said, her voice loud and sure, "the Great Mother laid an egg and that egg became our world."

The other women cooed, said, "Yes," in low, droning, singsong voices.

Miss Abigail snorted more powder, smiled wide at Mama. "You, Miss Lily, are the one we've been waiting for," she said. "Our missing piece. The fifth point of our star."

And Mama did not question. She nodded, like she, too, believed it was the Great Mother and fate that had pulled them together.

The next morning, she and Necco began work on building their own shack in the camp of the Fire Eaters. Over the next months and years, Mama learned to inhale the Devil's Snuff, to tend the secret patch of berries they used to make the snuff, to see visions, eat fire, and talk the snuff talk. They stayed at the camp by the river most of the year, and when the weather turned cold and the Fire Eaters scattered, Mama found them shelter in tunnels near the old mill—the Winter House—to hunker down and await spring.

Mama called the city Burntown, reinventing it, the way she did so many things. As if, by giving it a new name, she could turn it into a different place. And it was a different place. They were living on a different side of it, anyway, the underside, the fringe, the places most of the city residents didn't even notice. Up top, where the college was, where people went to work every day at the paper mill, that was Ashford. But down here under the bridge where the women did the snuff, saw visions, and ate fire, this was Burntown.

In time, Mama started painting again, making pictures of the visions the snuff gave her. She'd paint on paper shopping bags, plywood scraps, birch bark. She made her own paints from berries, leaves, roots, clay, sap, and even blood. Necco would watch her paint, see her get totally lost in it, the way she used to in their lives before, and think that in these moments, her mother actually seemed almost happy.

The longer they stayed with the Fire Eaters in Burntown, the more snuff Mama did, the farther away their old lives became, the more Mama turned into a completely different person. A woman whose paranoia seemed to creep after her, everywhere she went. She was sure that they were being watched by librarians, cops, bus drivers.

"The Jujubes are especially bad, Necco," Mama said, using her own special nickname for the cops (the flashing lights on top of the cruisers looked like candy to her). "They're looking for us, too. If they find us, we're done for." Whenever they saw a cop, they crossed the street, ducked down an alley out of sight. Necco always thought doing this made them look more suspicious, but there was no arguing with Mama.

"There is a man, Necco, who can take all the light out of the world. He's a walking shadow, a black hole man. And he has such power, he can do things you can only imagine. They say he can fly. He can come spying on you in your dreams. He's the King of Liars. A jackal-hearted man. He goes by many names: the Chicken Man, Snake Eyes . . . And here's the worst part of all: he's the one responsible for the Great Flood. Other terrible things, too. Like what happened to your grandparents."

"My grandparents died in a car accident," Necco reminded her mother, irritated. Sometimes it just exhausted her, trying to sift through her mother's stories and pick out what was real and what wasn't. It was like panning for gold, picking through all the mud and sand, trying to find the nuggets of truth. "And how can a man be responsible for a flood? It's not possible."

"Oh, but it is. It is for Snake Eyes. He's the one who killed your daddy and Errol. He meant to drown us, too, baby girl, and he's real unhappy we got away from him. He's searching for us even now. Every day. Every night. He's on our trail like an old hound dog, or a shark that's tasted blood. He won't rest until he finds us. We have to be on the lookout. Ever vigilant. He's sneaky, this man. He can change his face, his hair, his clothes. He can look like a businessman or a greasy-haired biker."

"Right," Necco said, exasperated. "And if all that's true, Mama, if there's really a human chameleon after us, how are we supposed to even know it's him?"

"His mark, Necco," Mama said, sounding just as irritated and frustrated with Necco as Necco had been with her. "He has a pair of dice tattooed on his left wrist—both with a single dot on top. You see that mark, that pair of snake eyes staring back at you, you run. You run as fast and as far as you can."

Maybe, Necco told herself, it was easier for her mother to have someone to blame; a mythical monster who was responsible for all the bad things that had happened to them, who lurked in the shadows of every alley. Easier than believing that sometimes truly terrible things happened for no reason.

The events of the flood—losing their home, Daddy, and Errol—had broken her mother in some profound way. The snuff just continued to fill what was left of her with tiny hairline cracks, making her fragile as a porcelain doll.

And eventually, that doll shattered. Mama's paranoia and frightening snuff-induced visions got the best of her, and she threw herself off the Steel Bridge. That was back in the spring. It's been months, but Necco misses her each and every moment, wishes she could turn back the clock and find a way to stop her.

If Necco closes her eyes now, she can picture her mama so clearly, hear her voice as she talked the story-talk down by the river after doing the snuff, the underside of her nose stained red as she told how the world was born like she was right there, seeing it for the first time. Sometimes, Necco imagined her mama to be the Great

Mother, eyes big and bright as planets, greenish brown ringed in yellow.

"In the beginning, the Great Mother laid an egg and that egg became our world. A bright and blazing orb, spinning through space." Mama would light the torch: a wad of cotton wrapped at the end of a straightened wire coat hanger, soaked in camping fuel from a red and silver can. It burned like a newly formed planet.

"Imagine it," Mama would croon, voice hypnotic, as she waved the torch through the air, swooping, doing careful figure eights. She'd put her fingers to the flame, pulling at it, teasing it, cupping the fire in her hand, making it jump, do tricks. She was that good.

Necco would be sitting, cross-legged on the ground watching. She'd lean closer, smelling the dirty brown river that raced behind Mama, and the thick, fuel-laden smoke that drifted from the torch. She could hear the cars roaring over the bridge above them. A whole other life going on up there, a life she and her mama were once a part of: a life of trips to the grocery store in the car, going to museums, visiting her daddy in his office at the college, doctor and dentist appointments. It all seemed so far away.

Mama would sway in her thin cotton dress. It was one she'd worn in their other life, one with sunflowers on it that Daddy said made her look like Queen of the Garden, and they'd dance as Mama stared into the flames with total focus, in a trance. There were blisters and scars around her mouth, her ragged red hair was singed, her eye-lashes burned off. And if you looked in just the right place, you could see the outline of the little revolver Mama kept strapped under her dress, just in case.

"Imagine the world as it first was—nothing but fire," Mama would say, eyes glassy, nos-trils red, lips blistered, her voice almost a song. "Then, things cooled. The rains came down. It rained and it rained for days and nights, season after season. There was water, one great ocean covering the whole planet. And the creatures! The creatures had fins, gills—that was life as it was then. Eventually, the Great Mother created land and the creatures learned to suck air into their lungs, to slither and squirm up out of the water onto the muddy banks and shores. They had webbed feet, damp skin. They hopped. They sang. They were our first ancestors, long before the monkeys with their sticky little fingers."

This part of the story always reminded Necco of the science lessons her daddy gave her and Errol; how he said all creatures shared one com-mon ancestor once upon a time. She'd imagined, back then, a creature like her mama described now, part fish, part frog, flopping its way out of the water, getting that first gulp of air.

Mama would raise the torch, continue on. "Life on earth is constantly evolving. The Great Mother sees to that. There is fire and water, water and fire. Destruction and life. The flood we lost your daddy and Errol in, that was only the beginning. The world is changing. There is danger all around." Here, she'd open her eyes, look right at Necco, face serious, tight with panic. "I have seen him in my dreams, Necco. I know he's coming. That's why we have to stay here, we have to stay hidden. But one day, he'll find us. One day, there will be no more running. No more hiding." At this, she would touch the gun under her dress, just making sure it was still there.

———————

"What'd you bring today?" Necco asks Hermes later that night, following him into the backseat. They've filled the space between the backseat and the front with cushions, making one large bed. "The nest," Hermes calls it, and she likes to cuddle up there with him at night, burrowed under the blankets, imagining they're creatures deep underground; rabbits in a warren, snug and safe.

Necco has added the latest gifts on the shelf above the backseat to the other treasures gathered there: candy, the jar she uses for making sprouts, pretty rocks, Promise the doll. The knitting needles and yarn sit next to the one thing of her mother's she's kept: a gold locket with her father's picture inside. But it's a funny photo, because it's Daddy as a little boy. Back before Mama even met him. In the photo, her daddy is a scrawny, dark-haired boy dressed in a Robin Hood costume, holding a homemade bow, a quiver of arrows strapped to his back.

"Did you get my necklace fixed?" she asks. She has a charm she wears around her neck—a little brass elephant that belonged to her father. He'd given it to her for her fourteenth birthday, just a few weeks before the Great Flood. The chain broke last week, and Hermes took it saying he'd get it fixed. He knew a jeweler, someone he took stuff to sell sometimes. This guy could fix the broken clasp.

"Not yet," Hermes says and frowns.

"Well, what did you bring, then?"

"News," he says, looking away for a second. "I have something to share with you. Something big. And it's going to change everything, but it's going to be good in the long run. I really believe that."

It almost sounded like he was trying reassure himself as much as her.

"What is it?" she asks, the worry making her throat ache.

"I can't tell you yet. Not now. I have to show you."

"Show me? Well, when can you show me?"

"Tomorrow. I'll take you tomorrow."

"Where?"

"You'll see." He strokes the hair away from her face, kisses her forehead, and pulls her into an embrace. "You'll understand everything then."

She leans into him, sees there's a string around his neck. She reaches for it, pulls out a funny-looking key. The shank of the key is a cylinder with little teeth jutting off the sides. The head is coated in bright orange plastic and has the number 213 engraved on it in black.

"What's this?"

"It's part of what I have to show you."

"But what—"

He puts his fingers to her lips. "Be patient," he tells her. "Tomorrow. I'll show you tomorrow."

She stares at the strange little key, watches him tuck it back inside his shirt.

"I can show you this now, though," he says, smiling, reaching into the outer pocket of his backpack. He pulls out a loaf of bread, a hunk of cheese, and two apples.

Necco is ravenous, but as soon as she gets one whiff of the cheese, her stomach does a flip.

"You okay?"

She nods, swallowing down the watery feeling in her mouth, trying not to throw up. "Fine," she says. She takes deep breaths.

She's been throwing up a lot lately, but hasn't told Hermes. Pretty soon she won't be able to keep her secret from him, though. She's been mulling it over for weeks now, trying to figure out how she should tell him. She looks over at the knitting needles, remembers sitting at her mother's feet with Errol in the warm living room, the comforting **click-click-click** sound. If Mama were here, she'd say those needles the girl brought were a sign, a symbol. Mama was a big believer in signs and messages. She had been even way back in their lives before the flood.

"I have a surprise, too," Necco says.

"Yeah?" he asks, ripping off a hunk of bread and cutting a piece of cheese to go with it.

"It's a big one and I'm not sure you're going to like it."

"What is it?" he asks, setting down the food.

"Well, the thing is—" she says, stalling like a coward. But she's no coward. She's the Fire Girl. "I'm pregnant." She lets the words fly out like sparks, watches the shock of it roll over him.

"Are you . . . are you sure?" he stammers.

"I wouldn't tell you if I wasn't."

"But we've been careful," Hermes says.

"Not careful enough, I guess," she tells him.

"Holy shit," he says, eyes wide. "A baby? How long have you known?"

"The past couple of weeks."

This seems to shock him more than the initial news. "Why didn't you tell me before?"

"I needed to think. To figure out what I want to do."

There's a pause. It feels like they're both holding their breath. "And?"

"I've decided I want to keep it," she tells him. "But I don't expect anything from you. I know the last thing on earth you want to do is be a daddy, especially like this. I'm thinking that maybe I should check in to a shelter, the Lighthouse or someplace like that. Get off the street, get checked out in a clinic."

She's been reading up on pregnancy at the library and thinks of all the things that can go wrong: ectopic pregnancy, miscarriage, various birth defects. She needs to give this baby a chance to grow and be healthy. She needs good food. A safe place to sleep at night. Vitamins. She needs to start taking special vitamins with iron and folic acid. That's what the books said.

Hermes smiles real wide. "You're going to have a baby."

"Yes," she says, her head spinning a little, because hearing it out loud like this, hearing someone else say the words, that makes it real.

He puts a hand over her belly. His palm is warm, fingertips calloused and rough.

"You're going to be someone's mommy," he says. "And I'm going to be a daddy."

And hearing those words, it's like a wave crashing over her, carrying her off to a land far, far away. A land of mommies and daddies and tiny babies and songs and cribs and nursery rhymes. **Hey, diddle, diddle, the cat and the fiddle, the cow jumped over the moon.** But then, another wave of memory comes, one that threatens to destroy anything that might bring her a taste of a normal life. That's what the Great Flood has done to her. She struggles her way back to the surface, her head aching.

"Yes," she says.

"Are you sure you want to do this?" Hermes asks. "Be a mom?" He says it like she's been given some mistake disguised as a gift that she might not want any part of—two left shoes, a teacup with a hole at the bottom.

"Yes, I'm sure. But like I said, you don't have to be a part of this. I can do this on my own."

"But **I am** a part of it," Hermes says, pulling her close. "I'm not going anywhere. I'll take care of you and the baby, and we'll be a real family. You'll see. And all this makes what I have to show you tomorrow so much more important. It's perfect really."

A real family. She's not even sure what that means. She remembers her own parents tucking her in at night, back before the flood, when she was just a little girl. Mama would brush and braid her hair, Daddy would read her a story. How happy and whole she felt with both of them there each night. Necco closes her eyes, concentrates, and the memory is gone. Banished, like all the others that came before it. She's tried so hard to put away all the memories of her own family, of growing up in the time Before the Flood. She keeps them all locked up in a box inside her, because it's just too painful to think about how things used to be. It's how she survives; how she doesn't let herself go crazy. Crazy like Mama went crazy.

She knows it's not fair, the life that she has right now to offer her baby—living in a car, eating fire for candy and trinkets. But she'll change things. She'll turn it around. She's got a reason now. And Mama's gone. There's no reason to keep living like this, like a girl on the run. The things that Mama said, they were paranoid thoughts from too much snuff. There was never any bad man after them. No one watching, lurking. It's time to move forward. To get off the street.

She'll go to the shelter, ask for help. And piece by piece, she and Hermes can build a real life together. Get jobs maybe. An apartment. A little crib for the baby. She'll learn to knit. Use the needles she got today to knit little baby booties, a tiny hat. **Click-click-click** will go the needles while she knits in a rocking chair, just like her own mama once did.

"It's going to be okay," Hermes says. "Hell, more than okay. I can make this work. I can even go to my family if I have to. My dad's a complete asshole, but my mom would help us. We'll figure it out."

Hermes rocks her, and she closes her eyes, feels the key around his neck press against her back. She imagines a baby tucked deep inside her, a tiny tadpole breathing fluid, a gilled thing.

She falls asleep and dreams she's pushing a baby carriage over a bridge. Then her skin gets clammy because she realizes it's not just any bridge, but the Steel Bridge, the one her mama jumped off, throwing herself into the muddy river fifty feet down.

But Necco's ripped a hole in time somehow and Mama's there, alive again, waiting, perched on the edge, looking down into the water. Her mouth is stained red, her singed hair in tangles. She's dripping wet, like she's just climbed out of the water. She's got Hermes's key strapped around her neck.

"Mama?"

Mama turns from the water, studies her.

"I've been waiting for you," Mama says, smiling, showing teeth the color of blood. "Let me see that grandbaby of mine."

Necco bends down to pull back the covers on the carriage, but can't. She's afraid of what she might find there.

"Sometimes," Mama says, her fingers wrapped around the key that dangles from her neck, "the truth isn't something you want to look in the face. Sometimes, you're better off not knowing."

Theo

~~~~

Theo walks along the sidewalk quickly, her left hand holding a cigarette, while the fingers of her right hand work their way over the neatly stitched rows of purple yarn, plucking at it worriedly. Will Hannah like it? Will she think a hand-knit scarf is stupid? It suddenly feels sappy, way too sentimental.

A moving truck rumbles by on the street: LET US HELP YOU WITH YOUR NEXT BIG MOVE, it says, its tailpipes belching diesel fumes. Someone coming or going—going, if they're lucky, moving far away from this stinking city.

Theo's on First Street, which is paved in old cobblestones and full of shops and cafés that cater to the college crowd. It's the part of the city that pretends to be something other than what it is, the part that says "Vibrant, fun college town!" when the reality is that walking three blocks in any direction will reveal just how economically depressed the whole city is. You'll see the closed storefronts with broken windows, or the guy begging for change on the corner holding a sign that says I'D RATHER BEG THAN STEAL.

Theo passes Blue Coyote Burritos; Lavender and Lace: Supplies for Body and Spirit; Pen and Ink Art Supplies; Two Rivers Books and Cafe (POETRY SLAM TONITE!); and Millhouse Coffee Roasters, where people are sitting at the little tables outside and trying not to let the stink of the paper mill ruin their lattes.

Theo sucks the last drag off her cigarette, stomps out the butt with her boot, then checks her watch. Three-thirty. Shit. She's going to be late. All because Luke made her go see the Fire Girl. He was too afraid to do the deal in school, so they'd done it as they crossed the street in a jostling crowd of kids. She handed him a brown paper grocery bag holding two ounces of cocaine wrapped in plastic; he gave her an envelope stuffed with two thousand bucks. Easy-peasy. She didn't think people even did coke anymore. She rarely sold it to anyone at school. Luke was going to resell the coke to his cousin downstate for a wicked profit, he'd told her, but Theo couldn't care less. The kid was a nasty weasel. As long as she got her money and didn't get caught with the drugs, she was fine. Having so much of it in her bag all day had worried the hell out of her, made her suspect she was pushing her luck big-time.

But then suddenly, the deal was done, and she felt such sweet relief that she went ahead and saw the Fire Girl anyway. Gave up her pink knitting needles to see the trick (it was okay, though, she had a couple other sets of size 8s—she'd bought a whole bag of miscellaneous needles and yarn at the church rummage sale last year). She'd been hearing stories about the Fire Girl for weeks, boys who said she was magic, could hold fire in her fingers and swallow it down. Someone said that she also gave blow jobs for ten bucks.

Theo didn't believe that. Not after meeting her. The girl was tougher than Theo had imagined, the kind of girl who didn't take bullshit and had a knife to back her up.

It makes Theo smile to think about it now. Maybe she should start carrying a knife strapped to her boot. Maybe Hannah would think it was sexy.

She smiles bigger, harder; a face-cracking smile. The worrying is over. She feels almost giddy. Alive in some new way. Like a kid who's just dived off the tallest rock at the swimming hole on a dare, then surfaced, alive and well. Now all she has to do is deliver the cash to Hannah and she's set. She'll tell her no more giving her huge amounts of product to carry around. Too stressful.

Her mind drifts back to the scarf. Maybe she shouldn't give it to Hannah after all, even though Theo has worked so carefully on it all week—knit a row, purl a row—sure that the very act of knitting Hannah a scarf would bind them together somehow, as if the little knots she made with the needles made a net that could hold them and keep them safe.

———————

They'd met three months ago at the Ashford library, in the biography section. Theo was looking at books on P. T. Barnum and Hannah was searching the shelves.

"You don't see anything on William Jensen, do you?" she asked.

"Who?" Theo asked, looking at the girl beside her. She was slightly shorter than Theo and wore jeans, flip-flops, and a black T-shirt. Her hair was twisted back in a painful-looking knotted ponytail, and there were sunglasses with mirrored lenses perched on top of her head.

"Jensen—you know, the guy who built the mill here in town? Did you know his wife and son were murdered?" She waited a beat, then widened her eyes, and said in a low, eerie voice, "Decapitated." She drew a finger across her throat to emphasize her point.

"Wow," Theo said. "I had no idea."

"Totally true. You'd be amazed at all the dark history this town has—stuff they don't teach you in school—you've gotta go digging to find it. I'm kind of an expert. The Jensen double murder was never solved. The police thought Jensen did it, but he had an airtight alibi. The poor guy was never the same. It ruined him. I'm doing research on old crimes of Ashford for a summer sociology class. But I don't see anything on Jensen in the biography section."

Theo glanced at the shelves. "Um . . . I think there's a local history section around the corner."

"Right . . . of course. Thanks!" Hannah wandered off around the corner, came back with a book, and sat down in one of the chairs. Theo sat across from her. Hannah cracked her knuckles while she read, pulling on one finger at a time, then folding them over, pushing them closed: **pop, pop, pop.**

"I'm sorry," she said, when she caught Theo looking at her. "It's an annoying habit, isn't it? It helps me concentrate. I'm not even aware I'm doing it half the time."

"It's fine," Theo said. "We've all got our bad habits, I guess."

Hannah looked at Theo a moment, taking her in, sizing her up. "Not you, though, surely. You don't look like a girl with a single bad habit."

There was something oddly flirtatious about

the way she spoke. Did she know somehow? Had she had a glimpse of Theo's most secret thoughts, the ones she hardly even admitted to herself?

Theo laughed, looked back down at the open book in her hands. "I've got plenty."

"Good ones? Juicy ones?"

"Maybe." Theo's heart felt light and fluttery as she wondered what might happen next.

Maybe that was that. The girl would get up and leave. Just as well, really, Theo told herself. This was real life, not some crazy novel or art house film. The girl would leave and Theo would check out her book, go home, and order takeout with her mom. The regular Friday evening routine.

The girl closed her Ashford history book, but kept her eyes on Theo. "You know what one of my bad habits is? Chocolate malts. Why don't you come with me? My treat, but in exchange, you have to promise to tell me at least one bad habit."

Theo felt her face flush. She set down the P. T. Barnum biography. "Deal," she said.

"I'm Hannah," the girl said, standing, then linking arms with Theo as they left the library.

———

Hannah was a sophomore at Two Rivers College studying sociology.

"The whole reason I came to Two Rivers, the

whole reason I got into sociology in the first place, was this guy who used to teach here. Dr. Miles Sandeski," Hannah explained over milk shakes.

They were sitting across from each other in a green vinyl booth at the Koffee Kup—an old aluminum landmark on the corner of Stark and Spruce Streets. Theo had never been before because her mom said the food was "a heart attack waiting to happen." The arched ceiling was painted turquoise, the walls were covered in orange and black ceramic tiles, and the floor had black-and-white checkerboard linoleum.

In addition to the chocolate malts, Hannah had ordered sweet-potato fries, which they were sharing.

"Dr. Sandeski wrote this book on how society and the stories we tell each other can create criminals and heroes. He weaves all this amazing stuff about culture and myth and the hero and the antihero into it. It's called **The Princess and the Elephant.** Have you read it?"

Theo shook her head.

"Oh my God!" Hannah's eyes were huge and her jaw dropped in this totally drama-girl way. "We'll go to my place right now. I'll give you a copy. You've got to read it! It's like the greatest book ever! Life-changing. I actually own two copies—hardcover and paperback."

So they walked back to Hannah's apartment,

which was in one of the big brick buildings across the street from the college. They were old row houses for the mill workers once upon a time and had been turned into apartments and condos, some of which were better kept than others. Hannah lived in a nice one, but even though it had been thoroughly renovated, the building smelled of old bricks and timbers. "The smell of history," Hannah said when Theo commented on it. "Or maybe it's the smell of ghosts. They say my building's haunted by one of the mill girls who used to live here, Anna Boroski. She was only sixteen and pregnant. She threw herself out the top-floor window." Theo shivered, and Hannah looked pleased with herself.

Hannah's apartment was small but tidy, decorated in pale colors. There were exposed wooden beams in the ceiling, some original brickwork in the living room. It looked like it had come straight from the pages of a Pottery Barn catalog. Pretty nice for a college student's place.

Hannah plucked a paperback copy of the book from her shelf and gave it to Theo. "You can keep it," she said.

Theo looked at the book in her hand, and the strange but captivating illustration on its cover. There was an elephant covered in jewels, but inside the body of the elephant was a beautiful young woman who appeared to be either sleeping or dead.

"What made you come to the library today?" Hannah asked.

"To see if I could find anything on P. T. Barnum. You know, the 'there's a sucker born every minute' guy?"

"But why today? Why that particular time?"

Theo shrugged.

"You know what I believe?" Hannah asked, stepping closer to Theo. "I think everything happens for a reason. I think we were meant to meet, Theo. I think fate led us both to the library this afternoon." She stroked Theo's wrist with her fingers. "Don't you feel it?" she asked.

Theo's pulsed raced. "Yes," she said. Her face flushed. She was breathing too fast, too hard. She tried to pull away from Hannah, but Hannah held tight.

"I'm going to ask you a question and I hope you say yes, but if you say no, I totally get it," Hannah said.

Theo nodded.

"Do you want to see what I think fate has in store for us?"

"Yes," Theo said, more of a breath than a word.

Hannah pulled Theo to her and kissed her. It was Theo's first kiss ever. The book slipped from Theo's fingers to the floor.

————

"So did you finish the book?" Hannah asked her the next week. They were in bed at Hannah's apartment. They'd been meeting almost every day. Going for coffee, browsing in the bookstore, eating sushi at Hannah's favorite restaurant, where there were huge fish tanks built into the walls. But they always ended up back at Hannah's apartment, in the bedroom.

It was a game they played sometimes, to see how long they could wait. How long they could put it off. It was a delicious sort of torture to be with Hannah out in the world eating, shopping, walking through the city, waiting for Hannah to lean in and whisper in her ear, "Let's go back to my place."

"Yes," Theo said. "I finished it. It was great. I really loved all the mythology and archetype stuff."

The truth was, she liked it fine, but thought the part about how each person was living her own myth, and it was the early events in our lives and our environment that shaped what this myth would be, was a little far-fetched. She didn't like the idea that people were all trapped inside some story created by events and circumstances they had little control over. She believed people were more powerful than that.

Hannah brushed a chunk of hair away from Theo's eyes. "Do you think it's true what he said, that we've all got good and evil inside? That we're all capable of doing something terrible?"

"Sure," Theo agreed. "Given the right circumstances. But ultimately, it comes down to choices, right? We have the power to say yes or no to a thing."

Hannah looked at her quizzically for a moment, then asked, "Have you ever done anything illegal?"

Theo laughed, running her fingers over the perfect curve of Hannah's shoulder. "What, like killed somebody or stole something? Um, that would be no."

Hannah stared down into the covers, disappointed, and Theo wished she hadn't been so quick to answer.

"Have **you**?" Theo asked, putting her lips right against Hannah's ear.

"Maybe," Hannah said.

"Tell me," she begged, voice low and full of awe. "You can tell me anything. Whatever it is, I won't care."

It was true. Hannah could say she had a body in the closet and Theo would find a way to help her get rid of it. Stupid, but true.

"Let's say I have a friend," Hannah said, still talking to the pillow beside her. "And maybe this friend gets me products to sell. Things people want. And maybe I sell them and make a little money."

Theo sat up. "What kinds of products?"

"He can get just about anything," Hannah said, still not looking at Theo. Smoothing the fabric of her pillow while she spoke. "Pills, heroin, weed. One time, he says he even got some of that new thing, the Devil's Snuff. There's a huge demand for that—you wouldn't believe what people are willing to pay! Some people, they don't even think it exists—but the people who've had it, they say it changed their lives. Gave them visions. Showed them things. You're never the same after you take it."

"So wait, you're a drug dealer?" Theo could hardly believe what she was hearing.

Suddenly, Hannah turned to look at Theo and smiled, ran her hands along Theo's naked back. "My friend and I, we were thinking it might be nice to branch out. You know, sell products to a different group. But it's not like I could go waltzing into a high school and set up shop, right? We'd need someone their age, someone who goes to school there, who blends in. Someone no one would ever suspect of being caught up in anything . . . illegal."

Theo had a sinking feeling then, that Hannah had planned their whole meeting, their whole relationship, around this one moment. Hannah had seen a lonely-looking high school girl and known that if she played her cards right, she could get Theo to do whatever she wanted. But the sinking feeling was followed by a realization—

Theo didn't care. She honestly didn't give a shit if she was being used. And even if she was, she knew what she and Hannah had was real. Theo felt it each time they were together; the magnetic pull, the desperate way they kissed as soon as they were first alone.

"I'm your girl," Theo told her, meaning it in every imaginable way. **Yours and yours alone.**

"I was hoping you'd say yes," Hannah said, pulling Theo to her. "It'll be perfect. You'll see. Maybe we can save our money and then, when we're sick of it all, we could go away together."

"Go where?" Theo asked, heart pounding.

"I don't know. Wherever. Just you and me."

And so it began. At first, Theo just sold a little weed—some nickel bags to the stoner kids at school. Then word got around. People started asking for other stuff—uppers, downers, acid, 'shrooms, painkillers, heroin. And the more orders she got, the more chances she had to meet up with Hannah, who took the money (always giving her a cut) and gave her more drugs. Theo never met the guy who gave Hannah the drugs, and when she asked about him, Hannah was vague and changed the subject.

"The less you know, the better off you are, right?" Hannah said. "It's really to protect you."

Each time she brought Hannah money, Theo imagined they were a little closer to going away together. She let herself imagine it: getting in

Hannah's little Volkswagen and just going, leaving everything else behind.

The longer the dealing went on, the more ballsy she got. Shit, she'd even sold speed to the overweight cafeteria lady, Mrs. Small. Theo had caught her crying in the bathroom once, and asked if there was anything she could do.

"No, thank you, Theodora. I'm just tired. Bone tired."

"I have something that will make you feel better, give you more energy. Heck, you might even lose weight." She'd given the woman two pills on the house, a little worried about the risk, but somehow knowing sweet Mrs. Small would never turn her in. And she was right—the next day, while Theo was in line for the world's crappiest lasagna, Mrs. Small had leaned in, whispered, "Can you get me more?" Theo had smiled. Oh, yes, she could. For a price, she could get anyone anything they needed.

Anything, that was, except for the coveted Devil's Snuff, which was like the Holy Grail of drugs, talked about only in reverent whispers. Theo wasn't even sure it existed. Kids asked her about it though. Could she get it? Had she ever tried it? Did she know anyone who had?

"I'd pay just about anything for one hit of the stuff," Luke had told her back when they were negotiating the coke deal and discussing what else she might be able to bring him in the future.

"You ever get your hands on some, call me first and name your price."

———

At 3:45, she's outside Hannah's brick apartment building, her thumb on the buzzer, and over the intercom comes Hannah's voice, "Is that you, Theo?"

Yes, yes, yes.

She loves the way Hannah says her name, making it sound like music.

Another buzz and the door clicks open and Theo races up the steps. Hannah's waiting in the open doorway, pulls Theo in, and they kiss. Theo takes off the scarf, wraps it around Hannah's neck. "I made this for you," she says, the words fast and breathy as Hannah pulls Theo's school blazer off and starts working at the buttons of her crisp white shirt.

"It's beautiful," Hannah says, guiding Theo to the bedroom. "Did it go okay today? Did the kid give you the money?"

Theo nods. "It went perfectly."

Later, when they're together in bed, Hannah coos, "I can't believe you made this for me!" as she drapes the scarf around her neck. "It's so soft!" It's the only thing Hannah has on, and it looks so perfect that Theo's throat feels tight. Hannah's skin is ivory white with a smattering of freckles. Theo likes to run her fingers from one freckle to another, inventing shapes, constellations, a whole universe of stories over Hannah's skin. The story of who she is, the little girl she used to be, the old woman she'll one day become—Theo wants to know all of it, every facet of Hannah.

"It's merino and alpaca," Theo tells her, remembering how long she'd spent in the knitting store downtown trying to pick out the perfect yarn.

"No one's ever knitted anything for me," Hannah says, running her fingers over the nubbly purple scarf.

Theo smiles and bites her lip shyly. "Not even a grandma or a dowdy old aunt?" she asks.

Hannah shakes her head, pulls the scarf around her tighter, covering her mouth and nose so that only her eyes are showing.

There's so much more Theo wants to say: **Stay with me and I'll knit you anything you'd like—sweaters, hats, mittens in thick yarn. You will never be cold.** But Theo's not an idiot—she knows how corny and ridiculous that would sound, and she's always afraid of appearing like a little kid to Hannah, who is three years older and in college.

"So it really went okay today? With the dropoff and pickup?"

"No problem at all. The guy's family is loaded. He's kind of an asshole, but he's really popular—gets good grades, the teachers all love him. No one would ever suspect that I just sold him two ounces of coke."

"So where is it? The money? Can I see?"

"Sure." Theo slides out of bed, goes to get her satchel. Her little purse is there on the floor, beside the pile of her clothes, the school uniform lying in a strange puddle, as if the person inside had suddenly vanished.

No satchel.

Theo's skin prickles. She'd had it when she came in, right? She closes her eyes, goes back in her mind.

"Oh God," she says, heart falling heavily into her stomach with a hard thud.

"What is it?" Hannah asks.

Fuck. Fuck. Fuck. The last time she'd seen her satchel was when she'd set it down on the Fire Girl's car. Then, she'd seen the girl pop the little ball of flames into her mouth, and that guy had come swinging his backpack at all of them, yelling, chasing them off.

She'd left it on the hood of the car. The bag with her books (including Hannah's copy of **The Princess and the Elephant,** which Theo carried with her everywhere), baggie of assorted pills, and two thousand bucks in an envelope.

How could she be so fucking stupid?

"I umm . . ." she stammers, not wanting Hannah to know what a complete fuckup she is. "I left my bag at school."

"What? With all the money in it?"

"I know, I know. Dumb. Don't worry, though, it's in my locker. It's just that I was in such a hurry to get out of there, to come see you, that I forgot all about it." She gives Hannah a weak, see-how-smitten-I-am smile.

Hannah looks ghostly pale. Even her freckles have faded. "But the money . . ."

"It's safe. It's in my locker."

"Can you go get it now?"

Theo thinks for a second, remembers the tall kid swinging his backpack, the Fire Girl with her knife, then shakes her head. "School's all locked up. I'll go get it and bring it back here first thing tomorrow."

"But my friend, he's coming tonight. I told him I'd have it."

Theo bites her lip. "Tell him the guy didn't have the money yet. But he's gonna have it tomorrow."

There's the sound of a key in a lock and the front door opening. "Babe?" a man calls.

Theo is still naked, standing over her clothes. She looks at Hannah, whose eyes are frantic as she shakes her head and puts a finger over her lips.

"You're early," Hannah calls out, then gestures at the closet. "Hide," she whisper-shouts. "Hurry!"

Theo scoops up her clothes, heart hammering. Hannah throws the scarf, and Theo takes that, too. She gets into the closet, shutting the door behind her just as the one to the bedroom swings open. The closet is dark and smells like Hannah. Theo crouches on a pile of shoes while blouses on hangers brush against her face. She tries to slow her breathing as she hears the man enter the room.

"What are you doing?" the man asks.

"Taking a nap," Hannah says.

"Without clothes?"

"I was hot."

"I'll say you're hot. Smoking hot. Come here," the man says, his voice low. There's the sound of kissing. Theo swallows hard, her eyes stinging, her nails digging into her palms.

Who the fuck is this guy?

Theo listens, wishing she couldn't hear. Wishing there was a back door to the closet, a window, anything.

The man whispers something Theo can't hear. She has never wanted to kill anyone so bad in her whole life.

If she had a knife like the Fire Girl, she just might.

"Jeremy, stop," Hannah says. "I'm not really in the mood."

"You sure look like you're in the mood."

"Looks can be deceiving."

There is the rustle of covers. "You feel like you're in the mood," the man named Jeremy says, voice low.

"Quit it," Hannah says. "Seriously."

More rearranging of bodies. The squeaking of bedsprings. Then a lighter being flicked. Theo smells the sharp tang of cigarette smoke.

"So did the little altar girl bring the cash?"

"Not yet. She called to say the guy couldn't come up with all the money today. But he promised he'd have it tomorrow. First thing."

"I don't like it. I don't like her walking around with all that coke."

"It's fine, Jeremy."

"How do you know she's not gonna bolt on us? Sell it and run?"

"She won't."

"Ahh, that's right. Because the poor little girl is in love with you, right? She's got it so bad it hurts. How could I forget?"

"Jeremy, don't."

"You're a heartbreaker, Hannah, you know that? Shame on you, really. Stringing the poor girl along just to make a few extra bucks."

Theo digs her nails more deeply into her palms.

"That's not how it is," Hannah says.

"You know, I get a hard-on just thinking about how bad that girl must want you."

There's another squeal of creaking bedsprings, more kissing, then the unmistakable sound of a zipper being unzipped.

Theo covers her ears. Clamps her eyes shut. Please, God, no. Don't let them start fucking. She can't bear it. She'll definitely have to kill him then. Maybe she'll kill both of them. Bash their stupid heads together again and again until they're bloody mush.

"Wait, Jeremy," Hannah coos. "Let's do this right. How about you go out and pick us up a nice bottle of Chablis? You know how a little wine relaxes me, right?"

"Only if you promise to stay just like that, waiting there in bed for me."

"Promise," she says.

"I'll be back in a flash," he says, footsteps hurrying out of the room. Theo waits for the sound of the front door being opened, then closed. The closet door swings open.

"You have to go," Hannah insists. "Before he comes back."

Theo says nothing and keeps her head down, not wanting to even look at Hannah. She pulls on her tights and skirt, her bra, white shirt, and blazer. Pulls on her boots but doesn't bother to lace them. She wraps the scarf around her neck tightly, almost choking herself, then hurries out of the room.

"Theo?" Hannah calls.

Theo stops, turns, and looks at Hannah. Hannah looks all wrong, older, her eyes not as blue; she looks like someone Theo hardly knows.

"I'm sorry," Hannah says.

Theo turns and makes her way to the door, legs feeling like rubber, an acid taste in her mouth.

"Theo?" Hannah calls once more.

Theo stops, waiting. Hoping. Hoping that Hannah will tell her it's all a mistake, will say, **Fuck Jeremy, he doesn't mean shit, let's you and I run away, let's go, right now.**

But that's not what Hannah says.

"You'll bring the money tomorrow? First thing?"

"Of course," Theo says, letting herself out.

————

Theo walks the streets for nearly two hours, then goes back to the diner where she and Hannah had sat together that first day, telling each other their bad habits (Theo confessed that she regularly cheated on tests but that her worst bad habit was getting crushes on the wrong people. She'd chosen the word **people** carefully, to make Hannah wonder).

Theo sits down in one of the green booths, orders a coffee. She flips through the songs on the jukebox, thinking about the songs Hannah might like: jazzy ballads, old blues, and country. She stops herself. Doesn't matter what Hannah would want to hear because Hannah's not here. Hannah's back at home fucking Jeremy.

Theo takes out her cell, checks for messages and texts, but there's only one, from her mom saying she's working late and can't pick up anything for supper. Theo texts her mom back: **No worries. I'm at the library studying for a test. I'll grab a sandwich on my way home.**

She knows what she has to do. She'll go back to the Fire Girl's car, find a way to get her bag back. She just prays that the girl and guy haven't hit the road with their new windfall.

She gulps down the rest of her sour coffee and walks toward the school. It's dark now and she keeps to the shadows. She'll get the bag and bring the money right to Hannah, dump it outside her door. No note. No sweet good-byes. Just one last fuck off and farewell. That will be that. She'll never talk to her again.

Theo sees it so clearly now, what an idiot she's been. She'd always half-suspected, of course, but it's so much worse knowing this dickhead Jeremy had been in on it. She imagines Hannah and Jeremy in bed together now, mocking her, laughing at her, calling her the little altar girl—so fucking clueless. So fucking pitiful. Their own cash cow. Ka-ching.

She's swallowing hard, trying not to cry, focusing her mind on what needs to be done. She puts one foot in front of the other, moving down the sidewalk, a girl on a mission.

Soon, she sees the big stone church, the school, and the vacant lot surrounded by crumbling brick walls across the street. The church and school are all lit up like something out of a movie set, while the lot is all darkness and shadows. She can just make out the outline of the walls, a pile of tires visible through an opening.

She creeps up slowly, finds a passage through the wall, stepping around piles of rubble, eyes on the car, looking for movement, listening for voices, but there's nothing. Her feet crunch on pebbles, broken brick, bits of glass before she reaches the clumps of weeds. Nature is trying to reclaim the space but not succeeding because the ground's no good; even the weeds are stunted.

Once she's right up against the car, she crouches down. Maybe they did look inside the bag; maybe they found the money and took off on the mother of all benders, unable to imagine their luck.

But no. Peering through the rear window, she sees that the Fire Girl and the boy are sleeping on the backseat, arms wrapped around each other, bodies under a thick pile of covers. Theo searches for her satchel but doesn't see it. She thinks of the Fire Girl's knife, imagines that'll be the first thing she goes for if she wakes up and catches Theo spying. And then there's the boy and his backpack. Who knows what weapons he has stashed in there.

She moves around to the front of the car, looking through the cracked windshield. There's nothing on the two front seats. She spots a random assortment of stuff on the dashboard—rusted metal gears, a broken glass bottle, dried flowers, a pair of goggles. But no satchel. The Fire Girl shifts, moans. Theo drops to the ground and holds her breath.

Shit.

After a minute, she dares to peek back in and sees that the Fire Girl is motionless again. Best not to push her luck.

Tomorrow. She'll come back first thing tomorrow, before the first bell even rings. Maybe the boy will be gone then. She'll have a better chance with the Fire Girl without him. She can offer the girl a reward of some sort if she has to. Give her some pills or whatever she wants on the house. Or maybe she'll just tell the Fire Girl the truth: **Without that bag, I'm royally fucked.** She imagines telling her the whole story, of how she met Hannah, was lied to and led on. She'll tell her that all she wants is to hand over the cash and cut all ties. She thinks that the Fire Girl just might understand. Sometimes life is about bad choices, downright shitty choices.

Theo pushes off, scampers away from the car

toward an opening in the wall that leads to the alley between the auto parts store and an abandoned bakery. She sees a hint of movement. An animal?

No, too big for an animal.

There's a figure in the alley: a person standing in the shadows, back to the wall, watching. Staring right at her. She can't make out any details— just the palest flash of a face as it ducks back into the shadows and the outline of a long coat.

Theo freezes, then turns on her heel and runs back across the lot, bounding over a section of low brick wall as she heads toward the church, with its brightly lit entryway. The crunch of her footsteps seems loud enough to wake the Fire Girl and her boyfriend, but she grits her teeth and keeps going. She doesn't risk a look back until she's on the sidewalk. Nothing. Whoever it is seems to have disappeared—maybe she scared him as much as he scared her. The Fire Girl's car is as still as ever. Theo starts jogging toward Summer Street, relieved to know her apartment is only minutes away.

Necco

〰〰〰

Necco is dreaming of her father. Of his workshop, the little aluminum-walled shed in the backyard that was one of her favorite places on earth despite being dark and airless.

Daddy is at his workbench, sitting amid a chaotic assortment of springs, gears, and scraps of metal and wood. The smell in here is comforting: grease, rust, and the smoke from Daddy's pipe.

One of Daddy's best creations flies in circles above them: a little mechanical bat with leather wings, tethered to the ceiling with a strand of wire. Round and round it goes, gears ticking like a clock, wings beating. Necco always wished she could clip the string and let the bat fly off into the night.

Her father's most frightening invention is laid

out on the worktable, covered in a white canvas tarp like a corpse. But he's not working on this machine now. Something else has his attention.

"What are you working on?" Necco asks.

The machine under the tarp gives a twitch, then begins to move with a slight rise and fall, as if it's breathing. She hears the dull pop and crackle of static.

She wants to run but instead forces herself to move forward, sliding one foot in front of the other, like she's walking on ice, as she comes up behind her father. He's wearing his leather apron, denim work shirt, and stained khaki pants. His right hand is visible on the bench: he's holding a large sewing needle. He's got something cupped in his left hand. Something she can't see yet.

"Daddy?" she says, placing her hand lightly on his back.

He turns to face her, and she tries to scream but no sound comes.

His left eye has been replaced with a thick, telescoping monocle that is stitched into the socket with heavy black thread, blood seeping down his cheek.

He holds out his left hand, opens his palm, and his eyeball is there—a smooth orb with a familiar brown iris—looking up at her.

"A way to keep an eye on you," he tells her.

———

Necco wakes, heart pounding, the sunlight hitting her face. It comes streaming through the Pontiac's cracked windshield, so bright it feels as if it's pulsating and flickering like a nearby fire. Necco lies there a minute, letting it warm her, letting the terrible dream images fade away. She hears the kids across the street hurrying to school. The church bell is ringing. **Ding dong. Ding dong.**

She's listening to the bells, thinking about the church and how she's never been inside, when something silly comes back to her in a flash: a metal bottle opener with a magnet on the back stuck on a glossy white refrigerator. They used it to open cans of juice, bottles of orange pop and Hires root beer, which was Errol's favorite. Mama called the opener a church key, which always seemed like a funny thing. Like church was a big bottle waiting to be pried open.

Then Necco remembers the key around Hermes's neck. The mysterious thing he has to show her. And she gets nervous, the hairs all over her body standing up—she doesn't like surprises. But maybe this will be a good kind of surprise. Maybe it's true what Hermes promised, that everything is going to be okay. She rolls over to wake the old sleepyhead up so he'll take her to see whatever this big secret thing is.

The scream escapes before she can help it. It's a shriek really, high pitched and crazy sounding.

A sound that can't possibly be coming from her. She's not a girl who screams.

Hermes is lying on his back, waxy and still like a piece of fake fruit. His face is covered in blood—its stickiness has soaked his shirt, the blankets, even her own clothes.

A pink knitting needle sticks out of his left eye.

Necco closes her eyes and feels water cover her in one great, powerful wave, making everything dark and cold, filling her mouth and lungs. Her screaming still sounds far off and dull. A voice underwater. A drowning sound.

Then there are other sounds. The kids are coming, the nuns and teachers, too. They surround the car, peer in through the windows like they're looking into an aquarium.

Their mouths move, and at first she can't understand what they're saying. Can't hear them above her own frantic screaming.

At last, the words tumble through.

"He's dead! She's killed him."

Someone else screams. Someone makes a retching, puking sound. One of the nuns starts to pray.

"That's one of the knitting needles Theo gave her yesterday," chirps a boy with glasses. "She murdered him with it! I always knew she was dangerous."

Someone else says the police are on their way.

Mama said never trust the Jujubes. Never tell them anything. If they come after you, run.

They tried to find Necco after Mama died. They asked around. Came to the little shack under the bridge where she and Mama camped out in nice weather and went through all their things. They questioned the other Fire Eaters. Necco watched them from the bank across the river. She watched them and knew she could never go back to the little house they'd built from old shipping pallets and driftwood. She also couldn't chance going back to their other home, the Winter House. She spent a few weeks going from place to place, sleeping under bridges, in old drainage tunnels. Then she met Hermes.

She can't let the Jujubes find her. Not now. Not like this. They'll haul her off to jail without even asking any questions. **Caught red-handed,** they'll say, and there she'll be, fingers sticky with blood, a girl no one would ever believe.

Necco takes in a breath, feels herself start to move in slow motion, all awkward and jerky, like her body's just a puppet and she's at the controls. She finds Hermes's backpack on the floor of the car, tucks Promise the doll inside. Remembers how the doll used to open and close her eyes and turn her head before the gears rusted. Now, she's got one eye open, one closed. Her face is dirty, her hair matted. Necco hears sirens in the distance, and moves faster. She grabs her gold locket with the photo of little-boy Daddy dressed as Robin Hood, a bow in his hands, a thick belt around his waist, his outfit brown and green like a tree. She pulls on her boots, reaches for her blade, and without looking at his face, carefully slices the string around Hermes's neck, pocketing the key.

She climbs up to the front seat, reaching under to grab the girl's satchel with the money and pills, and stuffs it into the backpack as well.

Knife in hand, she crawls out of the Pontiac, the kids around her screaming, scattering.

"Oh my God, she's got her knife!"

Some of them run back across the street, stand in the shadow of the church. Some just back away slowly, eyes still locked on the Fire Girl. They've never seen anything like this in their lives. A real-life monster in their midst.

She's got blood on her hands, down her front. It even soaks the back of her shirt, making it stick to her skin. She smells its sweet, iron scent and thinks she might be sick. She takes another deep breath.

The sirens are closer now. The Jujubes will be here soon.

Heart pounding, she shoulders the heavy black backpack and starts to run. She thinks they will try to stop her, but the kids and nuns fall back, away from her, parting like the sea for Moses.

Her legs are fast as she sprints, through an opening in the ruined brick wall, and down the alley between the auto parts store and empty bakery with busted windows. She zigzags between buildings, keeping to alleys and empty one-way streets, slipping through fences, sliding between dumpsters and tractor trailers pulled up to loading docks with early morning deliveries.

She cuts through the urine-soaked alley behind the Mill City Bar, and dodges the rusted, parted-out lawn mowers and snowblowers that are lined up against the crumbling brick walls of the small engine repair shop. She knows Burntown's secret shortcuts, its shadowy forgotten places that college students, nine-to-fivers, and comfortable families who walk these streets never see. There are two cities: hers and theirs, and she knows how to walk them both.

She makes it to Orange Grove Avenue (silly name, far too cold here for an orange tree to survive), drops over the low ledge on the east side, and takes the drainage tunnel under the street until, finally, she comes out down by the river.

There's plenty of cover here: bushes, scraggly trees, brambles. Other than the park across the river, it's the largest stretch of wild land in the city. There are bent apple trees with tangled branches, red and black raspberry bushes, cattails with roots that taste delicious roasted in the fire, fiddlehead ferns to pick each spring, wild onions with greens for salad and bulbs for soup, daylilies with orange flowers you can eat and shoots you can cook like asparagus, and sumac bushes with clumps of berries like fluffy torches that you can soak in water to make pink lemonade. One time, Necco caught a bear drinking down here. An actual black bear in the heart of the city. It was just after Mama died, and Necco wished more than anything that Mama had been there to see it.

Now, she rests under a gnarled tree with branches that brush the ground. She listens to the sirens, which are farther and farther away. She catches her breath, then pushes off again, making her way upriver, staying under cover.

Her mama taught her well.

If there is one thing Necco is good at, it's running.

Theo

~~~~~~

Theo's mom has already left the apartment by the time Theo rolls out of bed, gets herself dressed, and makes her way downstairs. Her mom works at the Ashford Bank and Trust. She was recently promoted to branch manager, which as far as Theo can tell just means she has to get there half an hour earlier every morning and stay late every night. Apparently, being obliged to work harder than ever is her reward for working hard.

There are two wrapped Pop-Tarts (unfrosted blueberry, of course) on the counter next to an empty coffee mug, and a note on the dry-erase board on the fridge: **One way or another I WILL be home for supper. Chinese takeout sound good? See you tonight, Love, Mom.**

A night at home with Mom and Chinese takeout sounds perfect. Just what she'll need to try to forget about everything with Hannah. And by then, she'll be done with the whole mess. She will curl up on the couch, eat shrimp lo mein, and tell Mom about how great school is going. She'll share how excited she is for college next year (she's already been accepted into Two Rivers and isn't even considering anyplace else because she's getting a huge grant for being a low-income student from Ashford) and all the other happy horseshit Mom loves to hear. It's always been a little too easy to play the good girl with Mom— the girl who gets straight A's, goes to church on Sunday, and spends her spare time reading, studying, and knitting. The girl whom boys might ask out sometimes, but who always says thanks, but no. "You'll find the right young man, eventually," Mom tells her. Her sweet, well-meaning mom with her sensible haircut and cheap, bank-friendly polyester pantsuits that are always pilling. "Maybe when you go to college."

"Maybe," Theo says, smiling and nodding. Sometimes she feels like an impostor in her own life.

Theo pours the lukewarm remains of the coffee into the cup Mom left for her, gulps it down, tosses a foil-wrapped package of Pop-Tarts into her purse, and heads out the door to get the satchel before the first bell rings. She walks briskly down Summer Street. The roads are crowded with commuters, delivery vans, buses, a few bicycles. No one looks anyone else in the eye. Everyone seems harried and unhappy. A kid zips by on a skateboard, his music so loud she can hear it pulsing through his headphones. An old woman pushes a shopping cart full of her worldly possessions along the shoulder of the road, oblivious to the cars beeping at her. She walks with a limp, using the shopping cart like a walker.

Theo's nearly there now, just four blocks away, when the phone vibrates in her blazer pocket. She pulls it out, knowing who it will be, telling herself she shouldn't answer. But Hannah's called twelve times since last night, leaving messages that say, **I need to talk to you, please call me back.** She sounds a little more desperate each time.

Good. Let her get good and desperate. Bitch.

Theo looks at her watch. Shit. Even if things go well with the Fire Girl and she gets the bag without a hitch, there's no time to get all the way to Hannah's and back before first period. She'll have to ditch Chemistry, her most difficult but also her favorite class. It'll be okay, though. Mr. McKinnon writes comments like **Theo is the kind of student a science teacher dreams of . . .** on her report card. She'll tell him she had a migraine, offer to stay after school to make up the lab work.

With shaking fingers, she pulls the pack of cigarettes from her purse and lights one. She tries to put Hannah out of her mind and concentrate on how she'll get the satchel back from the Fire Girl. She decides honesty might work best. She's sure the girl looked through it and found the money. "It's not really mine," Theo will tell her. "It belongs to this guy. If I don't give it to him, I don't know what he'll do."

Surely the Fire Girl will understand. She knows about danger. About the terrible mistakes people make. Theo got that just in the five minutes of being around her yesterday.

She turns the corner onto Church Street, and her smoky breath catches in her throat, the cigarette falls from her fingers.

There are half a dozen police cars, vans, even cops on bicycles. There's a news truck with a satellite dish, an ambulance, and a horde of people gathered along the edge of the street.

She moves forward, faster now. At first, she thinks something has happened at the school. A shooting maybe, some misfit kid gone wacko—but why so early, before the school day even starts? Then, she sees the yellow crime scene tape blocking off the vacant lot across the street. It's stretched across what remains of the old brick walls. She's almost there now, and she peers over a low pile of rubble along Church Street and sees that the Fire Girl's car is being searched by two men in suits with rubber gloves on.

No, she thinks, shaking her head, as if that will stop all this from happening. **No, no, no.**

"Theo." She feels a strong hand clasp her arm and turns to see Luke. He's pale and sweaty, and he's taken off his school tie and unbuttoned his shirt.

"What's going on?" she asks, her eyes on the car, the swarm of cops around it. Is that blood smeared across the open door?

"You're not going to fucking believe this! The Fire Girl, she fucking **stabbed** that guy who chased us away yesterday. She killed him and took off through the alley."

"No way!" Theo remembers seeing them sleeping tangled together under the covers.

"I saw it," Luke says, voice shaking. "I got here early. She was screaming—a bunch of us ran over. God, Theo, there was so much blood." Luke lowers his voice. "The cops are asking about you."

"Me?" she asks, but she knows why. The bag, of course. The cops had found her bag in the car. And it had her books, her student ID, a baggie of drugs, and all that cash.

Theo scans the scene, wondering which way she should go, which way has the fewest cops. She won't run, that would just draw attention. She'll walk away calmly. And go where? To Hannah? No way. Hannah's the last person who could help her now—when she heard the cops had the money she'd freak the fuck out.

"You can't say anything about how I was the one who brought you here yesterday, okay?" Luke is still talking, fast and quiet. "Not a word about anything that happened on our way over here yesterday." Poor Luke with his scholarship to Yale and perfect life that might all be ruined if anyone found out he'd just bought two thousand bucks' worth of blow. And, as usual, thinking only of himself when some guy had been murdered.

Murdered.

She still can't believe it. She thinks of the knife strapped to the Fire Girl's boot, a good six inches of blade. But why? What had he done to deserve it?

"Of course I won't," she snaps at Luke, turning from him, eyes on the sidewalk as she starts to cross the street.

She'll keep walking toward the school, then go around to the back, head south on Sycamore Street, and zigzag her way back home. She'll quickly gather up whatever cash she can find, pack a bag, and go. And where, exactly, are you gonna go? she asks herself. It's not like she has friends and relatives who would take her in, offer to hide her. She's got no one. Her mom. And Hannah—well, she used to have Hannah. That's really it.

She remembers the woman limping along with a shopping cart full of dirty clothes, an old blanket, and other treasures. She thinks of the Fire Girl—of what her life might have been like before she came to live in the car, what path might have brought her to that vacant lot. Was that Theo's future?

"Theodora?" a man's voice calls out behind her. "Theodora Sweeney?"

No! Her heart hammers in her ears. Running will make her look guilty, and she'd never get away—there are uniformed cops ahead of her on both sides of the street.

Slowly, she turns.

One of the men in suits is walking toward her. He's got short dark hair and big square Clark Kent glasses.

"Are you Theodora? One of the kids over there, he said that's you."

"Yes," Theo says. Caught. She's been caught. The whole thing feels so anticlimactic—no big chase, no drama. Just one question: **Are you Theodora?**

"I'm Detective Sparks. I have a few questions for you."

He's got a little notebook out and is holding a pen.

Theo nods. Her face is burning, her palms damp with sweat.

"Do you know the girl who's been staying in that old car?"

Theo shakes her head. "Not really. People call her the Fire Girl. I just met her for the first time yesterday."

"So you'd never talked to her before yesterday?"

"No."

"But you'd seen her around?"

"Sure. We all did. She lives in the car. She's been there since the school year started."

"Do you know where she came from? Anything about her at all?"

Theo shakes her head.

"And the young man who sometimes stayed with her? Did you ever meet him?"

"Not technically. He chased us off yesterday. When we were talking to her."

"What were you talking to her about?"

Theo's face burns. "I . . . if you bring her a gift, she'll show you her trick. She eats fire."

He scribbles something in his book.

"So you brought her a gift?"

"Yes. I mean I gave her some candy. And knitting needles and a little ball of yarn. It was all stupid really, but I was curious. I'd heard so many people talk about her, I wanted to meet her myself. I wanted to see the trick. And really, it was pretty cool. She had this ball of fire in her hand, then she just opened her mouth and popped it in . . ." She trails off lamely.

"Can you describe the knitting needles and yarn?"

The question is so unexpected, it takes Theo a second to regain her bearings. "Sure. Yeah. The yarn was dark purple, kettle-dyed—merino and alpaca. And the needles, they were pink aluminum. Size eight."

The detective nods. "Is there anything else you can tell me about the girl—anything you might have heard or seen?"

"I don't think so."

"And you've never heard her real name? She didn't tell you?"

"She didn't say a word. People say she can't talk . . . she's mute or something. They say her throat's all burned and scarred up from eating fire?" She's babbling now, passing on gossip.

"The last time you saw her was yesterday afternoon?" He looks right into her eyes, and she feels her throat tighten. She remembers seeing the Fire Girl and the boy last night, spooning. How peaceful they'd looked, his arm wrapped tight around her.

"Yes," she says, but she's sure he knows she's lying.

"And what time would you say that was?" he asks.

"Right after school. Three o'clock."

He nods. "I'm going to have to ask you to come down to the station later. You can bring your parents."

"Am I . . . am I going to be arrested?" she

asks. Her mother will be so disappointed, feel so guilty, think, **If I'd only been home more, if I'd been a better mother.**

"Arrested?" He looks amused. "Of course not! I'll just be asking you the same questions I asked now, only we'll be taping it."

"I don't understand," Theo says.

"It seems that one of your knitting needles was used in a crime."

"One of the **knitting needles**?"

"I'm afraid I can't say any more." He flips back to the previous page of his notebook. "The school has your address as Six Vine Street, Apartment 3B. And your phone number is 555-2949. Is that information correct?"

"Yes."

"Good. I'll be in touch soon to set up a time."

"Okay," Theo says, feeling numb all over.

"Thank you for your time," the detective says. He turns his back on her, heads back toward the crowd in the vacant lot. She stands frozen for a moment, then goes up the steps and into school, because suddenly that seems like the safest place she knows.

Necco

~~~~

At last, Necco reaches the spot where she and Mama used to bathe, right under the old bridge Mama jumped from.

In the days after her mama's death, Necco would visit this place, sit on the shore, gazing up at the Steel Bridge, picturing her mama there, perched on the edge like a great bird, and wonder why.

Why, Mama? Why?

And then, she'd replay their final moments together over and over, a loop of tape running through her brain, desperately trying to figure out what she could have done differently, how she might have saved her mother.

Necco had gone out early that last morning collecting cans and bottles, and found a good haul. Necco was the one who made and held on to their money, who figured out when supplies needed replenishing, when it was time to get more cash, shoplift another jar of coffee or box of sugar. Necco was the one who made sure they had enough food to eat. Mama no longer concerned herself with trivial things like food and water and where the next meal might come from. Anytime Necco expressed concern over their situation, Mama would say, "The Great Mother will provide." And Necco would secretly think, **Great Mother, my ass,** and go dumpster diving or on a shoplifting mission.

Necco and her mother ate well on what other people threw away: day-old bagels, wilted vegetables, soups from dented cans, bruised fruit. They stocked the pantry in the Winter House with crushed boxes of tea, ripped bags of flour and sugar, and cereal that was past its expiration date. They filled water bottles from sinks in public bathrooms and drinking fountains.

That last morning, Necco returned to the Winter House with over fifteen dollars from collecting bottles and cans and thought she'd treat Mama to a trip to her favorite diner, the Koffee Kup, where you could get a bottomless cup for one dollar. If they got one of the friendlier waitresses, they'd be a given a complimentary basket of rolls that came with little packets of jam and marmalade. Mama loved marmalade. They'd sit in a green vinyl booth, mix plenty of cream and sugar into their coffee, play the old-fashioned jukebox on the table. Mama knew all the songs, hummed along, remembering happier times.

But when Necco got home, she found Mama packing up their things.

"What's going on?" Necco asked.

"I thought we'd move down to the river today. Back to camp." Mama was pinballing around, throwing things in boxes and bags with no system whatsoever.

The Fire Eaters all scattered in the cold months, seeking refuge in drainage tunnels, abandoned buildings, anyplace out of the cold. Then once the snow melted and the trees began to get the faintest hint of green, they'd all meet back at the camp under the Blachly Bridge. But the trees were still bare and there were determined patches of snow in the shadowy places.

"But isn't it a little too early?" Necco asked. "The nights are still cold. And Miss Abigail and the others aren't back yet."

"I think it would do us good to be out in the fresh air again," Mama said. "We've been cooped up too long. The others will be back soon. And we can get things all tidied up for them."

The truth was, Necco missed the camaraderie of the other women, Miss Stella especially. Necco missed her walks with Miss Stella into the woods, fields, vacant lots, and down to marshy places along the river's edge to hunt for wild edibles.

"Why don't you bring this first load over?" Mama said. "Get a good fire going and we'll make fry bread. Get the big pot cleaned out, too, and start some baked beans. We'll have a real homecoming celebration. The others will smell the food and be back at camp in no time."

Necco agreed, loading up with supplies, including dried beans, brown sugar, molasses, and canned tomatoes, so she could start cooking.

"I'll be there in a little while," Mama promised.

But she never came.

———

Necco slips off the pack, removes her heavy leather boots, and eases herself, fully clothed, into the muddy river. The coldness startles her. The water is shallow here, and the bottom is sandy, easy on the feet, but you still have to watch for broken glass, rusted metal. She crouches down low, swishing herself around, rinsing the blood off her black pants and gray tunic—it was the only outfit she'd been comfortable in lately, as her body slowly grew out of her other clothes.

When she was a kid, back before the Great Flood, Necco loved to swim. Now she can't stand being in the water. She gets panicky if she's in water that's much above her knees. She'll get into the river to rinse off, but she never lingers.

She feels the icy current rippling around her, making her clothes clean. She reaches down and picks up fistfuls of sand and uses the grit to scrub away the stains. The brown water swirls, turns a murky red around her, and she thinks it's a good thing there aren't any sharks here. No fish at all. Not even a frog. The water's too polluted. There's an old paper mill upstream, and you can see the stinking, foamy, white sludge they dump right into the water.

Necco decides she needs to get in and out quick, not just because of the icy cold but because whatever's in this water can't be good for the little tadpole inside her.

She leans back her head to rinse her hair and looks up at the peeling green paint of the metal bridge frame, the enormous concrete supports holding it. She thinks of the lives going on up above, how the cars passing have no idea she's down here, in the underworld of Ashford. Then, a thought passes through her, one so unsettling, she pushes it away nearly as soon as she registers it. What if her mother had been right? What if there really was a bad man, Snake Eyes, after them? What if that's who got Hermes?

No, she tells herself. Impossible. She isn't going to let her thoughts turn crazy. She's going to stick to facts.

The tires of the cars above make a singing sound on the metal bridge each time they pass.

The Singing Bridge, Mama called it, not just because of the noise the cars make but because of the birds. Pigeons roost there, hundreds of them, thousands maybe, cooing gently—not a song exactly, but more a noise of contentment. When Necco looks up and squints, sees all those pigeons moving along the supports, it almost seems as though the bridge itself is a living, breathing, cooing thing.

Still, the metal supports underneath are slick with white pigeon shit. Guano, Mama called it. She had a way of making even shit seem exotic.

"Mama," Necco says, ears underwater, hearing only the rushing river. She knows it's useless to talk to the dead—this is best left to the Fire Eaters, with their heads clouded by snuff—but finds comfort in it anyway. "I wish you could tell me what to do next."

She remembers the machine her father built, Edison's Telephone to the Dead. She hasn't allowed herself to think of it, but now, she lets the memories come back. Once, when she was ten or eleven, she snuck down to her daddy's workshop in the middle of the night and turned it on, even though she wasn't allowed in the workshop when Daddy wasn't there and couldn't imagine the trouble she'd get into if she were caught. But she felt drawn there. She'd asked questions about the machine, begged her father to turn it on for her, just once, so she could see how it worked. But he only shook his head, said no in a way that told her it was never going to happen.

Could it really be possible? she had wondered. To talk to the dead?

She even knew just who she wanted to talk to: her grandmother Elizabeth, whom she had never seen except for in pictures.

Guided only by moonlight, she crept down to the workshop, stood in darkness until her eyes adjusted, then pulled back the tarp that covered the machine. She flipped the switches, watched the tubes glow, listened to static coming through the speaker. Then, she picked up the receiver that looked like an old-fashioned telephone in black-and-white movies, and spoke into it hesitantly. "Grandma? Elizabeth Sandeski? Are you there?"

She wasn't sure how this was supposed to work—did you just ask for a specific person?

"It's me, Eva. Miles's daughter. You've never met me, but I think about you all the time. I wonder about you. Are you there, Grandma? Please say yes." She whispered the words, embarrassed, even though she was alone.

Sounds rippled through the crackling. A steady ticking, like the second hand of a clock. A pulsing, drumlike beat, then laughter. Like hundreds of people were laughing at her. Then, she heard her name.

"Eva," a woman said, her voice far off, echoey.

Necco jerked back, every muscle in her body tight and thrumming. The old plastic receiver fell out of her hand. Heart hammering, she picked it back up, needing to use two hands because she was shaking so bad.

"Yes! Is that you, Grandma?"

"Yes," fainter this time.

"I'm sorry I never met you," she blurted. "Sorry about the accident."

"No accident," the voice said, then, there was something more, but it was too full of static to make out.

Necco fiddled with the dials, tried to get the voice back.

"Grandma!" she cried, crouching down, placing her ear against the speaker.

"What is it you want?" a man's voice asked, as crisp and clear as if there was an actual tiny man stuck inside the box. Maybe this was her grandfather, the jazz musician. Or her uncle Lloyd, maybe. She'd seen lots of pictures of him, even a few of him holding her. Uncle Lloyd had died when a fire broke out at his garage. Aunt Judith and their son, Edward, moved away and Necco never saw them again. She had no real memories of any of them as flesh-and-blood people; to her, they were only pictures in the photo albums on their living room shelves.

"Who is this?" she asked.

The voice came crawling through the tiny speaker like a snake, something foul and poisonous and full of danger: **I'm whoever you want me to be.**

Then laughter; a horrible, keening laughter. Just one person at first, then a whole ghastly chorus of hysterics: high-pitched, twittering giggles; low, rumbling guffaws; hissing, sniggering wheezes. She was sure she could smell fetid breath coming from the speaker, feel the warmth and moisture of it on her cheek.

She slapped the switches off, yanked the plug out of the wall, threw the tarp over the machine, and sprinted back to the house, feeling as if something was right behind her the whole way. Then she crawled into bed between her parents (although she was far too old to do such things), saying she'd had a terrible nightmare.

"My poor duckling," Mama said, pulling her close, kissing her head.

Mama, she thinks again now, as she lies back in the rippling water. **Mama, I need you.** Her ears and face have gone numb from the cold, but she doesn't lift her head until a figure appears on the shore, bathed in shadow and moving slow.

"That you, Necco?" it calls.

Necco stands upright in the waist-deep water, frightened at first, half-thinking she's summoned a ghost. Like she did that night in Daddy's workshop.

I'm whoever you want me to be.

But after Necco squints into the shadows, she smiles.

"Miss Abigail," she says, bowing her head, remembering her manners. She walks out of the river, water dripping from her tunic.

Though it's been months since she's seen the old woman, Miss Abigail hasn't changed. She's dressed in her usual layers of bright and mismatched colors that bulge out like a petticoat and make her look much rounder than she actually is. Her long gray hair is decorated with colorful bits of rag tied in bows.

Necco doesn't visit the Fire Eaters' camp much these days. Too many memories. Too painful. Though she thinks of them often—her second family—and misses them with a dull and steady ache.

"What are you doing bathing with your clothes on, girl?" the old woman inquires.

"They were dirty," she explains as the wind hits her, makes her shiver.

Abigail looks at her a long time, squinting through a filthy pair of half-moon glasses. "You in trouble again, Necco?"

It's ironic that someone with such poor vision can see so much.

"Tell me," Abigail urges.

Necco isn't sure where to begin. She closes her eyes, sees Hermes's bloody face and the knitting needle. "My friend, someone, someone killed him." She barely gets the words out, not wanting to break down in front of Miss Abigail. "And everyone thinks I did it. I was right next to him, I slept right through it somehow. I woke up and— Oh, Miss Abigail, there was so much blood! The Jujubes are looking for me right now. I'm not sure what to do. Where to go." Suddenly she's crying. She wipes at her eyes with her soaking wet sleeve, tries to steady her breathing.

Miss Abigail nods, squats down on her haunches, and looks up at the bridge above. She licks her lips, rubs at her nose. The skin underneath is stained red, permanently tattooed by the snuff.

"I used to come here after your mama passed. I'd come and I'd sit and I'd wait for a sign. I thought if she could find a way to come back, even if just for an instant, it would happen here, in the place she lost her life. And then, maybe somehow, she could tell me."

"Tell you why she jumped?" Necco asks.

Abigail looks at her a long time. "Child, your mother did not jump from that bridge."

"No," Necco says flatly, but she feels the ground moving beneath her. "She **did** jump. That's what the police said."

She'd gone crazy. Crazy from the snuff. Afraid of her own shadow.

"It's time you learn the truth. I thought that

keeping it from you would protect you, but now I see I was wrong."

"Learn what?" Necco swallows hard. She wants to climb back into the water, lay her head down so that all she hears is the roaring water, not whatever Miss Abigail is about to tell her.

Miss Abigail takes in a deep breath, looks back up at the bridge, at the birds gathered underneath. Suddenly, the entire flock swoops down, flies up the river—almost as though it were by Miss Abigail's command. Or maybe they just don't want to hear what she's going to say.

"Your mama was murdered. Dead before her body even hit the water."

"No," Necco stammers, but doesn't some part of her suspect it to be true? "Are you sure?"

"Yes. And there's something else I'm sure of. You're not safe, Necco. You're in terrible danger. You and that baby you're carrying."

Necco's hand flies to her belly. "How did you—"

"I know plenty, girl. You know better than to question my powers, don't you? To question the visions the snuff brings me?"

"Yes, ma'am," Necco tells her.

"I told your friend about it. That your mother's death was no suicide, that you were in danger. I tried to warn him, to tell him the best thing to do was to take you far away from here."

"Friend?" Necco's head is pounding. She doesn't like where this is going. Not one bit.

"Hermes. He came to see me last month, asking questions about you and your mama. He wouldn't let it go. He was determined to find out what really happened to your mother. To your father and brother as well. He's the one who was killed last night, right?"

"Yes," Necco says, just as a terrifying thought comes to her, catching her by surprise, nearly knocking her over with its force.

"Maybe they were all killed by the same person. My father and Errol, Mama, and now Hermes."

Miss Abigail looks up at the bridge.

"Could be," she says.

"Is it Snake Eyes?"

Miss Abigail looks at Necco knowingly, but doesn't answer.

Necco stares into the brown, swirling water and thinks back to the warnings her mother gave her: how Snake Eyes was out there, after them. That he was responsible for the Great Flood, for the deaths of Daddy and Errol. She even said he was to blame for the accident that killed Daddy's parents.

Necco looks up from the water now to the old woman before her. "Miss Abigail, I never believed my mother. I never thought we were actually in danger. I never thought there even was a Snake Eyes. Maybe if I had—"

It's like a cannonball in the gut—this new knowledge. If she'd only believed her mother, believed they were really in danger. And Hermes, his death was all her fault. If she'd known the truth, she could have warned him.

"Maybes do no good, child," Miss Abigail says. "What's important is that you know now. What's important is what you do with this information."

Necco nods, realizing that her own past is the key to all of this. Everything came back to the events on the day of the Great Flood, which her mother said Snake Eyes was responsible for. If she could remember what really happened that day, she might have a clue.

"What should I do?" she asks Miss Abigail.

The old woman thinks for a minute, gazing up at the pigeons who are returning to the bridge, like the answer might be there in their soft murmurs.

"You should go to the Winter House. You'll be safe there. You go and stay out of sight. Tomorrow night, when the moon is full, you come find me. We'll ask the snuff for guidance, to show the path you're meant to take."

"Okay," Necco says. She pulls on her boots.

"You hurry now, girl," Abigail says. "You run like it's the Devil himself on your trail."

Pru

~~~

Her father always told her, **You, Prudence Elizabeth Small, my tiny elf child—you are going to grow up to be famous.** And she came to see he was right. He was a clever man, a cobbler with a gift for predictions. Ronald Small died when Pru was nine, so he didn't get to see his little girl all grown up and the star of the show, but she pictures him sometimes, watching her from way up in heaven. She imagines he is one of those bright beams of light shining down from the peak of the big top, fuzzy with smoke and dust, a ray straight from God. She hears her daddy's voice mixed in with the applause and oohs and aahs when she comes out to do her tricks. The audience's voices shake from the thrill, the strange rush she gives them.

Rapture she calls it. The experience she gives them is something close to divine, and she controls every detail. Even when they laugh, it's because she means for them to. They've never seen anything like her, Pru Small, and she knows her daddy would be proud.

She hears him say, **Good girl. You made the big time.**

———————

When Pru does the hula hoop dance, she stands on tiptoes like some tiny ballerina, spinning and spinning until she's dizzy; dizzy with that sawdust, elephant shit, lion piss smell that's all mixed together with greasy popcorn, roasted peanuts, candy apples. It's the smell that keeps her coming back, brings her out, night after night, all ruffles and sequins. Sometimes she thinks she could live off it. She thinks she could live forever all alone on some desert island somewhere, no food or drink, if she just had some of that smell captured in a little bottle she could wear around her neck and pull the cap from now and then, just a little whiff to keep her going.

Some people think the star of the circus is the ringmaster, the lion tamer, or the lady who swings from the trapeze. But in Pru's circus, it's none of those people. In Pru's circus, she's the one who keeps them coming back for more. Her: the fat lady, Queen of the Big Top. When she puts on her pink tutu and sparkling silver tights, she knows the whole thing revolves around her, Pru Small—the brightest star, the sun in this solar system of her small traveling circus.

The irony of her name does not escape her. She thinks that being born with the name Small was just a challenge to grow large. To be as big as she could. Her name is a constant taunt that reminds her to never stop growing, to be her own force of nature. A woman so big that there's always the threat that she might just gobble everything up: the tiny bright clowns, the kids in the audience sucking candy apples, the lady who hangs by her hair. One good suck, and they'd all disappear somewhere deep inside of her and there'd be nothing left at all. She thinks she's like that small, bottomless car the clowns get out of; they just keep coming and coming, carrying suitcases, dogs, picnic baskets, even the kitchen sink. She knows she is limitless. She can never be full.

The elephants are lined up behind her swaying their trunks, smelling pleasure. Mr. Marcelle, the strongman, with his striped suit and handlebar mustache, is right beside her, and when she stops her ballet spin, he takes her hands in his and they dance, move together across the center ring. With him, she feels weightless. There is no such thing as gravity. He knows he is lucky to be touching her, he whispers how beautiful she is, how she is more woman than any man could possibly deserve, could ever hope to hold. They lean this way, then that, and the crowd is laughing, like the whole thing is a joke, not synchronized perfection, not love at its finest.

Wayne, the ringmaster, all decked out in his tailcoat and top hat with a red bow tie, is blowing his whistle to announce it's time for the parade. "Ladies and gentlemen, boys and girls, children of all ages, welcome to the magic that is the circus! A world where anything is possible."

Mr. Marcelle doesn't let her go but leads her over to Sophie, her favorite of the elephants, and up the ramp she climbs onto Sophie's back and you'd think she'd be too fat for the elephant to carry, but Sophie never seems to mind.

Up jumps Emmett, the trick dog, into Pru's arms, and when she sets him down, he does flips on Sophie's great gray back, a ruffed polka-dotted collar around his neck, something Pru herself sewed for him, for in addition to being the fat lady, she is seamstress of the circus. It is just one of the many reasons she knows they could not go on without her. She is indispensable.

The big gray elephant leads the parade around the ring, Pru on her back, waving and smiling like a glamour girl—Miss America, Miss Universe—but she is so much more than those girls. She is the lady who swallowed them for breakfast then belched them out because she didn't like the taste. Skin and bones, they know nothing of life.

Of **this life;** her life of fresh-baked pleasures: a soft buttery loaf of bread for breakfast, another for lunch, a third for dinner. Those girls are hard and dry as melba toasts.

In the circus it is possible for fifteen clowns to get out of a tiny car, for a man to put his head inside the mouth of a lion, for a 350-pound woman to be a star.

———

The children line up in the cafeteria for lunch, and Pru tips them each a circus wink as they come through. "How are my little acrobats today?" she asks them. The little boys want to run away with the circus. The little girls want pink tutus and silver tights. Gravy on their mashed potatoes. Some want more, others less. She's not supposed to give them a choice, all plates are supposed to come out the same, but Pru Small understands hunger. She's learned that hunger is like the biggest, most dangerous lion in the cage. You think you can tame it, you think you can make it your friend, but it's still a wild beast, a thing of its own. Her stomach grumbles as she places perfect round balls of mashed potato on plates using an ice cream scoop. Ladles the beef and gravy over the top. String beans on the side.

Sometimes it's a game the children play, to see how much food she will give them. They ask for more, more, more, a Pru Small–size portion, and she does not disappoint. She holds nothing back. There is always plenty and plenty more where that came from.

Pru Small has worked at Our Lady of Hope Catholic School for twelve years now. She is the lady in charge of the cafeteria. They call her Mrs. Small, although she has never been married. Some of the teachers they call Miss, but her, she's a Mrs. to them and she's gotten used to the title, and to the secret life they must think she leads with Mr. Small and all their kids, like the little old lady who lived in the shoe. Different from her life at school, where she plans the menus. Cheeseburger casserole. Fish sticks on Fridays. She places the orders for cases of frozen meat, huge cans of wax beans. She makes sure they stay within budget. Makes sure there is always enough.

Some of the children know her secret, although others go through all thirteen years without knowing. Some learn in the first week of kindergarten, when they come to lunch in tears, crying for Mommy, wanting to go home. Pru brings them an extra cookie, leans down, and whispers in their ears, "Do you want to know a secret?" And they give a sniffly nod.

"I come from the circus," she tells them, and the crying stops, the child looks up at her with wonder in his eyes as they are both transported to a place where magic can happen. Pru tells a circus story, and soon the child is smiling, smelling the popcorn and elephants, holding his breath as the tightrope walkers dance overhead. The circus is a universal language, and Mrs. Small is gifted in its tongue. She describes Mr. Marcelle, Emmett the trick dog, the lady who swings by her hair. She talks and talks until it's time to go back behind the counter, back to cleaning up the hot table; restocking the bins for the older kids, who come during second and third lunch period; refilling the potatoes and meat gravy, the green beans that none of the kids seem to like.

———

Pru's plate is piled high, mountains of potatoes with firm, sculpted peaks. The gravy is good today, salty and full of fatty meat. The doctor tells her to lay off the salt, to stay away from all these potatoes, all this bread. **Carbohydrates are death to the dieter,** he tells her, but she butters another slice, sops up the gravy. The fat lady's got to eat to stay in business. The circus would fail if the fat lady got thin. Pru's secret goal is to reach five hundred pounds. Her plan is to eat a little more each day. To keep going even after she is finally full. To take just a few more bites.

Her doctor prescribes blood pressure pills and inhalers for her asthma; he suggests thick black elastic socks for her swollen ankles and feet, and hands her page after page of photocopied menus full of fresh fruit, black coffee, cottage cheese, and melba toast. He is a good man. He means well. He just misunderstands. Underestimates. It is clear that he is a man who has never been to the circus.

Still, she has been tired. Leading a double life has taken its toll. But she's found the cure. A magic pill to help get her through her days, put a spring in her step, give her plenty of energy for the circus after being on her feet for eight hours in the cafeteria. It makes her feel like a teenager again. One of the senior girls, a girl with a kind face and a lovely old-fashioned name—Theodora—has been getting them for her. Five dollars each. "The cost of a good latte," Theodora had pointed out.

"But what are they exactly?" Pru had asked.

Theodora had looked at her and smiled. "Special vitamins."

Pru had nodded, knowing these were no vitamins. But it didn't matter. Pru didn't care if they were the ground-up horns of the Devil himself—they made her feel better. They helped her forget her pain, move beyond it into a place where she could be the circus star she truly was.

The only trouble is that she has been out since yesterday and her body feels it, hurting in all the familiar places and some new ones as well. Theodora was supposed to bring her more today, but Pru hasn't seen her at lunch.

"Pru! Where are you, Pru?"

It is Mr. Marcelle coming through the back door, wheeling in boxes on his dolly. She wipes the gravy from her lips, pushes herself out of the wide chair, and walks as slowly as she can, not wanting to give him the impression that she's hurrying. She wants him to think that she doesn't even remember today is Thursday, that she hasn't been thinking of it, planning for it all week. That she doesn't think of Thursday as Mr. Marcelle's day.

The navy jacket he wears says PAGLIERI & SONS FOOD SERVICE and underneath that, his name: FRED MARCELLE. Pru has never called him by his first name. It wouldn't be right somehow. He is Mr. Marcelle, a large man; stocky some would say. He's shaved bald under his stocking cap, but baldness becomes him. She would tell him this if she didn't think it would be rude.

He gives her a wink as he rolls in the frozen tubs of ice cream, and boxes of hamburger patties. Her heart flutters in her chest like the largest of butterflies.

"How's Pru today?"

"Fine, Mr. Marcelle. I'm just fine." She dabs at her forehead with the back of her hand, and watches as he slides the boxes off next to the freezer before turning back toward her.

"I heard there was quite a commotion across the street this morning," he says.

She nods. The homeless girl is all anyone's been talking about. "A terrible thing," Pru says, lips drawn up tight.

"I guess the kid she murdered turned out to be the governor's son."

"Really?" Pru says. She's been so concerned about trying to spot Theodora, about getting more vitamins, that she hasn't been paying much attention to what people have been saying.

"Yeah, the governor and his wife have been on TV. They're offering a reward for anyone with information leading to the capture of the girl. Ten thousand dollars. My brother's been doing some poking around, asked me to give him a hand."

Mr. Marcelle's brother is a private investigator, and Mr. Marcelle works for him on weekends and some evenings during the week. "Mostly I'm just the muscle," he's told Pru. "If there's an ugly case he sometimes needs someone to watch his back."

It sounds terribly exciting, working for a private investigator. But Mr. Marcelle says it's mostly just a lot of sitting around watching people, waiting for them to do something interesting. Most of their work involves trying to catch unfaithful spouses or untrustworthy employees.

"Will you?" Pru asks now. "Help look for the girl?"

Mr. Marcelle shrugs. "I don't know. Depends

what he asks me to do. Ten thousand dollars is a nice chunk of change, even split with my brother."

"Yes," she tells him. "I suppose it is."

"You don't know anything about her, do you, Pru? Do you think she's a kid who used to go to this school?"

"I didn't even know she was living out there until all the commotion this morning. It's sad, though. The idea of a girl with no better place to go than an old stripped-down car."

Mr. Marcelle looks a little disappointed, and Pru is truly sorry she doesn't have anything to tell him. She thinks of making something up, some invented bit of gossip, the girl's name maybe—**I heard she was called Anne**—but lying to Mr. Marcelle is out of the question.

"I've got something special for you today, Pru." He gives another wink, wheels the dolly back out to his truck.

They give each other little gifts, Mr. Marcelle and Pru. Circus gifts. She gave him mustache wax and a little comb, and now he wears his mustache curled at the ends, just as she once suggested. Maybe he wears it that way only on Thursdays. Maybe he gets in his truck after this delivery and cleans it off, smooths it back down. She isn't sure. She thinks maybe it's only something he does to please her. Humor the fat lady. She tries to imagine him curling his mustache each morning in the mirror like he's getting ready for a big-top show. Sometimes, she thinks of this as she is at home, standing before the mirror herself, getting ready for her own day. She thinks of her strongman curling his mustache and smiles.

Sometimes she saves him a sweet: a cupcake or an extra-large cookie. A comic strip cut from a newspaper that she thinks he'd enjoy: **Peanuts, Garfield, The Wizard of Id.**

And what does he give her? Things for the circus, of course. Bright-colored papers, tin cans with pictures of Chinese fruit, bits of wire and string. She's told him what she needs and he understands, though he has never seen. He brings her empty spools of thread and fruit packing crates with labels from South America. The words are in Spanish, the weights metric, and pictures of cartoonish, lizard-green avocados smile in the sun: **aguacates.**

He's got something extra special for her today. She can tell by the way he fiddles with it in his pocket while they talk. She looks over the invoice, checks off all the items that have been delivered. Cartons of saltine crackers in little plastic packets, cans of beef broth, boxes of instant potatoes.

He asks her what's new at the circus, and she smiles at him over the great wealth of food, the neat stacks of boxes he's left. She's aching to tell him. She describes the new girl who spins plates, tells him about the bear who has learned to ride a unicycle. All the while he's working this gift around in the pocket of his navy jacket, smiling wistfully like a little boy because you're never too old to forget circus pleasures.

Finally, he pulls his closed fist out of his pocket and holds it out to her. His hands are large and covered in wiry black hair like the man is part bear. She smiles at the thought of Mr. Marcelle on a unicycle as he unfurls his fingers to show her his surprise.

"Ooh," Pru says, but it comes out as more of a gasp than a word. Mr. Marcelle has a small golden elephant in the palm of his hand. Pru just stares at first, not quite daring to touch it. She studies the way it glows, even under the kitchen's flickering fluorescent lights. When she reaches out to touch it, she finds that it's still warm from Mr. Marcelle's body heat, and a little moist, too. Made of metal, most likely brass, it has a little loop at the top that suggests it was once part of a piece of jewelry. It's been polished to a shine.

"Where did you find her?" Pru asks.

"Damnedest thing. My brother gave it to me last night. Said it came from one of his clients. I thought of you right away. I cleaned her up and put her on the dash of my truck, saving her for you."

She pictures thick-bodied Mr. Marcelle scrubbing at the elephant with a toothbrush covered in Brasso. Making that pachyderm shine.

"She's perfect," she tells him. "She's just what I need. Priscilla, I'll call her. Priscilla the golden elephant."

It's the best gift he's given her. And although he doesn't know it, could never guess, Mr. Marcelle with his mustache waxed and curled has saved the circus once again.

Necco

~~~~

Necco's clothes are still damp, but they're drying, feeling stiff and sparkling a little from the silt in the river. Necco, the glimmer girl. She hurries along the streets, through alleys and abandoned buildings, making her way to the Winter House as quickly and carefully as she can. She'll hole up there, as Miss Abigail instructed, until tomorrow night. She'll go through Hermes's backpack, take some time to try to wrap her mind around all this new information: try to remember everything her mother ever said about Snake Eyes, look to her own past for clues.

"He's a trickster," Mama said once. "A man who is never what he seems. And he's terribly clever, Necco. He fooled me. He outsmarted your daddy even, and you know that couldn't have been easy."

Necco has pulled a wide patterned scarf from Hermes's bag and used it to cover her head, disguising herself in case she's seen. When she's on the sidewalks, she chooses the most crowded ones and blends in, losing herself among the groups of students and mothers trying desperately to keep track of young children. She passes the VFW, smells beer and cigar smoke, hears laughter and the dull murmur of a television through the open door. She sneaks around the side of the old brick building, cuts through the parking lot of the Chinese restaurant, comes out by the Laundromat, where a man is taking a smoke break while his clothes wash. Necco turns, heads along the back side of the City Hall park.

"Never follow a straight path," Mama would say. "And never take the same route more than once. Vary your routine. Keep people guessing. That's the key to survival."

After all the seasons on the street with her mother, Necco knows the safest routes across Burntown. She's also learned the best dumpsters for food, clothing, whatever they might need. And they knew which ones were watched by the roving eyes of security cameras. Mama hated cameras of any sort.

"They'll steal your soul," she warned. "It's

important that you and I are never seen, Necco. We have to live like ghosts, like shadow people. To have our image captured by one of those cameras means we ourselves might be captured next."

Necco cuts through an old warehouse now (empty, fortunately), comes up behind Laverne's Bakery on State Street, where she stops to check the dumpster: there are often bags full of rolls and bread, sandwiches, too, sometimes, and today she's in luck: ham and Swiss on rye with tomato. Necco doesn't eat meat, not since she once got food poisoning from fried chicken that had looked and smelled fine, so she pulls the ham out, leaves it on the ground for a lucky dog or cat to find. There are strays all over the city, scrounging for food, making the best of things, just like she is.

Necco gulps down the sandwich as she walks, realizing this is the first she's eaten since the hunk of bread and cheese last night. Her stomach is in knots, but she knows she needs her strength. And she's eating for two now. She's got to try to start eating regular meals. Pick up some prenatal vitamins. Eat plenty of leafy greens so she doesn't get anemic. She needs to start drinking milk so the baby will have strong bones.

But her first priority is to get off the streets. Drinking milk and eating spinach aren't going to make a damn bit of difference if some wacko decides to put a knitting needle through her eye or throw her off a bridge. Even though she's being careful as she ducks and weaves her way across the town, she can't help feeling like she's being followed, like Snake Eyes is out there watching, waiting, biding his time. The knot in her stomach grows when she realizes this is exactly how her mother felt all those years. Her mother, whom she never believed. She wraps up the rest of her sandwich and tucks it into the backpack for later, starts walking as fast as she can without breaking into a run.

There are two entrances to the Winter House: the one on the west side behind the old woolen mill, where you have to pry up a round metal cover and climb down a ladder, and the one she heads for now: the door in the rocks on the other side of the river.

To get there, she travels north on Canal Street, passing the brewery with its warm roasted-malt smells. Beyond the brewery is the area Mama called the Ghost Trains: an old switchyard with a roundabout; rows of old freight cars sit rusting on the tracks that extend out from a big circle in the center. The trains quit running before the mills did. Now, people squat in the cars, which are tagged with graffiti, and she's always careful crossing through here—you never know who might be lurking in the shadows. She reaches down, draws her blade just in case, but all is quiet.

She leaves the old train yard, climbs the hill to the Millyard Bridge, which takes her right over the dam.

She hears the deafening roar of water charging at the concrete wall, spilling over the top. It's here the old canal system started, channeling the water to power the mills.

Once she's across the bridge, Necco finds the path that leads down to the water's edge. It's slow going; the woods are overgrown and tangled, the path hard to see in the dark. She thinks of pulling a flashlight from the pack, but doesn't want to risk being spotted. The trail is rocky and steep, slippery in places. She grabs on to saplings and vines to keep from falling. This area is loaded with bittersweet vines that pop open each fall, revealing a red berry covered by yellow pods. "A beautiful plant," Miss Abigail once told her, "but one that doesn't belong—an invasive species. See how it girdles the trees, crowds out the native bushes; it's a plant that is determined to survive."

At last, Necco reaches the bottom, and begins to creep along the narrow path between the river and the wall of rocks. Her eyes are searching.

She finds the entrance easily enough, even in the dark. There, about ten feet up—above the old, bricked-over tunnels that were once part of the canal system—is a small door set into the stone. A magic door. A fairy door. A door that makes no sense at all, is almost impossible to believe in. When you first see it, you blink, sure you're imagining things.

She looks carefully in all directions and sees no one, nothing, so she starts to climb. The climb is not easy—there are only a few places to put her hands and feet, which slip easily on the damp, mossy stone—but her body remembers the way. There are places where stones protrude just enough to get a handhold and foothold, little brick ledges around the old canal tunnels. She used to do this several times a day back when she and Mama lived here. Hermes's pack is heavy on her back, and her limbs ache from the hours of walking she's done today, but still, she climbs.

No one was sure what the Winter House was, exactly. They heard rumors that the tunnels went back to the days of the bootleggers smuggling whiskey from the north and rum from the south. Local historians said the Jensen family ran rum and had numerous speakeasies around the city during Prohibition.

Necco reaches the door and is relieved to see it has the same old broken lock hanging from the hasp. She pushes it open and heaves herself into the cement and brick tunnel, quickly pulling the door closed behind her.

Flicking on Hermes's flashlight, she shines

the beam down the tunnel, startling a rat, which runs in the other direction. She doesn't mind rats. They're intelligent. Focused. Survivors, like her. They've just got a bad reputation.

The tunnel is arched overhead, wide enough only for people to walk single file. It smells like damp brick, old wood, mildew, forgotten things. The smell hits her like a punch in the gut.

This was once her home. Hers and Mama's.

She moves forward and is relieved to see carefully woven spiderwebs crisscrossing the tunnel—a sure sign no one has been here for a while. About twenty yards in, the tunnel forks. You can go right or straight. Straight takes you another hundred yards or so, then you hit a brick wall. Necco had always wondered what's behind the bricks; she had even started chipping away at the mortar, revealing glimpses of wood heavy and thick like ship timbers. Before she got very far with her excavation project, however, Mama died.

She takes the tunnel to the right, a strange excitement building as she gets closer. Another ten yards and she sees the heavy metal door with a rusty ring handle. Holding her breath, she tugs on the handle, pulling the door open.

Nothing has changed: as Necco moves her flashlight around the room, she sees it's exactly the way it was when she left that last morning.

It's not a large space, maybe ten by sixteen

feet. At the far end are their beds: wooden pallets with mattresses piled high with blankets. There is a low row of shelves between the two beds stacked with paperback books, magazines, and newspapers—mostly from the free box at the library. Her mother's paintings and drawings are scattered around the room. They are brightly colored and heavy on the reds given how many were inspired by her snuff-induced visions—a berry-covered vine that reached high up into pink clouds, where a pair of eyes looked down, watching; a fish with red-feathered wings flying up over the Steel Bridge; and fire, with images hidden in the flames, faces, a pocket watch, a little girl holding a doll.

The kitchen area has a big blue water jug with a spigot up on a shelf above the table and a plastic dishpan they used for a sink. Under the table is a five-gallon bucket for the dirty water that came from washing dishes. Every morning and evening, it was Necco's chore to go dump this and the bucket they used as a chamber pot into the river.

Pots, pans, bowls, plates, cups, and silverware live in a dented metal cabinet between the sink and the old Coleman propane camp stove. They used to steal small cylinders of propane from the hardware or outdoor supply store. Across the room from the kitchen area is the table they used for eating, cobbled together from broken-down shipping pallets. The chairs around it are mismatched, scrounged from the roadside. Everything they owned had been cast off, rejected. But it suited them fine.

When Necco was a little girl, her father used to read her a wonderful book called **The Borrowers,** about little people who lived beneath the floor and within the walls of an old house. Necco liked to think of herself and her mother as Borrowers of a different sort; larger, human, but still, surviving in the shadows off of things no one will miss.

To the left of the little table area is their second entrance: a tunnel that leads down a long passageway that goes past four other doorways, all bricked up, until it reaches a metal ladder bolted to the wall. If you climb up and lift the metal plate on top, you'll find yourself out behind the old woolen mill, a crumbling brick building on the edge of town that has been closed now for over half a century. While it was rare that anyone would trespass, she and Mama had camouflaged the round metal plate as best they could, painting it with a thick, smelly glue and covering it with dirt, stones, and pieces of brick. If you didn't know it was there, you'd never find it.

Still searching with the flashlight, Necco spots Mama's old red sweater draped over the chair. Two empty cups on the table hold the last bit of tea they drank together. She half-expects Mama to be lying down on the mattress, to sit up when she hears Necco enter, to say, "What took you so long?"

But there's no movement. No sound. Only more cobwebs.

Necco goes over with her light, lifts up Mama's cup. There's a dead moth at the bottom—brown, dried, and dusty.

"Oh, Mama," she says, letting herself cry for the first time all day. The weight of everything that has happened bears down on her, roaring like the water at the dam.

She sinks to her knees, clutching the empty mug.

————

Once she's cried herself out, Necco finds a box of matches and lights the candles and oil lamps. She spends a few minutes tidying up, and it feels good to be busy—she sweeps, washes the two mugs, and makes sure that there's plenty of water and propane left, as well as a few things still in the pantry. After putting the kettle on, she makes herself a cup of tea with plenty of sugar, and helps herself to a stale cookie from a dented metal tin.

She sees the easel her mother cobbled together out of sticks and scrap wood in the corner of the room. It holds the last painting her mother was working on, the whole thing draped in an old white sheet like some misshapen ghost. There is the coffee can lid she used as a palette, but the paint, a swirl of earthy colors Lily mixed herself using clay, coffee grounds, and berries, has hardened, the brush sitting in it ruined. Necco walks across the room, pulls back the sheet; and studies the unfinished painting for the first time; when Mama was working on a painting, Necco was never allowed to look until it was finished.

She sees right away that this one is different, breaking away from her mother's usual style. It's a painting from the time Before the Flood. She's painted Errol and Daddy in their old living room. Daddy and Errol are sitting on the oval braided rug in front of the fireplace, playing cards. Necco looks closer, sees the cards in Errol's hands; they're more like tarot cards, each with a creepy image: a giant wave, a pair of dice with one dot on top of each, a Chicken Man, a terrified little boy standing behind a wall of flames.

The image of Errol on the living room floor is so like him, it startles Necco. Mama has captured the mischievous sparkle of his eyes, and the shaggy dark hair that always hung across his forehead, nearly covering the scar above his left eye. She can almost hear Errol's voice: "Want us to deal you in, Little E?"

She reaches out, touches his cheek, feels the brushstrokes on wood. Remembers how he was Big E and she was Little E. "Together, we're **E** squared," he used to say. "Together, we're so much more than just **E** plus **E**. The whole is greater than the sum of its parts," he said.

Suddenly, she feels tired. Dead tired. But there is one thing she needs to do before letting herself sleep.

Setting Hermes's black backpack up on the table, she begins unzipping all of its various compartments and pulling everything out. Hermes never went anywhere without the pack, and it seemed, to Necco, to be almost magical. Whenever she needed anything—a safety pin, a candle, a piece of candy—he would reach in and make it appear.

She works slowly, but determinedly, touching each object with reverence and then sorting them all into neat rows. A pencil is not just a pencil, because the last person who touched it was Hermes. Hermes when he was alive.

She doesn't find the one thing she was hoping for most—the elephant charm with its broken chain he'd taken from her to have repaired.

It can't be gone. It was the one thing of her father's she had left.

Necco blinks back frustrated tears, tells herself not to think about the lost elephant now. Nothing she can do. She looks at the first row of things she's pulled from Hermes's pack.

In addition to Theo's school bag with its pills and money, there are two flashlights, a soldering iron, a metal canteen, clumps of wires, screwdrivers, a circuit board, batteries of various sizes, a pry bar, a Zippo lighter, gum and butterscotch candies, a stack of index cards and a pen, a tiny sewing kit, a bundle of black nylon cord, half a dozen stolen cell phones, an assortment of various electronic cords and cables, and, zipped into a padded case, Hermes's laptop.

She opens the laptop. It asks for a password. She guesses HERMES, NECCO, even tries his real name, MATTHEW. None of it works. She closes the screen, then looks at the next row of items she's pulled from the pack.

A small first-aid kit, a roll of electrical tape, a roll of silver duct tape, three different sorts of pliers, a folding knife, and finally, the little leather pouch he used as a wallet. Inside, she finds four dollars and twenty cents, a bus pass, and a handwritten receipt from the Westmore Lanes Family Fun Center. She looks at the receipt carefully. He'd paid fifteen dollars—ten dollars plus a five-dollar key deposit—to rent a locker for the month. Locker number 213.

She pulls the strange key with the round shaft and orange head out of her pocket.

213.

It's going to change everything.

She reties the string it's on and slips the key around her neck. After digging the tattered paperback copy of **The Princess and the Elephant** out of the tall girl's satchel, she curls up on Mama's bed and buries her face in the pillow, trying to catch a trace of Mama's smell. But there's only dust. She opens the book to the dedication page: **For Lily, who is my everything.** She closes the cover, tucks the book under her pillow, pulls her knees to her chest, and wills sleep to take her, to carry her away.

Theo

~~~~~~

I just talked to Jeremy. He's really pissed, Theo. Please call.

Theo has her phone pressed against her ear, listening to her messages.

She had gone to her morning classes in a daze, unable to focus on anything but the missing bag and money. She wondered what had happened to the Fire Girl, and she had to stop letting herself imagine her knitting needle impaled through some guy's chest or else she was going to puke all over the pale yellow student desk. While her teachers droned on about derivatives and allegory, she nervously drew spirals and question marks and dollar signs in her notebook. At last, just before lunch, she realized she had to get out of there and work on a solution to her problem.

Besides, if Hannah and Jeremy decided to come looking for her, they'd come to the school first. She imagined them hanging out by the front steps, waiting for the last bell to ring and for their chance to accost her as everyone skittered out the main doors like bugs.

No way she was walking into that trap.

After stopping off at her locker to grab her phone, she snuck out the side door into the bright sunshine, walking quickly, hoping no one would notice a student going AWOL. Now that she's safely around the block, she continues to listen to the messages from Hannah, throat tight, heart pounding in her ears.

It's after nine, where are you?

Theo? What's going on?

I just talked to Jeremy. He's really pissed, Theo. Please call.

The last call came in an hour ago:

Jeremy's on his way. If you're not here with the money, I don't know what he's gonna do. I'm scared. Please call.

Theo tells herself she is not going to feel bad for Hannah. Not going to be worried. Not going to imagine Hannah being slapped around by some money-hungry, drug-crazed asshole.

"She made her choices," Theo says out loud. She swallows hard. Remembers tracing her fingers over Hannah's collarbone, down her neck into the small valley at the base of her throat.

She remembers resting her fingers there, feeling Hannah's pulse, being unsettled at how strangely vulnerable Hannah had seemed, naked in her bed, blood thumping under her pale, freckled skin.

"Forget it," she tells herself and hurries home. She starts desperately looking around the house for money knowing it's hopeless, that she won't find more than spare change, but she's got to try. She tries the pint-size kitchen first, searching the junk drawer, which is full of rusted screws, dead batteries, broken pencils, and some change (pennies mostly); then moves to the hall closet, where she looks through the pockets of coats (she finds an expired bus pass, thirty-two cents, and half a roll of breath mints); and goes to her room and empties her piggy bank (six dollars and twenty-two cents). She's got the debit card she and her mom share, but that's linked to Mom's checking account, which never has much in it at all. Theo is supposed to ask before she uses it to buy anything over ten dollars.

She opens her closet, reaches for the cowboy boots way in the back that she never wears, and pulls out the plastic bag tucked into the left one. It's where she stores the drugs she doesn't bring with her to school. There's not much left—a handful of uppers, a little weed, a couple of eighths of mushrooms. If she sold it all, she'd get maybe a hundred bucks, tops. There's a small roll of cash stuffed into the toe—the money she's been saving up to go away with Hannah. She counts it. Sixty-three dollars. She was sure she'd had more. But she'd used it to buy some yarn. And a necklace at the hippie gift shop that Hannah had said looked cute on her. And sweet potato fries at the Koffee Kup. And all the other stupid nickel and dime crap that added up.

"Shit!" she hisses, heading back to the living room.

She starts scanning the apartment for anything of value she might be able to pawn, but there's nothing. No family silver, no antiques. The jewelry she and her mom wear is all from the dime store and craft fairs, and their TV is old and crappy. Her laptop is pretty ancient, too.

She and her mom don't have much, but they've learned to do just fine in spite of it. None of their dishes match. Their kitchen table wobbles unless you put little squares of cardboard under one of the legs. They've had the same couch all her life—a crappy old futon that's always sliding off the frame and is leaking stuffing in places. Still, she thinks, there are people who have less. Like the Fire Girl. She'd probably walk into the apartment—see the beds, the TV, the food in the kitchen, the warm clothes in the closets—and think Theo had everything.

Theo lets herself imagine the Fire Girl in her apartment. She'd get her bag back. Ask why the

Fire Girl killed that guy. Say that she was sure he must have deserved it. "Guys can be such assholes," she'd say, as if she had experience with such things.

Theo's cell phone rings. Another call from Hannah.

Deciding she can't put off the inevitable, she picks up. There's nothing to do now but tell Hannah the truth: **I've lost the money. What now?**

"Theo?" a male voice snarls.

"Yes," she says robotically. She knows this voice at the other end. She doesn't know his face, doesn't have a clue what he looks like, but his voice she knows. Jeremy. Jeremy, who called Hannah Babe. Just hearing his voice makes her stomach feel like it's full of snakes. She remembers being in Hannah's closet, the feel of the clothing on hangers brushing her face and shoulders as she crouched there, listening to this man with the voice kiss the girl she loved.

"Where the **fuck** is my money?" She can practically feel his spit hit her face, his breath hot as a bull's.

She takes in a breath. "I don't have it. It got . . . lost."

"Do you think I'm stupid?" Jeremy snarls. "Do you think I'm some kind of fucking idiot?"

"No."

"Here's what's gonna happen, Theo. You're gonna get me my money. If it's lost, you're gonna find it. If you can't find it, you're gonna borrow it, steal it, sell your fucking left kidney for it, whatever it takes. Do you understand?"

"Yes," Theo squeaks out. Her legs have turned to rubber and she lets herself sink down onto the couch.

"I knew you would. Hannah says you're a smart girl," he says, and the snarl has left his voice; now his tone is teasing, cocky. "You have until tomorrow morning. Ten o'clock. If you're not at Hannah's with the money by then, I'll come looking for you. And trust me, Theo, you **do not** want me to come looking for you." He hangs up before she can respond.

Her heart pounds so hard she can feel her whole body vibrate with each beat.

What is she going to do?

She could tell her mother. Go find her at the bank and tell her the whole story, ask her mother to help her come up with the two thousand. Her mom has no savings, but maybe she could apply for a loan, use her credit cards for cash—something. But telling her mother would mean admitting to everything: the drug dealing, having an affair with a college student she'd met at the library (a girl college student, even). It would destroy her mom, who has such a perfect picture of Theo in her mind. Theo, who's always such a good sport about the long hours Mom has to work to keep the two of them afloat, to keep paying for Catholic school because it's so much better than sending her to the public schools, where she'd meet the wrong sorts of kids and get a less than wholesome education.

So where does that leave her?

A girl who's out of choices. A girl who's got to get herself out of town, as far away as possible. She'll pack up some things, and disappear. It's the only way.

She goes into her room, turns on the music, and throws her backpack on the bed.

She starts to pack on autopilot: socks, underwear, jeans, a couple of T-shirts, wool sweater, rain parka, notebook and pen. Ancient, cranky laptop. Her felted knitting bag with her favorite needles, pouch of knitting notions, and assorted yarn. She takes the photo of her and her mom out of the frame and tucks it into the notebook. She grabs the bag of drugs from the boot and pockets the cash. Then she heads to the kitchen, grabs a spoon and fork, can opener (her mom won't miss it—there's an electric one on the counter), and a steak knife, which she wraps in a cloth napkin. It doesn't have the same deadly weapon look the Fire Girl's knife had, but it's the best she's got for now. She searches the cupboards, comes up with a couple of old granola bars, a can of cling peaches, a sleeve of saltine crackers, and an unopened jar of peanut butter. Into the backpack go all her kitchen finds, along

with her cigarettes and lighter, lipstick, deodor-
ant, toothpaste, and toothbrush.

She hoists the bag onto her back and is unpleasantly surprised by its weight.

She'll head to Aunt Helen's for the night. Aunt
Helen is her mother's aunt, and lives alone in an
old house at the edge of town—the house her
mom grew up in. Helen never locks the door and
is deaf as a stone. Theo is confident she'll be able
to creep right in and find a dark corner to sleep
in—Helen will never know. She feels a little bad,
taking advantage of an old person, a person she's
related to even, but what choice does she have?
And it's not like she'll be harming Helen in any
way.

She heads for the front door, pausing in the
kitchen at the dry-erase board on the fridge—
this is where she and her mom leave each other
notes. Should she write something? What would
she say?

Her eyes tear up, and before she can change
her mind about all of this, she marches her ass
out of the apartment, down the stairs, and out
onto the sunlit street; a girl on the run.

Pru

〜〜〜

More. More. More. This is the vague threat looming at the edge of the horizon. The crowd is always pleased with how the circus dazzles them, but next time, they want more. Something bigger, better, with stunts even more death defying. They want to see that the fat lady has put on weight and learned to play the accordion. The woman who hangs by her hair has to spin longer, have a few more sequins on her costume. And there must be new acts. Without them, the circus goes stale.

When Pru is at work in the ring, she forgets her other life. She forgets the cruel whispers of the teenage girls on the number 10 bus she takes home from work, how they laugh and sometimes say things like **If I ever get even half that size,**

shoot me. She forgets climbing the two flights of stairs up to her apartment. Her knees screaming; bone on bone, rubbing, grinding. Her chest heaving, her breath whistly, musical. She sweats. God, does she sweat. And her whole body aches. If she had only one of the tiny red pills, then the pain would go away, she'd have energy to do shows all night.

But there are no pills. Pru poked her head around while kids were leaving for the day, scanning the halls, but she never caught sight of Theodora. Pru snuck into the office and got Theodora's phone number from the files, but it would seem so . . . so desperate to call her, wouldn't it?

She doesn't need the pills after all, she tells herself as she begins her climb up the apartment building stairs. She can do fine without them.

"Rent was due yesterday, Pru," comes a voice from the first floor. Tiny Wayne, mouse of a man, sticking his head out the door of his apartment. He's in a stained white undershirt and smells of the Old Grand-Dad bourbon that he sips all day out of a coffee cup.

"Payday's tomorrow, Wayne."

"Tomorrow, then. Got to pay the bills, Pru. Got to keep the creditors off my back. People don't pay their rent, I can't pay my bills. There's heat, electricity, insurance, trash. It's a well-oiled machine. Everyone's got their role to play."

"Yes, Wayne. I understand. Tomorrow's payday. I'll bring the rent then, I promise."

Wayne nods up at her and shuts his door. She takes the key from the string around her neck and lets herself into her apartment. Her home. Her haven. Pru's own little big-top house.

Emmett dances at her feet, warming up. Does his flips, thinking it might earn him a treat.

"Wait a minute, sweet boy. The show's just about to start."

Emmett is a black-and-white Jack Russell terrier named for Emmett Kelly, the famous clown. Pru has a picture of Kelly on the wall in the hallway, and sometimes she points to him, tells her little Emmett, **This is the master. This is who you were named for. Do right by that name.** The circus is full of such legacies.

She has taught Emmett several tricks. He can sit, dance on his hind feet, jump through a hula hoop, and do flips. The flips were the hardest to learn, but now it seems he can't get enough. He seems to crave dizziness, her Emmett. And he'll do anything for a hot dog. Oscar Mayer, cut up into little bits. She's even taught him to do his business in a cat box. Smartest little dog that ever lived.

Pru leaves the golden elephant and the ringmaster to get acquainted and follows Emmett into the kitchen, where she fixes them both a snack. Emmett gets Mighty Dog. Pru has a box of jelly donuts and two glasses of milk. The whole time she eats, she's thinking of the pills. Of the number at the bottom of her purse.

"Stop it, Prudence Elizabeth Small," she tells herself in a voice as close to her father's as she can make it.

"Come on, Emmett," she calls. "Time to put on our costumes."

Pru changes in front of the full-length mirror in the bedroom, proud of how easily she fills it. She has caught her breath. Regained her stature. Getting ready for a show always gives her a rush of energy. Her knees feel springy, strong, well oiled. She puts on the tutu and feels light as air. She takes the accordion from its case and straps it across her mammoth chest, pushes a few keys, forces the bellows closed. The note is loud and sure.

The circus has begun.

Pru dances out into the living room to start the show, Emmett at her heels in his ruffed polka-dotted collar and pointed hat with chin strap.

She is a giant, her own kind of God, towering over the three rings she has built in her living room. They are up on a series of tables side by side. It is a perfect model, each detail surviving Pru's careful scrutiny. All the players are clothes-pins with painted faces, wire arms, wooden legs, and tiny costumes that Pru has sewn by hand. The cages are wood and wire. The high wire is a string running across the center ring, held up by wooden dowels with matchstick ladders for the acrobats to climb. The two trapezes hang from the chandelier above the center ring. Pru has put colored bulbs in the chandelier for circus ambience. The walls of the living room are covered in circus art she's collected and collages she's made. In her favorite, a replica of an actual poster, a fat lady is sprawled on a chair. THE LARGEST LADY ON EARTH! proclaims the sign, and Pru has taken a photo of her own face and pasted it over the other woman's. The other woman is bigger than Pru, but Pru knows this is nothing. There's still time. She's getting there.

"Ladies and gentlemen, children of all ages," shouts the ringmaster, Wayne, who sways in Pru's right hand, four inches tall, body of wood, wire, and cloth. "Tonight's special attraction, the newest addition to our circus family, all the way from the Far East, land of mystery and intrigue, the world's only golden elephant, Priscilla, a baby, a miracle calf. There is none like her."

Pru takes the elephant and walks her around the ring while the audience applauds. The vibration of their clapping fills her ears, her heart and lungs, and she breathes easy. She plays a few notes on the accordion, does a clumsy pirouette, and the golden elephant trumpets beside her. Pru squints up at the lights and thinks, See, Daddy, you were right. I'm a star.

She's off today, missing her cues, not so light on her feet. **More! More! More!** the crowd chants in her ears, a dull rhythmic throb that starts to make her head and teeth ache.

She stumbles, catches herself on one of the tables, sending an earthquake through the center ring. The lion falls from his perch. The clowns collapse. Even Wayne the ringmaster has toppled. He peers up at her from the ground, a disappointed look in his painted-on eyes, his hat oddly askew.

"Intermission time," she calls, righting the center ring, picking up Wayne and apologizing, bringing out the clothespin vendors with their carts full of peanuts and popcorn, and bundles of tissue-paper balloons wired to their hands.

She backs away, dabbing at the cool sweat on her forehead. Her legs wobble.

Water. She needs a glass of water. And to sit down for a minute.

And a pill.

Just one pill and she'd be good to go.

She can see it so clearly in her mind, the tiny red dot, like bright candy. Like the candy buttons she used to buy by the roll when she was a child. She can practically taste the pill on the back of her tongue, bitter and slick.

She finds her purse, digs Theodora's phone number out. Thinking it would be best to call her on her cell, that's the number she copied from the records in the office. She goes to the phone on the kitchen wall and punches in Theo's number before she can talk herself out of it.

"Hello?" the girl says. She sounds frantic. Out of breath.

"Theodora? It's Mrs. Small. From the cafeteria at school."

She waits. The girl says nothing.

"I was wondering if I could get another delivery. You know, of the vitamins?"

Theodora blows out a breath, hissing like a dragon into the phone. "Sorry, Mrs. Small, but it's not a good time."

"Please," Pru says. Sweat trickles down her cheeks, tiny rivers cutting through the thick powder she's put on for the circus. "I could meet you somewhere. I could pay extra. I've got money. Whatever you need."

It's quiet for another beat. Pru watches as a drop of sweat falls from her forehead to the linoleum floor.

"See, the thing is, I'm kind of in trouble, Mrs. Small."

"Trouble? What kind of trouble? Tell me, I might be able to help."

"Bad trouble. There was . . . an incident. I owe a man some money. And if I don't get it to him . . ." Her voice cuts off.

"I can help," Pru says. "I can get you money."

Can she? Where? Where on earth is Pru going

to get the money? Payday isn't until tomorrow, and then all of it goes to rent, bills, food for her and Emmett. It's always so sad, watching it go so fast. Here one minute, gone the next; its own magic trick.

"I don't think you could get me enough," the girl says. "Thanks though."

"You don't know that," Pru says. She's the circus fat lady. Not to be underestimated. "You'd be surprised what I can do. Let me help you. I can give you a loan. A loan in exchange for more vitamins. Let's at least meet to discuss it. It's a business proposition. I'd become a sort of silent partner in what you do." She can hardly believe the words that are coming out of her mouth, but they flow so naturally. And she knows about business. About budgets and numbers. She knows enough to not be taken advantage of. She can help this girl and in the process, help herself. It's a win-win proposition.

"I don't— Yeah, okay, maybe," the girl says. "We could at least meet to talk about it."

"And you'll bring more vitamins?"

"I've got some on me, and I could probably get more."

"Do you want to meet tomorrow at school?" Pru suggests. "In the ladies' room near the cafeteria?" She's pacing, walking circles around the three-ring circus.

"No," Theodora says. "Someplace else. You live on the west side of the river, right?"

"On Canal Street. Not far from the college."

"There's a little market and café over on First," Theodora tells her. "Natural You, it's called."

"I know it," Pru says. She's passed it a million times, never been inside. The windows advertise sales on organic spelt, wheatgrass juice, toasted seaweed—things that sound horrid.

"Meet me there tomorrow."

"What time?" Pru asks.

"Can you come in the morning?"

Pru thinks it over. She can go in, pick up her check, and cash it at the twenty-four-hour place; they charge, but still, she'd have the cash. She'll tell the other cafeteria ladies she has a medical appointment. They'll be fine without her for one morning. And if she hurries, she can make it back by lunch.

"Nine o'clock?" Pru suggests.

"Perfect. I'll see you then."

"And you'll bring the vitamins?"

"Yeah. I'll bring whatever I can get."

Necco

〜〜〜

Necco pauses outside of Natural You, her stomach rumbling. She woke up ravenous and found
only a few stale cookies, sugar, and tea in the Winter House. She knows it's a terrible risk, coming
out of hiding, but she needs to see what's in the
locker Hermes rented. Whatever's in there might
help her. If it was digging around into her past
and family that got Hermes killed, maybe he'd
actually found something useful, something to
prove who Snake Eyes was and what he'd done.

Natural You is on the way to the bowling
alley, and inside are bulk bins full of dried fruit,
nuts, trail mix. She and Mama used to come here
because it's easy to fill your pockets from the bins
and there are always lovely samples of cheese

and fresh bread and smoothies with wholesome ingredients.

She'll get in and out quickly, she tells herself as she pushes open the door, her hunger overriding her better judgment. The store smells like patchouli, warm bread, and spices. As she heads toward the bulk bins, she feels a pang of guilt. She doesn't really need to steal, not with the wad of cash in that girl's satchel. But she needs to save that money for true emergencies. She stuffed the whole bag into the cavity behind a couple of loose bricks in the Winter House. It was a secret hiding place Mama created—where she saved cash when she had it, and left her pouch of Devil's Snuff. When Necco had pulled out the bricks to put the girl's bag there, she'd found a single pearl earring tucked way at the back. Mama had found it on the sidewalk, and thought that it might be worth something. But it was clearly cheap costume jewelry, the gold plate peeling, the pearl yellowing and plasticky. Still, Mama had held on to it. She was a dreamer that way. A spinner of stories. She said things, then believed them because she had to. Necco understands that now.

Necco works her way down the aisles of Natural You and slips a handful of almonds into her pocket, some dried apple, working from the bins at waist level. The store is crowded and no one seems to notice.

Necco is wearing Mama's red wool sweater,

with her hair braided and pinned up. She had grabbed Hermes's sunglasses with the mirrored lenses, but she can't see inside with them too well, so they're up on top of her head. She catches a glimpse of her reflection in the glass door of the freezer that contains organic sorbets and soy ice cream bars; she looks like any of the other slightly disheveled, hippieish shoppers here, maybe a college student picking up some hemp shampoo between classes.

A dreadlocked man in a Natural You apron catches Necco's eye.

"You need any help, miss?"

More than you could know.

She shakes her head, flashes him a big, warm smile. "Thanks, I'm fine."

Always smile, Mama used to tell her. **Be the gray man,** Hermes would say. The gray man is the guy who passes right by but no one notices. Be invisible, avoid confrontation, don't do anything to draw attention to yourself.

She presses on, passing the dairy section, and a cooler full of tofu and tempeh and all other kinds of fake meat. She's on her way to the front doors when she spots an area for supplements.

Fish oil. Green tea extract. Vitamins she's never heard of.

Vitamins! That's what she needs. For the baby.

Necco scans the shelves, studying the labels of the amber-colored bottles. One of them has a silhouette of a pregnant woman, belly swollen as the moon. PRENATAL PLUS, it says. A COMPLETE SUPPLEMENT FOR MOTHER AND BABY.

Perfect. In one quick motion, she grabs the bottle, tucks it up into the sleeve of her chunky sweater. Then she turns to go. Walking slowly, blending in. If one of the cashiers catches her eye, she'll smile.

"Excuse me, miss?" A voice behind her, gentle, but insistent.

Her heart hammers but she doesn't slow, pretends not to hear the voice or the footsteps behind her. She walks faster now, her eye on the front doors. But first she has to pass by the cash registers, where two bored clerks are looking her way.

A hand grabs her shoulder. "Slow down," a man's voice says.

She turns. It's Dreadlocks. He has no smile for her now.

"Are you going to pay for that?" he asks.

"What?" she says. She doesn't have to fake her confusion; she never gets caught. Mama would be so disappointed. If they call the cops, it's all over.

"The bottle of vitamins in your sleeve."

A small crowd of shoppers circles closer, excited by the spectacle.

She freezes, thinking over her options. She could say she was going to pay for it then pretend to have left her wallet at home. Deny having any bottle of vitamins, make a show of being out-raged by his accusation. Or, she could do what her gut is screaming at her to do: run. Break away and run as fast as she can.

Dreadlocks keeps his hand on her shoulder, tightens his grip. "I'm going to have to ask you to come back into the office with me."

"There's . . . been a mistake," Necco says slowly, just as a voice behind them chirps: "Jessy! There you are! I've been looking for you every-where. Did you pick up my vitamins?"

A girl hurries forward, linking arms with Necco.

It's the girl from yesterday, the one who gave her the knitting needles. Necco turns and smiles at this girl—Theo, Necco recalls—relief flooding through her like sunshine, and lets the vitamins drop from her sleeve into her hand.

"Got them," she says. "Just like you asked."

Theo takes the bottle, glances at it for a sec-ond, and smiles, then moves toward the cashier, already pulling out her wallet.

But Dreadlocks does not let go of Necco's shoulder.

Theo turns back. "Is there a problem?"

"Your friend was hiding those in her sleeve. Looks a lot like shoplifting to me."

Theo returns to them, smiles indulgently at Dreadlocks, says, in a low voice, "Here's the thing, they're for me. I asked her to get them for me."

"But that doesn't change the fact that—"

"Do you see what kind of vitamins they are?" Theo says, exasperated now, holding the bottle out. "Prenatal. And in case you hadn't noticed, I'm not **exactly** supposed to be needing these." She gestures to her school uniform. "My friend Jessica was just trying to not draw any attention to our purchase. Now, since the damage is done, I'd like to go ahead and finish said purchase before we get any more people gawking and whispering and judging." She turns to the small crowd and waves the prenatal vitamins at them. "Teach your kids safe sex. Condoms. Abstinence, even."

Necco bites her lip to suppress a smile.

"So, can we go now or what?" Theo asks.

Face red now, the man nods. He lets go of Necco's shoulder.

Thank you, thank you, thank you, Necco sings inside her head.

Theo links arms with Necco once more, and they head toward the register. Necco thinks of her mother, remembers her warning, To put your trust in another, that's a dangerous thing. Trust no one. That's the only way to stay alive out here. We've got to live like ghosts.

Live like ghosts, Necco thinks now as she slips her arm gently from Theo's and watches the cashier—an older woman with a long, untidy braid—ring up the vitamins. Theo swipes a debit card and punches in a number.

"Do you want a bag?" the cashier asks, not taking her eyes off Necco.

"No, thank you," Theo says.

The woman takes her time finishing the transaction, pushing buttons on her machine. She finally moves her gaze from Necco toward the front of the store. Necco sees what she's looking at and feels her heart drop like a cold stone.

There's a rack of newspapers, and there, on the front page, is the headline GOVERNOR STANTON'S SON SLAIN. Below it, a picture of Hermes. It's probably his high school senior photo; there he is with short hair but his familiar smirk. Next to this photo is a drawing of Necco that bears a remarkable resemblance, really. The bold line of print above her sketched face reads: REWARD OFFERED FOR ANY INFORMATION LEADING TO THE SUSPECT'S ARREST.

Necco can't move. Can't breathe.

"Jared?" the cashier calls, and Dreadlocks walks their way—he hadn't gone far, has been watching this whole transaction with his arms crossed over his chest.

"What is it?"

The cashier looks at Necco, then nods in the direction of the rack of newspapers.

"**What,** Renee?" Dreadlocks says, irritated, not getting it.

"Come on," Theo says, grabbing Necco's hand, pulling her away, past the newspapers, out the front doors, walking fast. Theo looks left, then right. There is a large woman down at the cross street, moving their way. She seems to recognize Theo.

"Oh, there you are," she calls, waving her arm, the sleeve of her red coat flapping like a flag.

"Mrs. Small," Theo says. "We have to go. Now."

"Go? Go where? Who's this?" she asks, eyeing Necco suspiciously.

"Is your place far?" Theo asks, casting a glance back behind her shoulder. Dreadlocks is outside now, watching them, talking into a cell phone.

"Around the corner," Mrs. Small says.

"Let's go," Theo instructs, taking the lead now as she pulls Necco along, Mrs. Small behind them, hurrying to keep up.

Pru

~~~~

Pru has never had guests. The only one who ever comes into her apartment is Wayne, and that's when something needs fixing: a clogged drain, a leaking radiator. As she and the two girls made their way down the street, she started to argue, to tell the girls they couldn't possibly go to her place, that she's due at work in half an hour, lunch won't wait, the other cafeteria ladies are depending on her, but Theodora cut her off and said simply, "Look, if you want your vitamins, this is the way it is."

And Pru **did** want her vitamins. So Pru told them which building it was, led them up the dark wooden stairs, down the hallway that always smelled like dirty feet and boiled cabbage, and unlocked her door. Now Emmett is dancing around their feet in the kitchen.

"Where did you get that newspaper?" Pru asks Theodora, who is holding a paper in a plastic bag that she hadn't had before.

"I borrowed it from one of your downstairs neighbors. But I'll put it back when I'm done. They'll never even know. No worries." She sets the paper on the kitchen counter.

"But . . ."

"Cute dog," Theodora says, cutting Pru off, bending down to stroke Emmett's head. She's got a heavy backpack on, as does the other girl, the quiet one. This new girl is older, college age maybe. She's wearing black leggings, big black boots, a rusty-red wool sweater. Her auburn hair is braided and pinned up in a messy bun. Her face is pale and her green eyes look dazed. Pru wonders if she's on drugs, this girl.

Theodora cuts through the kitchen and into the dark living room, where she pulls back the blinds and looks down at the street. "All clear," she says, the relief in her voice audible. "No cops. No store manager."

"Are you . . . you're being chased by the police?" Pru asks, watching uneasily from the kitchen. It's awful enough to have these two outsiders in the big-top house, but now the idea that they might be in trouble with the law puts a new weight on her chest. Her legs are heavy; she feels light-headed and achy all over. She wants, more than anything, to ask Theodora for the pills, to slip one onto her tongue right now and swallow it down, but she doesn't want to seem desperate. She's not an addict, after all.

"Hey, Fire Girl," Theo calls, still looking out the window. "Yesterday, when I came to see you, I had a bag with me. An old canvas army satchel with pins on it?"

"Yeah, you left it on the hood of the car," the girl says. "I've still got it."

Theodora turns to the other girl, looking shocked, like she can't quite believe what she's hearing. "Now? Is it with you?"

"It's not here, with me, but it's someplace safe."

"And the money?"

"The money's all there. And your books . . . and all the other stuff. I haven't touched a thing."

Theodora lunges forward and hugs the other girl, who seems startled, frightened even. She lets herself be embraced, but looks as uncomfortable as if it were an octopus doing it.

"Thank you, thank you, thank you! You have no idea the shit I'm in because I lost that money," Theodora says into the girl's shoulder. "There's this guy, Jeremy, and the money is his. He's going to hunt me down and gut me if I don't get it to him ASAP."

"Well, you can have it all back," Necco says.

"I can't believe it," Theodora says, smiling as she pulls away. As soon as she does, the other girl scuttles toward the back wall.

"Let's get some light in here," Theodora says, flipping the wall switch. She looks around the room, taking in the circus. "Holy crap!" she exclaims. "What is all this?"

Pru bites her lip, wishes she could turn out the lights, drag both girls back into the kitchen. She's never shown the circus to anyone. When Wayne comes up, she puts what she can away and covers the rest with sheets. She's told Mr. Marcelle about it, described it as best she could. But no one has actually seen it. She imagines how it must look to these two girls: tables pushed together and covered with three red-and-white wooden rings, the clothespin people in bright sequined costumes, the caged animals made from junk held together with glue and wire, the string high wire crossing the three rings; the sad hobby of the lonely fat lady. They must think she's cracked. Bonkers. The most pathetic thing they've ever seen. She's still trying to catch her breath from all the walking and the stairs.

Theodora's eyes move from the center ring to the poster of the fat lady on the wall, Pru's face pasted on. Pru holds her breath, wants to say something, to try to explain, but how can she? Where would she start?

It's all I have, she might say. Or, **I don't have to tell you anything.**

Theodora steps forward, reaching for one of the trapeze artists, gently touching her to send her swinging. "This has to be the most amazing thing I've ever seen," she says and smiles. "Did you do all this?"

Pru nods. She nods so hard and fast that she can't stop, she's like one of those bobble-head dolls.

"Isn't it incredible?" Theodora says, looking at the other girl, who has stepped forward now. Theodora touches the bear on the bicycle, the lions in their cage.

"It is," the other girl says, only half-looking. She glances nervously toward the window. Touches her belly. Pru wonders if she's seen this girl somewhere before. She's not a student at the school, Pru's sure of that. She knows all the kids; she makes it her business to learn each of their names and faces.

"By the way," Theodora says. "My name's Theo. You got a name other than Fire Girl?"

The girl nods. "Necco," she says.

"Necco?"

"Like the candy," the girl says.

"Candy?" Theodora says.

"The wafers," Pru adds. "I love those wafers. When I was a girl I would walk to the store with my daddy and he would let me pick one thing.

I sometimes chose those. A chocolate bar, that would be gone in a minute. But those candies, I could make them last and last if I sucked them, one at a time."

Necco smiles. "I like them, too. They were always my favorite. When I was a kid."

Theodora goes back to watching the trapeze artist swing. "I can't believe you did all this, Mrs. Small. It's amazing. So intricate. Do they have names? The performers?"

Pru reaches for the tiny figure in a top hat and coat with tails. "This is Wayne, the ringmaster. And over there, Mr. Marcelle, the strongman." She smiles as she pets her strongman—Mr. Marcelle in miniature. "We've got Miss Veronica Larrs, who does a whole act hanging by her hair. The Flying Kosomovs. Sergei the Lion Tamer."

Theodora takes everything in. She touches the little performers, rolls the lion cage and clown car, helps the tightrope walkers glide over the center ring. She oohs and aahs and can't seem to stop smiling.

It's true magic, the circus is.

But the other girl is still sticking to the shadows, watching Pru and Theodora rather than the circus. She has the look of a trapped animal—a real-life lion in a cage. She glances toward the window like she's contemplating making a break for it, even though they're two flights up.

Pru picks up her tiny brass elephant, enfolds it in her hand—her good luck, courage-giving pachyderm. Then she asks the question that has been throbbing through her brain since she first set eyes on Theodora on the street.

"Do you have them? Do you have the vitamins?"

Necco steps forward, looking puzzled. "My vitamins?"

Theodora shakes her head. "Different vitamins. I've got them." She unshoulders the backpack, unzips it, and starts rummaging around for what feels like an eternity.

At last, Theodora holds out her hand. Cupped in her palm are four little red pills. She hands them over to Pru.

Pru takes one of the red pills and slips it into her mouth as casually as she can, slides it over her tongue, swallows it down. Necco watches her, her eyes filled with understanding, but no judgment.

Not wanting to seem ungrateful, Pru thanks Theodora before asking, in a timid voice, "But is this all? All you could get?"

Theodora blows out a long breath, looks down at her scuffed black boots. "It's all I have on me," she says at last.

"But I've got money, see. Whatever you need. I left school, cashed my check. Brought you to my home. I was hoping . . . hoping for more."

More. More. More.

She doesn't want to seem desperate. Or pathetic. She sees the two girls watching her, judging the fat lady. But she's used to being judged, has learned that people will think what they will, often the darkest, cruelest things, and there's nothing she can do about it. And she's tired. Tired of making do with what's given her. It's time to stand up for herself. To say what she wants. To demand that she get it. "Our . . . **arrangement** was that I would lend you money to help you out of whatever trouble you're in and you would bring me more vitamins."

"I brought you what I have right now."

Pru licks her lips. "It's just that the vitamins make me feel so much better, and four pills, well, they won't last long."

Theodora looks Pru right in the eyes. "Mrs. Small, I understand," she says. "If I had more, I would have brought them."

"Are there any in the bag you left behind?" Necco asks, stepping forward. She's got one of the lions in her hands, is gently stroking its yarn mane. "There's a bag of pills in there."

"Yes, totally!" Theodora says. "There's a bunch more. I still can't believe you have it and that the money and everything is there. I was sure you and that guy had spent it. I came back the night before last to ask for it, but you were both asleep."

"Wait. You came to the Palace?"

"The Palace?"

"To the car. You came to my car that night?"

"Yeah, but like I said, you were both sleeping. I didn't want to wake you. I was afraid your friend would go ballistic. And you've got that knife."

A knife? Pru thinks.

"What time? What time did you come?"

"Around nine. A little after maybe."

"And Hermes was okay?"

Theodora nods. "Sleeping like a baby. He had his arm wrapped around you."

The girl seems to flinch, clenching the clothespin lion with wire legs in her hands. "You didn't see anything? Anything at all?"

Theodora rummages around in the backpack again, pulls out a pack of cigarettes.

"Can't smoke in here," Pru snaps. "It's against the rules. No-smoking building. My landlord will evict me. He's real strict."

Theodora settles on just holding a cigarette in her hand. "Actually, yeah. That night, when I was by the car, there was someone in the alley. Watching."

"What'd he look like?" Necco asks, eyes huge, frightened. "Did you see his face? Did he have any tattoos? Anything on his wrist?"

"I have no idea. He was in the shadows. I'm not even sure it was a guy. Just someone in a long coat, and when he saw me, he stepped back into the alley. Disappeared."

"Then what?" Necco seems almost frantic now.

"I was spooked, so I ran. I decided to come see you early in the morning to look for my bag. But when I got there . . . One of the police found me and asked me about giving you the knitting needles."

Necco turns away so that her back is to them.

At last, Pru understands. She knows who the girl with the candy name really is.

"Wait a minute," Pru squeals. "You're that girl! The one they're all looking for. The one who killed her boyfriend in the abandoned lot across from the school!" She takes a step back, moving toward the kitchen phone. She'll call the police, that's what she'll do. Say, **There's a murderer in my house.** And Mr. Marcelle had told her there was a reward. Ten thousand dollars. Think what she could do with all that money! Instead of calling the police, she should call him! He could come over, grab this girl, bring her to the police. They could split the reward money, the two of them . . . heroes.

Necco's eyes are steely. "I did not kill him."

She says this so ferociously that Pru takes another, bigger step back.

"Hermes was all I had," Necco says, quieter

now, voice cracking. "Why would I hurt him? I've got no one now."

Pru freezes. She knows about being alone, understands that it's not something you would choose if you didn't have to.

Pru also understands that things are not always what they seem. Knows it's not wise to judge by appearances.

"Okay," she says, suddenly remembering that she's the adult here. The authority figure. It's up to her to get to the bottom of things. "If you didn't kill him, who did?"

"I don't know. But I'm going to find out. Because the whole world will think I did it until I can prove different."

"But how?" Theodora asks. "How are you going to figure it out? I mean, just say the person I saw was the killer—someone in a long coat is hardly a workable clue."

Necco nods. Rubs the back of her head like it hurts.

"I'll start by trying to figure out what Hermes has been up to lately. He'd been gone all the time, said he was working on a secret project. I think he was looking into my past—into bad things that happened to my family. He was keeping something in a locker at the Family Fun Center—I found the receipt in his bag." She reaches into her shirt, pulls out a locker key on a string around her neck to show them. "He was going to take me there yesterday and show me what he'd found. He said it was going to change everything."

"What do you think it could be?" Pru asks, completely drawn in. A real-life mystery. Like the BBC program she loved with the handsome detective.

"Something he didn't want to carry around with him, obviously," Theo guesses. "Maybe because it put him in danger."

Necco nods. "I have to see what's in that locker. I've gotta get there. Today."

Theodora rocks back on her heels, twirling the unlit cigarette between two fingers. "I don't know, Fire Girl. You saw the paper—you're front-page news. The whole city thinks you're a deranged killer." Then, as if just remembering, she smacks her forehead, sticks the unlit cigarette behind her ear. "Oh, crap, that's right! The paper! Let's see what it says."

She goes to the kitchen, comes back with the newspaper. Sure enough, there's a drawing of Necco on the front page beneath a photo of the poor boy who was killed.

Theodora whistles. "Shit! Did you know he was the governor's son?"

Necco shakes her head, her pasty-white face going paler still.

"Matthew Stanton, age nineteen. The governor's offered a ten-thousand-dollar cash reward to anyone with information leading to your capture." She scans the article another minute, then reports, "The good news is that they don't seem to know a thing about you. At least not that they're mentioning. They just call you an 'apparently indigent young woman' and give a physical description. Some of the kids from school helped the sketch artist with the picture." She holds up the paper. "It's a pretty good likeness, huh?"

"And now you've been spotted by the people at that health food store!" Pru says. "There are probably police combing the whole neighborhood!"

Necco fingers the key around her neck. "I have to see what's in that locker."

Theodora sighs, carefully folds the newspaper, and tucks it back into its plastic bag. "If I help you get what's in the locker, will you take me to where my bag's stashed?"

The girl nods.

"Do you have a car, Mrs. Small?" Theodora asks.

"Well, yes, but—"

"We need to borrow it."

No way. No way were these girls taking her car anywhere. In all honesty, Pru isn't even sure if it still runs. It's been parked in the lot behind the apartment building for ages. She hasn't renewed the registration or insurance. No money for such things. And no need—not when the bus that takes her to and from school is so close. Once a week, she stops at the market on the way.

"No one borrows Mabel," she tells them.

"Mabel?" Theodora says. "You named your car **Mabel**?"

"There are pills in the bag, ma'am," Necco says. "Let us borrow the car and we'll go to the bowling alley, then to where I hid the bag. Theo gets her money, you get more of your . . . vitamins."

"And the guy I have to go see, the one all that money belongs to? He can get more vitamins," Theodora adds. "Lots and lots of vitamins."

Pru considers, pleased that her head feels clear, the fog has lifted. The vitamin is working already. She feels less achy. More alive. Ready for anything.

"So can I have the keys, Mrs. Small?" Theodora asks. "I have a license. I'm a good driver. We'll be back in a couple hours. And we'll bring more vitamins. I can leave something of mine here if you like. As collateral."

Pru thinks for a minute. "Like I said," she tells them. "No one takes Mabel."

"But, Mrs. Small," Theodora protests, "I don't think you—"

"I'll drive," Pru says. "I know just where that bowling alley is. I'll call work and tell them I won't be back in today."

"Excellent," Theodora says, a wide grin on her face. "We've got ourselves a plan!" She turns and looks at the other girl. "Before we go, maybe we should do something to disguise Necco. Do you have some makeup? A scarf or wig maybe?"

Pru smiles. She's feeling good now. Back in her element. "This is the circus, dear. We have a thousand disguises."

Necco

〜〜〜

The smell of the Family Fun Center assaults Necco as soon as she walks through the door: floor wax, popcorn, beer, the disinfectant they spray in the shoes. Although it opened only an hour ago, the place is bustling, and already Necco's head aches from the noise.

There are twelve bowling lanes, one of which is occupied by a birthday party full of small boys, all wearing cardboard crowns and whacking each other with cardboard swords. There's an indoor playroom with a huge climbing structure, and a pit full of colorful balls in which half a dozen children are swimming, cackling and cawing.

Kids and adults plunk gold tokens into video games, Whac-A-Mole, the claw. There is a fortune-telling machine in the corner with an old witchy mannequin head: LOVE? FORTUNE? LET MADAME ZELESKI READ YOUR FUTURE. A room with a thick red theater curtain on the door promises LASER TAG.

"Over there," Theo says, pointing to the lockers down at the end, near the bathrooms. Theo's long blond hair is mostly tucked up into a black felt bowler hat. She's wearing big round glasses with rose-colored lenses from Mrs. Small's costume trunk and looks more like a character from a play than someone from real life. Necco is wearing a dirty-blond, shoulder-length wig, a blue suede jacket with fringe, and huge amounts of makeup; the foundation has turned her pale skin an orangey tan color, and they've topped it off with sticky mascara, bright red lipstick. She has on Hermes's big sunglasses with the mirrored lenses. They calm her, help tone down the brightness and noise, help her to feel safe, help distract her from how her face feels itchy and tight. When she'd caught sight of her reflection in the door, she'd hardly recognized herself. Theo had begged her to stay in the car with Mrs. Small, to let her get whatever was in the locker, but Necco had refused. She wasn't trusting this to anyone. Opening Hermes's locker was something she needed to do. But now that she's actually here, inside, she doesn't like this place. The closeness of it. The noise. The feeling she has that everyone's watching her and can see right through her ridiculous disguise.

She follows Theo by the snack bar, where a teenage boy with bad acne is filling a display case with greasy pizza.

"Help you?" he calls out to them.

"No thanks, we're all set," Theo calls back cheerfully. Necco feels his eyes on them as they make their way to the bank of bright orange lockers. She scans the rows until she spots it: 213.

2 plus 1 is 3. If it were a sequence, it might be followed by 314, 415, 516.

Necco remembers that her father used to give her and Errol math puzzles like this. Find the next numbers in the sequence. She closes her eyes, recalls how she would lie on her belly on the living room rug and fill whole sheets with the answers. She could work on this for hours, so focused on the numbers that everything else melted away.

Errol grew bored, asked for proper math problems. "You know," he said. "Something that will teach us things we might actually use in real life."

"This **is** teaching you useful skills," Daddy said.

"Yeah, maybe if we're going to grow up to be code breakers or spies or something."

"Your sister seems to enjoy it," Daddy said.

Errol smiled. "Gonna grow up to be a spy, Little E?"

"Maybe," she said. "But if I do, I won't be able to tell you, so you'd never even know it."

Errol laughed. "You'd never be able to keep a secret like that from me, Little E."

Taking the key from around her neck, she bends down, fits it into the lock, and twists. The door springs open like something's pushing from the other side. A snake in a can. She's seen that trick before.

No snake here, though. A large manila envelope sits in the middle of what is otherwise an empty locker. She picks it up, surprised by how light it is. She'd been expecting something with more substance. She undoes the clasp and reaches inside. Her fingers tremble.

"What is it?" Theo asks, leaning in for a better view.

"I don't know," Necco says. "Papers."

"We should take them with us. Get out of here. You can read them in the car."

Necco is only half-listening. These papers were last touched by Hermes, and she imagines that they are covered with the faint ghosts of his fingerprints, the loops and swirls that were his and his alone. Matthew Stanton, the governor's son.

She pulls out a stack and flips through: on top is a note that says: **Meet at Ashford Library,**

1 pm, Mystery section. Yesterday's date was scrawled at the bottom and circled. This was part of his surprise. He was taking her to the library, taking her to meet someone, it sounded like, but who? Now she'd never know.

Beneath this are photocopied newspaper articles, sheets of legal paper covered with the familiar scribble of Hermes's handwriting (**your handwriting looks like tiny bird footprints,** she'd told him once, **like a little sparrow has danced across the page**), and a photograph of a blue house with a stone walkway. Necco recognizes it immediately. She lets her finger trace the stone path, knock, knock, knock on the front door. Hello, anybody home? If she opened the door, she'd see Daddy's favorite chair and the little table with his pipe and tobacco, the couch with the sagging springs where Errol might be curled up with a comic book.

"What is it?" Theo asks, squinting down at the photo.

"It's my house," she says. Her voice feels like it doesn't belong to her. She thinks of Promise the doll, of how she used to speak, sing a little song, and imagines her own voice small and hollow, like Promise's once was.

"Wait, you have a house? I thought you lived in that old car."

"It's the house I grew up in. It was destroyed in the Great Flood."

"Great Flood?" Theo says, eyebrows raised questioningly.

"That's what my mother called it. The flood that destroyed our house, killed my father and brother. When the dam broke?"

Theo shakes her head. "I don't think that dam has ever broken. I did this whole project on it. It was originally built back in 1836 to provide power for the mill, then the Army Corps of Engineers rebuilt it in 1939. That dam is totally solid. There's never been a single problem."

"My mother . . ." Necco says, frowning. "She had a funny way of looking at things, kind of reframing them. When she told a story, you had to work hard to pick out pieces of the truth."

She flips to a photocopy of a newspaper article from June 17, 1975, about a murder-suicide. She scans the article. Realizes this is about her father's parents. They weren't killed in an accident at all. The story she picks out is horrific. Her eyes catch on a quote from a neighbor: " 'Miles came to our house covered in blood, hysterical. He said a man in a chicken mask had killed his mother,' Mrs. Richardson told reporters."

Necco takes in a startled breath.

He's the King of Liars, her mother said. **A jackal-hearted man. He goes by many names: the Chicken Man, Snake Eyes.**

And here's the worst part of all: he's the one responsible for the Great Flood. Other terri-

ble things, too. Like what happened to your grandparents.

Necco feels the room getting smaller. Everything falls to the floor, papers scattering. And there, all pixelated and strange in a photocopied newspaper article, is her daddy's face looking back at her.

LOCAL PROFESSOR SOUGHT FOR QUESTIONING IN THE DISAPPEARANCE OF HIS WIFE AND DAUGHTER FOUL PLAY SUSPECTED

"Is everything all right here, girls?" A man wearing a Family Fun Center polo shirt has approached them. He's looking down at the scattered pages, at the article with her daddy's face on it.

Is

Everything

All right

A lightning bolt of pain starts at the old scar along the back of her head and radiates through her skull. Necco feels the waves wash over her, pull her under; she's coughing, gasping, but there's no fighting it. She lets the dark water take her down.

Theo

~~~

Necco's face is slack, her eyes unreadable behind the mirrored sunglass lenses. The papers she was holding are scattered at her feet.

"Necco?" Theo says, but the girl doesn't respond, does not seem to hear her.

Shit. This is so not the time to go all catatonic.

Theo takes the glasses off Necco's face. Her eyes are flat, staring down at the papers on the floor.

"Hey, Fire Girl, you there?"

"The Chicken Man," Necco says. "He was real."

"Has she been doing drugs?" the bowling alley man asks Theo. His skin is yellow in the flickering fluorescent lights. He's got a bad comb-over and smells like last night's vodka covered up with cheap cologne. "Is she on drugs, or what?"

"No sir," Theo says, heart pounding. "She's okay. She's just tired. And she didn't eat breakfast this morning. Low blood sugar, you know?" She remembers the prenatal vitamins—didn't pregnant women get funky blood sugar? Was that part of morning sickness?

———————

"Come on, Necco." Theo strokes her face, marveling again at how bizarre she looks with all that orange makeup Pru put on her. Like an Oompa Loompa.

"Necco?"

Necco shifts, turns Theo's way; her eyelids flutter. "Yeah?"

"See," Theo says to the bowling alley guy. "She's okay."

"She don't look okay to me. I'm calling 911," the man says, pulling out a cell phone and punching the numbers in.

"No, please," Theo says. "We're leaving. She's totally fine. Really."

But the man is talking, describing the situation to a dispatcher, saying they'd better send both the cops and an ambulance. "Looks like drugs," he says with authority.

Theo hurriedly gathers up all the papers scattered across the floor and tugs at Necco. "We've gotta go," she says, looping her arm around the frozen girl and steering her toward the exit, through the bowling alley doors, and down the ramp to the parking spot, where Mrs. Small waits in the car. It's an ancient Chevy Impala, with a tan exterior covered with rust. Theo opens the door to the backseat, and Necco crawls in, her wig crazily askew. She leans against the opposite door, closes her eyes.

"What on earth happened?" Pru asks.

"I don't know, exactly. She just kinda checked out. The guy inside just called the cops. We've gotta get out of here. Now."

Sirens wail in the distance.

"What was in the locker?" Pru asks, turning the key.

"A bunch of papers. Newspaper articles mostly." She jumps into the giant bench front seat beside Pru, still clutching the papers she'd gathered up from the bowling alley floor.

"Necco, dear, where to?" Pru asks, leaning her head into the backseat. "Where do we need to go to get Theo's bag and the vitamins?"

Necco doesn't respond.

"Just drive, Mrs. Small," Theo says. She looks at the papers in her hands. The photo of the house has something on the back. An address.

"Okay, I'm driving, but where are we going?" Pru asks, wheeling out of the parking lot.

"One ninety-eight Birchwood Lane," Theo tells her.

"Where's that?"

"The east side of the river somewhere. Take Franklin to Chandler, then head over the Steel Bridge."

"I've got an old map in the glove box," Pru says. Theo fumbles with the latch as she slips and slides on the cracked vinyl seat; of course there's no GPS in this beast of a car. The ashtray is full of dusty potpourri. One of Pru's wire-bodied acrobats with a papier-mâché head hangs from the rearview mirror.

"What's on Birchwood Lane?" Pru asks while Theo pulls out the map and starts to orient herself.

"It's where Necco grew up. There's a photo of it here in the papers Hermes hid in the locker."

"So why do we want to go there?"

"I don't know; have you got a better idea? Maybe there's someone there who knows her. Family or something."

"There's no one there," Necco whispers. "The house is gone."

Theo turns and looks at Necco in the backseat. "Good to have you back among the living, Fire Girl," she says.

"The house is gone," Necco repeats. "Lost in the flood."

"What?" Pru asks. "What on earth is she talking about?"

"Necco told me her house was destroyed in some big flood. She said the dam broke."

Pru shakes her head. "I've lived here my whole life—not just me but generations of Smalls before me, including men who helped build the dam and factory. That old dam has never broken. If it had, I'd know about it."

"Right? That's what I told her," Theo agrees. "I bet the house is still there."

"We're not going there!" Necco springs forward, leaning into the front seat space. "I promised I wouldn't! We **do not** cross the bridge!" She says this with such intensity that Theo feels a little afraid.

"Okay, okay," Theo says. "Whatever you say."

Necco sinks into the backseat again, goes back to staring out the window.

"Whatever **she** says?" Pru hisses. "Why is she the one calling the shots? I don't mind saying I think your friend here has a few loose screws."

Pru looks at Necco in the rearview mirror, and Theo glances back, too. Necco is gazing out the window, seemingly oblivious to their conversation, but Theo knows she's listening carefully.

"And don't forget," Pru goes on in a too-loud whisper, "she's wanted for murder! I know she looks innocent, and I'm all for giving people the benefit of the doubt, but what if she did it? What if she's actually dangerous? Maybe the best thing, for all of us, would be to drop her off at the police station. Let them sort it out."

Necco flinches slightly, puts her hand on the door handle like she's thinking about bailing out.

"No," Theo says firmly. "She's innocent. And remember, if we do that, I'll never get my bag back and you'll never get your vitamins."

Pru purses her lips. Then, at last, she says, "So where to, then?"

"Just drive," Theo says. "And don't cross the river."

Necco takes her hand off the door handle. "Go to Old Town," she says. "That's where the bag is."

Pru nods, steers the car back along the river, avoiding downtown.

Theo returns to the stack of papers on her lap. She picks up the newspaper article on top, the one Necco had been staring at in the bowling alley, and starts to read it out loud:

Dr. Miles Sandeski, a sociology professor at Two Rivers College, is being sought for questioning about the disappearance of his wife and daughter. Police were alerted when Sandeski's sister-in-law, Judith Tanner, arrived at their home on Birchwood Lane, after receiving a panicked phone call from Sandeski's wife, Lily. Ms. Tanner was greeted by Dr. Sandeski, who tried to send her away, explaining that his wife and daughter had to leave town unexpectedly. Ms. Tanner

said that there were signs of a struggle in
the house: overturned furniture, a broken
lamp. And Sandeski's clothes were muddy
and had what Ms. Tanner believed to be
blood on his shirt. Ms. Tanner left and
notified police, who have thus far been
unable to locate Dr. Sandeski, his wife or
daughter. Detective Samuel Glover gave the
following statement: "The disappearance
of Mrs. Sandeski and her fourteen-year-old
daughter is very concerning and we have
reason to suspect foul play. Dr. Sandeski is
wanted for questioning and anyone with any
information about his whereabouts should
contact police immediately."

Dr. Sandeski's supervisor, Dr. Bruce
Nessler, issued a statement earlier today:
"We at Two Rivers College are very taken
aback by this news. Miles is an outstanding
teacher, much loved by his students and
colleagues. The idea that he may have
harmed his wife and daughter is baffling
to all of us here at Two Rivers. We are all
praying for their safety."

"I don't understand what this has to do with
anything," Pru says.

Theo turns to Necco in the backseat. "This
article is from four years ago. The professor, he's
your father, right? And the fourteen-year-old girl
is you."

Necco keeps her head pressed against the window, doesn't look at Theo. "My father would never have hurt us," she says. "My father loved us. It's all wrong. That's not what happened."

"Miles Sandeski," Theo says. "He's the guy who wrote the book, right? **The Princess and the Elephant?**"

"Yes," Necco says, turning to look at Theo.

"I read it."

"I know," Necco says. "I saw the copy of it in your bag."

"Her father wrote a book?" Pru asks. "What kind of book?"

"It's all about good and evil, and myth and stuff. How we are shaped by our experiences and how it is that some of us grow up to be killers and some of us are the good guys. But really, what he says is that it's not so black and white, you know? We've all got good and evil inside us."

"So what happened to Dr. Sandeski? Is he still missing?" Pru asks. "Is he still on the run?"

Theo shuffles through the papers again, pulling out another photocopied newspaper article, and skims it. "Oh, shit," she says. "I'm so sorry, Necco."

"He's dead," Necco says. "Mama told me he and Errol drowned in the flood."

"I don't know about the flood part, and I don't see any mention of anyone named Errol, but yeah, I'm sorry—your father did drown. This article is from a couple weeks later." She clears her throat and reads it out loud:

DROWNING VICTIM IDENTIFIED

The human remains found on April 27 by a fisherman in the north branch of the Lacroix River have been identified as 45-year-old Dr. Miles Sandeski of Ashford. Dr. Sandeski, a professor at Two Rivers College, has been missing since April 12, and has been wanted for questioning regarding the disappearance of his wife and daughter. Police are calling Dr. Sandeski's death a suicide but have not released further details. His wife, Lily, and fourteen-year-old daughter, Eva, remain missing.

Theo looks back at Necco.

"Eva Sandeski," she says. "That's you."

Necco nods, looks out the window. "It was," she says. "Once."

Necco

~~~~~

Eva Sandeski.

So strange to hear someone speak her true name again.

She repeats it again and again in her head, can hear her mother and father calling to her: **Eva, Eva, Eva.**

Then Errol: **You there, Little E? Anyone home?**

She'd worked so hard to put all that away, to bury the details of her past deep inside her. But now, now she understands that if she wants to make sense of what happened to Hermes, of who killed her mother, she's got to unlock that box and try to remember everything she can. She begins at the beginning:

My name was once Eva Sandeski. I lived in a house at 198 Birchwood Lane. My mother was a painter and had a studio at the back of the house. My father was a professor. He wrote a book about the Princess and the Elephant.

These are things she remembers. And if that's not enough, it's all here in these papers Hermes collected.

Necco is skimming through them, trying to absorb all this new information. Trying to understand that everything Mama told her was a lie.

It was ironic, really. Necco never really believed Mama about Snake Eyes being after them, about them being followed, watched, in constant danger. But all that was true. And yet the biggest lie her mother told, about the Great Flood, Necco bought without question.

"Tell me what you remember about this Great Flood," Theo says now. They're driving across town, taking back roads to avoid congested areas. Pru doesn't want to risk someone recognizing Necco despite the fact that she's straightened up her wig.

"Not much," Necco admits. "Most of what I know came from things my mother told me after."

"But you must remember something," Pru insists.

Necco shuts her eyes, tries to go back to the

day of the flood. Maybe she's got something that might help locked up inside her: like the princess in her father's story.

It was raining hard. The rain, it had a pattern to it as it drummed on the roof, hammered against the windows. She would sit for hours, hypnotized, as she tried to decode it, to discover the meaning behind the constant taps, some light, some heavy and pelting as the BBs from Errol's rifle.

They'd been watching the river rise behind their house, talking about it as if it were a living thing, unpredictable and dangerous.

Her father had put sandbags around his workshop.

"Maybe we should build an ark," he'd joked to Mama, casting a wary eye at the rushing water. Objects floated by: boards, a basketball, some poor kid's plastic rocking horse.

"I just hope the dam holds," Mama had said, her small voice coming from under a black umbrella. Mama was beautiful then: flawless ivory skin, her flaming hair in a thick braid, hand-knit sweaters and tailored pants.

The water had an angry look, a roaring voice. It was the backdrop they lived with those last few days, the sound that nearly deafened them, dimmed out every other noise. They had to shout at each other to be heard over it, yell at the top of their lungs to ask to have the maple syrup passed at breakfast, to say, **Good morning, how did you sleep, what did you dream, what are you going to do today, no going out because the roads are closed, shut down with a big orange barricade and flashing lights, the river got too high.**

It makes her head ache, all this remembering. "There was a flood, I'm sure of it," Necco begins. "I remember water all around me. Being pulled under then carried off by it. Hitting my head on something: a rock in the river, I think. Then my mother finding me by the river the next morning. She said it was a miracle I'd survived."

Necco remembers her mother saying, "Look what I saved for you," and pulling Promise the doll out of the duffel bag she'd hurriedly packed with things from the house: a few changes of clothes, her and Daddy's wedding photo, the locket that had the tiny picture of Daddy as a little boy dressed up as Robin Hood.

"Maybe your father tried to kill you," Pru suggests now. "Maybe he went crazy or something and your mother took you on the run."

"No," Necco says. "That's not what happened." There's not much she's sure of about that day, but she knows, knows in her heart, that her daddy would never have hurt her. He loved her. He shared things with her. Secret things. Like his invention. His terrible invention. And the voice that came out of it:

I'm whoever you want me to be.

And that laughter, that horrible chorus of laughter.

Necco closes her eyes, tries to think back to that day. She remembers running out to Daddy's workshop in her yellow rain slicker, her father right behind her. They were going to check for leaks. Errol had gone down the road to see if the river had washed it out by the bend.

She got to the workshop first and found something frightening there. But what? Daddy's invention. It was under the tarp. But it had made a noise. It was **alive.** She'd screamed for her father, and he came running, opened the door to his workshop, and for just an instant, as he stood in the doorway, he was a perfect silhouette, a shadow man. She remembered a drawing Errol did of her once, shining a light on one side of her face, with a piece of paper pinned to a board on the other. He traced her silhouette, then when he was done, said with a very pleased voice, "Look, it's you."

But it wasn't her.

There was the slope of her nose, her familiar chin, the tousled hair, and even the hint of eyelashes—but this was a ghost version of herself. An empty shell.

That's what she'd thought of then, as she watched her daddy's shadow stand in the door of his workshop.

"What is it?" he had asked, stepping in.

And what happened then? She strains to remember and can't. Her poor, cracked head aches.

Necco tucks all the papers back into the envelope, slides it to the seat next to her, and rubs at the back of her head, fingers finding the ridge of a scar hidden under her hair.

"So where is it we're going, exactly?" Pru asks now from the front seat of the car.

"Turn left up here," Necco says.

"Does that even go anywhere?" Theo says doubtfully.

"It leads to the Jensen Mill," Pru says. "But I'd imagine it's in sorry shape. Hasn't been open for decades now. Is that where you have the bag stashed?" Pru asks, turning to Necco with a worried look, like it isn't a safe place to leave the precious vitamins.

"Just keep going," Necco tells her. "When you get to the building, pull up right at the front."

The road is in bad shape, completely washed out in places. They bang and bump their way along. Pru navigates the big car around the worst of the potholes and washouts, but the shocks are gone and they keep bottoming out. The old brick mill comes into view—a hulking behemoth, four stories high, it stretches along the river's edge. Its tall, arched windows are smashed, and its crumbling smokestacks reach for the sky. Faint outlines of the words JENSEN WOOLEN MILL whisper beneath them.

"Stop the car," Necco says. "I need you guys to wait here. **Do not** follow me. **Do not** come in. Just wait. I'll be back in fifteen minutes."

They have to think she's hidden the bag in the building. They can't see her go into the back entrance to the Winter House.

"But how do we know you'll come back at all?" Mrs. Small asks.

"I will," Necco promises.

But will she? What does she owe these people? Yes, they helped her, saved her even, but really, wasn't it all because they both want something she's got? It's the only thing that's kept the circus lady from turning her in, she's sure.

But she'll keep her end of the bargain. They took her to the bowling alley. She'll give them the bag. Then be done. They'll part company, she'll figure out her next move.

"Because she's leaving us her backpack and all the stuff she got at the locker," Theo says.

"No way," Necco starts to argue. "If you think I—"

"Look," Theo cuts her off. "It's either leave your stuff as insurance or I come with you. That's just how it's going to be."

Pru gives an enthusiastic, satisfied nod. "Good idea," she says.

Necco thinks a minute. She doesn't want to

compromise the safety of the Winter House. She can't let anyone know where the entrance is. Even bringing them here, this close, is stupid and dangerous. She knows her mother would not approve, can almost hear her asking, **What are you doing, Necco? Didn't I teach you better than this?**

"Okay," Necco agrees, hesitantly. They have no reason to run off with her papers; Necco's the one with the upper hand here—she's got what they both need. But they've still gotta follow the rules. "But you stay here, in the car. No matter what." She unzips Hermes's bag and takes out a small metal-barreled flashlight.

"Deal," Theo says. "Now pass me your backpack." Necco does, and Theo takes it and hugs it on her lap.

"The backpack stays closed," Necco orders. "I'll know if you've looked through it, and if you have, our deal is off. You get no bag, no money." She turns to Pru. "No **pills.**"

Theo nods in agreement. Necco opens the door and hops out. She scans the area, sees it's deserted, and runs for a side door that has been broken for years. She slips through it into the dusty, cool mill. Even though the mill hasn't run in years, the building still smells like oil, heat, and friction. She can almost feel the thrum of the looms. The brick walls and wooden ceiling were once white but are now a dusty gray, and tagged with graffiti. The junked remains of the old looms lie in rows, sad, piano-size machines of iron and wood with notched gears and wheels; some are still loaded with rotten thread.

She's never spent much time in here, knowing it was often populated with kids getting high and fooling around; they'd heard stories about the Jensen Mill ghost, a little girl who once worked at the mill and died, sucked into a cutting machine, before she was eleven. They said if you went late at night and called to her, she might answer. That on certain nights, you could hear the noise of the machines, a vibrating thrum so loud you couldn't hear yourself think, and then, on top of it, one voice—the little ghost girl looking for her missing arm.

Necco doesn't believe in ghosts. But she believes in danger.

Walking quietly, she pauses by the remnants of an old loom, listening. She hears something far off, from the other end of the building. A small scuttling. Rats probably, dragging off the remains of some stoner kid's sandwich. Just to be sure, she draws her blade. Somewhere in the distance, from the floor above her, maybe, she hears what sounds like crickets chirping.

Necco creeps through the ruined building, trying to shake off the feeling she isn't alone, and climbs out through a busted window on the other side. She slides her blade back into the sheath and sprints down the overgrown road until she gets to the camouflaged metal lid that marks the back-door entrance of the Winter House.

After checking to make sure Theo hasn't followed, she leans down, finds the handle, and pulls the hatch up. She lowers herself onto the old metal ladder, closing the hidden door over her head.

The cool, damp air comforts her, smells like home. She flips on the flashlight and scuttles along the stone tunnel to the Winter House door, which is closed, just as she'd left it early this morning.

As soon as she pushes it open, however, she knows that something isn't right. She does a sweep of the room: the bed she had neatly made this morning has been stripped bare, the covers tossed in a heap on the floor. The dishes, pots, and pans have been pulled out of their places on the makeshift cupboard and piled on the floor.

She detects a familiar, sweet scent. Pipe tobacco. Like her father used to smoke. The scent brings her back to such a clear vision: her father standing in the doorway to his workshop, just a silhouette. He'd come because she'd yelled for him. Because the thing on the workbench, the machine under the tarp, had made a noise.

"I heard a voice," she'd told him.

And her father had stepped forward, pulled back the tarp, and the machine, his terrible machine, was on, the tubes glowing like fierce eyes, the static humming like a voice. And then, a voice had come through, an actual voice, and it had spoken to them.

Danger, it said. **You're in danger.**

Then, **He's here!**

She shakes away the memory, continues scanning the room, sees no hint of movement from the shadows.

She hears the voice in her mind again: **Danger. You're in danger. He's here!**

Remembering what she came here for, she runs to the bed, pulls it back from the wall, and discovers that the loose bricks that covered her secret hiding place have been pulled out, revealing an empty cavity.

Theo's bag is gone.

How could anyone have found that hiding spot, or even found their way into the Winter House? Had she been followed yesterday without realizing it? Had she been careless in her panicked state? Or was it just an accident that someone found the place now? But her mama had taught her better than that—there were no such thing as accidents.

Her mama had also taught her to check behind her, to be extra careful of blind spots, but Necco had been so absorbed with getting Theo's bag, and distracted by the memories of her father and his machine, that she'd forgotten. So when the figure who has been hiding behind the open door springs forward and tackles her, Necco is not prepared. She has no time to go for her blade. The flashlight is knocked from her hand, and the next thing she knows, her face is pressed down into the cold stone floor, her right arm grabbed and twisted up high behind her, making escape impossible.

Fred

〰️

There are few things Fred hates worse than rats. And this place is crawling with them. Fred has seen only one, but he knows that where there's one, there are more. Many, many more. He's sure he can hear them, scuttling around in the dark corners, hiding under the wrecked machines. The old mill is in horrible shape—floorboards rotten, bricks crumbling. He imagines falling through the floor, being knocked unconscious. No one would find him. The rats would eat him.

He breaks out in a cold sweat just thinking about it: their little orange teeth ripping through his clothes.

Then he worries about his birds. Who would take care of the birds if he disappeared down here, became rat chow?

It's comical, really—he can bench-press three hundred pounds and here he is all freaked out because he saw one stinking rat.

He tells himself, **Get yourself together, my friend.**

He takes a breath, looks around. There's no one here.

Un-freaking-believable.

His brother had given him simple instructions: "Follow that guy. Do not let him out of your sight."

Fred had gotten a call from his brother earlier that day telling him to come to the library right away—the guy they'd been looking for was back.

James had been hired by the governor to track down his son, Matthew. James had followed Matthew around town for a few days, saw him meet with this kid a couple times (always in the library, in the mystery section). The last time was the same day Matthew ended up dead.

Fred's mission was simple. Follow the kid out of the library. Don't lose him. Find out all he could.

And somehow, the kid had disappeared. Like a magician. Now you see him, now you don't. Poof.

Maybe the rats got him. Or some magic porthole opened up and the guy walked straight through into another dimension.

Fred shakes his head. He doesn't like unsolved

mysteries, and he sure as hell doesn't believe in magic or other dimensions. This makes no damn sense at all. The kid had spent hours at the library, then headed out on foot across town. He didn't take any buses. Just hoofed it down to the river, crossed at the Steel Bridge, and made his way to the old mill. Fred, sensing that the squirrely kid now suspected he was being tailed, backed off a bit. James had said the kid might be dangerous, might even be armed. That he was somehow connected to the governor's son who got a knitting needle through his left eyeball. Shit. What a way to go.

"Follow him. Try to figure out who he is. Where he lives. What his connection to the governor's kid might be. Why was Matthew meeting with him? Right now, other than finding the homeless girl Matthew was shacked up with, this mystery kid is the biggest lead we have. Who knows, maybe he can even lead us to the girl. Or give us a name. Anything."

Fred didn't carry a gun. James did, but he was the real PI and totally got off on the image. He had a fancy silver PI badge that he flashed whenever he could (especially at pretty women) and a concealed carry permit. Fred was just the hired muscle. The one who did the grunt work and showed up when James, who was a skinny guy—and kind of lacking in the balls department when push came to shove—needed backup.

James is across town meeting with the governor, giving him an update. Probably being served some kind of fancy coffee in a huge office with a view.

Fred's phone rings out his text tone: chirping crickets. He takes it out of his pocket to see a text from James.

You still got eyes on the kid?

James loves talking the PI talk, which Fred suspects he mostly got from TV.

Fred's the younger brother, the one who makes shit money driving a delivery truck for Paglieri and Sons and lives in a hole-in-the-wall apartment; the quirky brother with the cockatoos (the damn noisy pigeons, James calls them). He doesn't want to be seen as a failure by his older brother, who, if truth be told, is really kind of a prick even if he does make a ton more money and gets to have coffee with the governor.

Yes he types back and then gets another chirp in response.

Good.

"Shit," Fred mumbles as he sticks the phone back in his pocket. He bites the inside of his cheek, thinking.

He'd seen the kid go into the old mill. Fred had waited a few minutes, then followed him in. That was nearly half an hour ago now, and Fred has searched the whole godforsaken place and found no trace of the kid. Had he backtracked and left?

Had he taken another way out? But why come in here at all? The mill itself is massive, and now Fred is all the way at the other end of the building. He's up on the top floor, where machines he can't identify lie in ruins, and wooden bobbins loaded with faded thread are piled here and there. Long bolts of fabric, chewed through by generations of rats, lie moldering on the old wooden floor. The air is thick with dust and decay. He's also found an old porno magazine, some graffiti tags on the wall, a few smashed beer bottles, and the burned-out remains of a small campfire.

Fred wants to give the kid up for gone, get the hell out of this creepy place and head back home to his birds. His stomach rumbles. He never even had lunch. He'll pick up a double bacon cheeseburger on the way home. His mouth waters thinking about it.

The crickets chirp again, and out comes the phone.

Get me the kid's name and there's an extra hundred bucks in it for you.

Right. Sure. Fred can feel the hundred slipping through his hands just like the kid has. Like a damn eel.

Feeling like the upper level has been sufficiently searched, he descends the rickety circular stairs back to the main factory floor, keeping one hand on the crumbling brick wall, the other on a banister that doesn't feel very sturdy. His footsteps echo on the stairs. He tests each one before putting his full weight down. When he gets to the main floor, he hears it: music. Ducking down, he holds perfectly still, listening hard. It's coming from outside. He jogs over to peer out a broken window in the front of the building. There's a car parked right in his line of sight: a big old rusted-out Chevy Impala. His hopes rise. Maybe the kid came here to meet someone. He gets out his phone, starts snapping pictures, but when he zooms in, he sees it isn't the kid in the car. There's a girl in the front passenger seat; she has long hair, and is wearing a Charlie Chaplin hat for God's sake. She's fiddling with the car radio. The driver shakes her head. When she turns to the girl, Fred gets a good look at her face. He knows who she is in an instant.

But what the hell is Pru Small doing out here?

Theo

〜〜〜

It's been sixteen minutes and Theo is getting antsy. She's flipping around stations on Pru's radio: Top 40, jazz, a preacher talking about the power of prayer.

And when you are in your darkest hour of your darkest day, he's saying, right before Pru turns to Theo, says, "Change the station. I'd rather hear anything than this ding-dong."

Theo laughs. "Ding-dong?" She raises her eyebrows. "Not a religious person, Mrs. Small?"

"My daddy, he would have called that man a charlatan, and he would have been absolutely right."

"How do you know?"

"I'm from the circus, Theodora. I know all the tricks showmen use."

Theo flips the radio off, pulls out her knitting bag, and takes stock.

"You knit?" Pru asks, voice full of surprise.

"Yeah," Theo says, pulling out some yellow angora yarn she'd bought once because she loved the soft texture and bright, lemony color. "My aunt—well, she's actually my mom's aunt—taught me when I was a kid. Then I kinda forgot about it. I started in again last year 'cause I couldn't find any leg warmers I actually liked so I had to make my own."

Pru is smiling. "What else have you made?"

"Hats, scarves, mittens. I made this bag." She holds up her patchwork felted bag with its bright colors and odd shapes. "I haven't tried a sweater or anything big. I'm not into complicated patterns. I'm more of what you'd call an intuitive knitter. I start projects not even knowing exactly what they're going to be sometimes. Like my bag. I thought I was going to make a blanket of patched-together squares, then I had the idea to do the bag."

"Amazing," Pru says. "I've always wanted to learn to knit."

"It's easy," Theo says. "I can show you if you want."

Theo's phone rings. It's her mom. Calling for like the 212th time since she got home last night and found Theo missing. Theo hasn't picked up. Hasn't answered any of her mom's frantic **WHERE ARE YOU????** texts. Theo doesn't know what to say, and the longer she waits, the worse she feels about it. Her mom probably thinks she's dead in a ditch. Other than Aunt Helen, Theo is all her mom has. Theo's dad died when she was a baby—she doesn't even remember him. Her mom never remarried, has dated a little, but never anything serious. Most days, she still wears her old wedding ring.

Her phone rings four times, and Theo doesn't pick up, lets it go to voice mail, guilt gnawing at her insides. Her mom calls again, leaves a second message. Theo silences her phone. Then she calls three more times, the phone buzzing quietly in Theo's hand like a large, angry insect. Her mom doesn't leave any more messages.

"Someone wants to get ahold of you pretty bad," Pru says, looking worried.

"I guess," Theo says, pushing the message button and putting the phone to her ear to hear her mother on the verge of hysteria.

Theo, my god, where are you? Where did you spend last night? I've been worried sick. I stayed home from work. I called the school and they said you weren't there. A young man named Jeremy came by looking for you this morning. He says you have something that's his, that he needs it back. I didn't like the looks of this boy, Theodora. And he's much older than you. Then, just a few minutes ago,

a policeman came. A detective. He asked a lot of questions, honey. About you and some girl who was living in a car? A girl who is wanted for murder. For killing the governor's son. Detective Sparks said . . . he said they have a picture from a store of the two of you together this morning. Her voice faltered. Please call me. Whatever trouble you're in, I can help.

Shit. Jeremy came to the house. He knows where she lives.

Theo's stomach knots up so tight she's afraid she might throw up all over Pru's front seat. She swallows hard. Takes a breath.

And the police have a picture of her and Necco together. Necco, who is wanted for murder. Fucking wonderful. Maybe Natural You had a security camera? Just as likely, some concerned citizen snapped a picture with their phone once they recognized Necco.

Theo listens to the second message from her mother: Call me, Theo. I'm begging you— this is way more than you can handle on your own. You don't have to handle it on your own. I know a lawyer. Ray. Remember him? I can call him.

Theo remembers Ray. Her mom dated him for a few months: a short man with thinning hair. He's a tax attorney; not exactly the kind of guy to seek advice from when you're wanted for hanging around with a murderer, or especially when you're the one who gave her the goddamn weapon. Wasn't that called being an accessory?

"This is bad," Theo breathes.

"What's that?" Pru asks.

The police probably think she was in on it the whole time. Part of some sick love triangle.

She looks at her phone with a sudden bolt of fear. She's watched enough late-night crime dramas to know that you can be traced with your phone. She imagines that detective from yesterday morning putting in a call, someone tapping a keyboard, using satellites or whatever it is they use, looking at a monitor with a little blipping light on it—**There she is, sir.**

Her heart is racing now.

How long till they find her?

"Fuck!" she says. "Fuck, fuck, fuck."

Pru looks mortified. "Theodora, what on earth—"

Theo pushes open the car door, throws her phone on the ground, and stomps on it as hard as she can with her boot. She smashes it again and again, until it's cracked and in pieces. Then, she scoops them up and runs over to the river's edge, throws them into the water.

"Let me guess," a man calls from behind her.

Fuck. Too late. They've found her. She's been caught. She knows when she turns, it will be Detective Sparks, and he'll have a little gleam in his eye that says, **I knew you were up to no good.** She could run, but the riverbank in front of her is too steep. No place to go.

She spins around. This isn't Detective Sparks or some uniformed cop with a gun drawn. It's a large, bald, thickly muscled man with a curled mustache coming out of the old factory. He doesn't look like a cop at all. He's dressed in jeans and a dirty white shirt.

"Boy trouble?" he asks.

"What?"

"You just busted up your phone, dumped it in the river. How come?"

Theo's heart pounds. Then she straightens her hat, thinks for a second.

"My boyfriend," she says. "He's this total dumb-ass. I'm sick of it. Sick of his lies, his stupid promises. It was his phone, actually. Well, one he got me. So he could always be in touch, know where I was and stuff."

The man smiles. "He's gonna be pissed."

"I hope so." She smiles back.

"This boyfriend . . . you meeting him here?"

The question catches her off guard. "No." Then, she starts to panic. Maybe she should have said **Yes, and he's a big strong guy with a gun and a temper.** She takes a step back, dangerously close to the edge of the river.

Suddenly, Pru is out of the car, coming toward

them. Her hands are fluttering around, straightening her hair and billowy dress. "Mr. Marcelle? What on earth are you doing here?"

The big man turns and looks at Pru, flashing her a smile so warm it makes her cheeks pink.

Pru

～～～

"I was just about to ask you the same question," Mr. Marcelle says. "You're about the last person I expected to see here."

It's the first time Pru's seen him out of his delivery uniform: he's wearing faded blue jeans and a white button-down shirt that's smudged with dirt. She'd like to wash it for him. She imagines treating the stains, letting it soak in her sink while he waits around in his undershirt. She feels her face heat up even more, so she looks down at the ground.

"Not that it isn't a pleasure," Mr. Marcelle adds. "Running into you like this."

Always a gentleman, Mr. Marcelle is.

"I'm sorry, but who the hell are you?" Theodora asks, sounding all tough-girl.

"Mind your language, Theodora," Pru scolds.

Mr. Marcelle sticks out his hand to shake The-odora's. "Fred Marcelle, at your service."

He gives a little bow, which Pru knows is for her benefit. Theodora is clearly a girl who doesn't appreciate chivalry, but Pru does.

"Wait," Theodora says, turning to Pru. "He's the guy from your circus, right? But he's a real person?"

Mr. Marcelle looks from the girl to Pru, bushy eyebrows raised.

Pru's chest gets tight. She's told Mr. Marcelle about the circus, about some of the acts, even, but has neglected to mention that he is one of the stars.

"Mr. Marcelle delivers food to the cafeteria," Pru explains. She wishes she could say more: **He's my friend. He brings me gifts. Gifts for the circus, where he is my strongman.**

"Well, I'm just making a wild guess here," Theodora says, "but I don't think this abandoned old mill is in need of any food deliveries. Not for the last eighty years or so."

Mr. Marcelle chuckles. "I'm actually out here doing my second job."

"And what's that?" Theodora asks. Pru wishes the girl would tone it down a bit, be less rude and abrasive. Kids these days don't know a thing about manners. That's the problem with the world today; people just aren't cordial enough.

"Mr. Marcelle works for his brother," Pru

explains. "He's a private detective." She delivers this bit of news with a certain sense of pride. She knows things about Mr. Marcelle. She knows he moonlights for his brother. And that he has cockatoos. He's shown her pictures of the birds on his phone, beaming like a proud father. Funny little birds with crested heads. He's always building things for them: new perches, bigger cages, swings. He's a handyman, Mr. Marcelle. A jack-of-all-trades.

Theodora's face twists in panic, and she glances over at the old mill. At last, Pru understands that her strongman's mysterious, sudden appearance could mean trouble for Necco.

"That's right," Mr. Marcelle says, his eyes on Theodora.

"So what brings you out here?" Pru asks, trying to keep the suspicion out of her voice. Does Mr. Marcelle carry a gun? She looks for the bulge of one hidden under his white shirt, but is distracted by the way the shirt strains at the seams around his bulky strongman shoulders. She'd like to make a him a custom shirt, one that fits perfectly. She could do that. She's a talented seamstress.

"Well," he says, straightening his shoulders, "I'm not supposed to talk about my work. But I can tell you this much: I was following a man."

A man! Thank goodness. It's not Necco he's after.

"A potentially dangerous man," Mr. Marcelle adds. "And he led me here."

"Dangerous?" Pru exclaims, nervous. "Here?"

Mr. Marcelle puts his great paw of a hand on her arm. "Not to worry, Pru," he says. "He's not here anymore. He slipped away. We're safe." He gives her arm a little reassuring squeeze.

Theodora hasn't taken her eyes off the building, but now she throws Pru a desperately worried look that Pru has no trouble reading: **Necco.**

"A dangerous man?" Pru can't help but repeat.

Mr. Marcelle nods. "This is all hush-hush, but he may be connected to what happened to the governor's son. My brother has a picture of the two of them meeting last week. They're connected in some way. The poor dead kid and this mystery man I've been tailing all over town."

"But who is he?" Pru asks.

"That's all I can say." He holds up his hands in a what-can-I-do? gesture. "Now, you haven't told me yet what you and the young lady are doing out here." He looks pointedly at Theodora.

"Oh," Pru says. "I'm afraid it's not nearly as exciting as your story. This is my niece, Theodora. She's staying with me for a few days. And she's writing a paper for school on old New England mills. So I thought she'd be interested in seeing the Jensen one."

Pru smiles, proud of her easily fabricated

story. Maybe if life in the circus doesn't work out, she can start writing novels—mysteries maybe, where things aren't always the way they seem. A private detective series starring a man who might just resemble Mr. Marcelle. A man with custom-made shirts sewn for him by the woman who loves him.

"A paper, huh?" Mr. Marcelle smiles, but Pru can tell that he's still skeptical. "Well, my advice is to look from the outside only. The building's in bad shape inside. It's not safe. And there are rats ... big nasty ones." He looks genuinely distressed.

"Oh, not to worry, Mr. Marcelle, my niece and I aren't going anywhere where there might be rats. We're going to stay right out here, maybe take a few pictures of the mill, then head out."

"Well, I've got to get going," Mr. Marcelle says. He reaches into his pocket, pulls out his wallet and a pen, and writes something on a business card. "This is my cell number," he says, handing it to Pru, his fingers brushing hers. "I'm sure my guy is long gone, but you call me if you see anything strange here. And like I said, don't go into the building, okay?"

"Of course not."

He winks. "Good. I wouldn't want anything to happen to you. And don't stay too long. It'll be dark soon. Things much worse than rats come around after dark."

"We'll call if we notice anything strange," Pru says and shivers.

"Anytime, Pru," Mr. Marcelle says, and she nods, lets herself imagine calling him just because she feels like it, just to hear his voice before she goes to sleep. He has such a lovely voice.

"Nice to meet you, Theodora. You've got a very special lady for an aunt," Mr. Marcelle calls as he walks back down the driveway. "Take care now."

"Sure," Theodora says, just a trace of teenage sarcasm in her voice.

"How about if we take a quick walk around the building before we go?" Pru booms while Mr. Marcelle is still within earshot. "Maybe you can teach me a thing or two about mills."

"Absolutely, Aunt Pru," Theodora responds, equally loud, as she links arms with Pru. Then she whispers, "Two big questions, Mrs. Small: When's the wedding with your strongman there? And where the hell is Necco?"

Necco

～

"Who are you?"

The man's voice roars in her ear. He's panting; his breath smells sweet, pepperminty, like candy canes. Santa Claus breath. He twists her arm up higher. Ho-ho-ho. Beneath the smell of minty breath, she detects the undeniable scent of pipe tobacco. Her father's smell.

"No one," she says, the pain bright and all-encompassing. She is no one. She is everyone. She is the Fire Girl, but the Fire Girl is face-down on the floor about to have her right arm torn off.

"Are you the one who trashed this place? Who tore it apart?" he asks.

"No," she tells him.

"Where are the people who live here?"

"No one lives here," she tells him.

"You're lying!" he snarls. "There's a woman. One of the Devil's Snuff group."

Necco pauses, heart thudding. **Mama.** How does he know Mama?

"She's dead."

"What?" He relaxes the pressure on her arm but doesn't shift his weight. She's still trapped, and there's no way to reach for her blade.

"She's been dead since spring."

"How?" His voice cracks a little.

Necco considers, not sure how much she should tell this stranger. If this was Snake Eyes, she'd probably be dead already. Whoever this is, he knows Mama. He seems shocked, upset, by her death.

He yanks up on her arm again. "How did she die?"

"She was murdered."

"Oh my God," he says, his voice much softer now. He loosens the pressure on her arm.

Necco lies still beneath him, breathing in the damp smell of stone, waiting to see what he might do next.

"What about the girl? Her daughter?"

Necco tenses. "I don't know anything about a girl."

He jerks her arm up hard. "Bullshit. Tell me what you know or I will seriously hurt you. You think this hurts now?" he asks, pulling on her arm. "This is nothing. It can get worse. Much worse."

"Look, I can't help you, can we just—"

"What did you do to her? Did you hurt her?" he asks, furious.

"No," Necco pants.

"Then where is she? Where is the Fire Eater's daughter?"

"Okay, okay, it's me!" Necco admits. "I'm her daughter."

Her arm is tugged tight again, a wishbone about to snap. Necco cries out.

"Bullshit! The girl I'm looking for has red hair."

"It's a wig. A . . . a disguise," she tells him, panting through the pain.

Keeping her arm twisted, he uses his other hand to snatch off her wig, pulling at her hair where Theo and Pru had bobby-pinned it.

Then he lets go, shifts his weight from her back.

"Eva?" he says, and it's like someone's calling to her from a dream, a name she only half-remembers, but she hears it now the way her father used to say it. As this man is pulling her up, helping her to turn over, she thinks it might just be her daddy's face she finds looking down at her. Daddy with cherry pipe-tobacco smell, his inventor's hands, the fingers thick with calluses and scars.

But it's not Daddy. He's dead. The newspaper said so. It's . . .

"Errol?"

He's older, a man himself now, and his hair is cut short and bleached, but she recognizes his pale blue eyes, the funny cowlick in his hair, the jagged scar over his left eye.

"Oh my God, Little E!" He pulls her up, takes her in his arms, and holds her tight.

"But Mama said you were dead," Necco says, tears coming to her eyes. She clings to him, buries her face in his shirt. It smells like campfires and roasted marshmallows and happy memories of the two of them sleeping out in a tent in the backyard. Errol used to teach her the names of the constellations, telling her that space went on forever. It felt impossible, yet thrilling.

"I guess I kinda was, in a way," he says.

She pulls away, studies him. He's been in the sun a lot—his skin is a warm bronze. He's wearing a faded black tank top, black jeans worn through at the knees, and old sneakers that have seen a lot of miles. Tattoos encircle his bare arms: fish, dragons, tribal designs, and a dagger with one word in neat calligraphy: REVENGE.

"After . . . after what happened," he goes on, "I just ran. I ran and didn't stop running. I stayed as far away as I could. I knew my life depended on it."

"Did you hear? About what happened to Daddy?"

He gives a solemn nod. "I knew the same thing would happen to me if I came back. I'd end up in the river, floating like some kind of scum. Is that . . . how it was with Mama, too?"

Necco nods. "They said it was suicide. And I believed it. I couldn't understand how it was possible, what would make her do such a thing, but I didn't think anyone would kill her. She told me people were after her, after us, but I never believed."

"How did you figure out that it wasn't suicide?"

"Miss Abigail told me. One of the Fire Eaters."

He springs up on the balls of his feet. "Does she know more? Does she know how it happened? Who did it?"

"I'm not sure. I'm supposed to go see her tonight. I'll find out all I can. Maybe . . . maybe you can come with me! She'd love to meet you! She and Mama were so close. Oh, Errol, Abigail is wonderful. She and the other Fire Eaters took us in, taught us how to survive out here. I'd be dead if it wasn't for them, I'm sure of it."

He doesn't say anything, just looks sad and worried. It's all too much for him, she supposes.

"How did you know about this place?" she asks. "That me and Mama stayed here?"

He looks away, then back at her. "Mama showed me."

"What?"

"She brought me here once. Just once. It was last year, in the fall. You and she were living with the Fire Eaters when I found you. Mama hurried me off, took me here to talk."

"But . . . she never told me," Necco says, hating how hurt she sounds. Like she's a little girl again, complaining to Errol about some imagined mistreatment from her parents.

"She thought it was safer that way. For you to keep on thinking I was dead. She said I could never make contact with you."

"But why? I don't understand."

He considers her a minute. "Mama said you don't remember anything from that day. Is that true?"

"Not much." She reaches out and touches his hand. "Errol, tell me what really happened that day. Tell me everything you remember. Mama said there was a flood. A flood that destroyed everything, but that's not what happened, is it?"

"A flood." He grins, but it's sad, and regretful. "I can see why she'd call it that. And she sure was right about one thing—everything we knew and loved was destroyed that day."

"Tell me," Necco begs.

Errol shakes his head. "Not here. Not now. This place isn't safe. Whoever did this—came here and tore your place apart—they might be back. And there was a man following me earlier. I think I lost him, but I can't be sure." He shoots her a worried look. "The last thing in the world I want is to lead him right to you. Especially not now, when everyone in the state is looking for you."

She stiffens. "So you know? You know what they say I did?"

"Yeah, I know. That's why I came looking for you. I saw it in the paper. But I also know you didn't do it."

"I think the man who killed my friend also killed Mama. Maybe Daddy, too. Mama called him Snake Eyes. Sometimes she called him the Chicken Man. Do you know anything about him?"

Errol flinches a little. "We can't do this now. I'm sorry, Little E, we just can't. It's too big." He reaches into his back pocket and pulls out a piece of paper and pen. He tears a scrap off, scribbles on it. He hands her the paper. "Meet me tomorrow at noon here. Come alone, Eva. Don't even tell anyone where you're going. And wear your disguise."

She looks down at the address and recognizes it immediately. She just saw it printed neatly in Hermes's handwriting on the back of a photograph. "Home? You want me to go back home?"

"Yes. Tomorrow at noon."

"But Mama said it wasn't there anymore. The house was destroyed."

"Eva, the house is still there. You'll see for yourself." He turns away. "I've gotta go."

She grabs his wrist, holds it tight. "No! I just found you. I thought you were dead!"

She's sure if she lets him go, she'll never see him again.

"Trust me, Eva, it's safer if we're apart right now. We have to be really careful. I think you're right—it is the same man who killed Dad and Mom and your friend Matthew. And now, he's looking for us. It's us he's after this time."

"Us? Why?"

"He thinks we have something. Something of Dad's."

"But what? Is it that machine? The Edison invention?"

He nods again.

"But I don't have the stupid machine. I don't have anything of Dad's. Why would he think we have it?"

"I'll tell you everything tomorrow," he promises, then turns to go. He stops, faces her again. "Little E, you can't tell anyone you saw me, understand? You've gotta swear."

She nods. Satisfied, he scurries off down the tunnel.

She thinks of going after him. Of tackling

him, making him tell her everything. But she stands alone in the Winter House, listening to his footsteps fade, trying to catch her breath and still her mind, which is running in fast, swirling circles, one word at their center: **Errol.**

Her brother is alive.

Fred

~~~~

After Fred leaves Pru and Theodora, he walks
down the driveway until he knows he's out of
sight, then cuts around in a big loop, following
the river back until he can see Pru's car again.
It's tricky going along the riverbank: the slope
is steep, covered in brambles and stones. More
than once, he nearly loses his footing and ends
up in the murky brown water. He imagines Pru
and the girl hearing the splash, running over just
in time to see him hauling his soaking wet self
out of the filthy water. Not very suave.

After creeping slowly up the bank, he finds
an old willow tree with a good view of the mill
and Pru's car. He hides, making himself comfortable as he watches Pru and the girl circle the old
building. They end up back at Pru's car. They're

arguing. He's too far away and the water roaring over the dam is too loud, so he can't hear exactly what they're saying, but it sounds like they think someone has run off on them.

Could it be his guy?

". . . not coming back," Pru says, her voice angry. "Shouldn't have trusted . . . should have gone with . . ."

Theodora says something about a bag. Pru shakes her head. Theodora looks at her watch.

Then, Fred's eye catches on movement off to the left, behind the factory. A figure is moving quickly along the tree line. Pru and Theodora can't see it; they're too close to the front side of the building.

"There you are," Fred whispers. It's the kid. No doubt about it. Pale blond hair, black tank top, black pants, messenger bag slung over his shoulder. Tattoos all up and down his arms. Fred waits, thinking the kid is going to make his way back to the car, to Pru and the girl. Surely that's what they're doing here, really. That girl Theodora is somehow involved with the mystery man. Has to be. Maybe she's his sweetheart. But Fred's gut tells him it's more complicated than that. And this ain't no lovers' lane. Besides, what is Pru doing here? He doesn't buy that the girl is her niece. Pru Small may be a sweet and charming woman, but she's a god-awful liar.

But the guy doesn't cut over to the car. In fact,

he seems to be doing all he can to avoid it and stay out of sight. Determined not to lose the kid a second time, Fred leaves his perch behind the tree and starts walking along the river again until he finds a spot where he can cut back up farther along the driveway. He sees the kid turning left on the road, back toward town. Fred takes one look at Pru and Theodora just in time to see a girl coming out of the mill. Shit—how many people were hiding out in there? This girl's got long wavy blond hair, sunglasses, and is wearing a blue cowgirl jacket trimmed with fringe. Where on earth did she come from? Was it possible she'd been hiding in there when he'd searched the place? He doesn't think so. He'd been careful, methodical.

He watches as the three of them stand talking—Theodora seems agitated; she's waving her arms around and talking loudly. He catches only one word because she yells it: "Gone!" Then they all get into Pru's car. Fred jogs ahead, finds a big rock at the very end of the driveway to hide behind as he waits for them to drive past. After they pass, and take a right, he comes out of hiding, sucking in a lungful of dust and car exhaust. He catches a glimpse of the kid crossing the Millyard Bridge over to his left. Good. He'll be more careful now. He's not going to lose him again. But he doesn't want to spook him either. He follows a good distance behind, thinking.

Fred worries Pru may be in some kind of trouble and not even know it. She's too good-hearted and naïve, Pru is. All caught up in her tiny circus world.

Visiting with Pru has become one of the bright spots in his dull delivery week. All the other stops he makes, people are friendly, sure, but there's something special about Pru—the sparkle in her eye, the lively way she talks about her circus—that makes his heart feel a little lighter. She reminds him that there is goodness in the world. And innocence still, even in these far-from-innocent times. It's the same feeling he gets being with his birds—that he's in the presence of a being who is truly honest and pure.

He gets to the bridge, still watching the kid, who's reached the other side and has turned left onto Canal Street. He's walking along the sidewalk with his head down, eyes on his phone. Fred pulls out his own phone, calls his brother.

"You still tailing our guy?" James asks.

"Yup."

"Learned anything?"

"No. He's just walking all over the city. Went out to the old Jensen Mill, had a look around, and is heading back downtown now."

"The mill? Weird."

"Yeah." Fred leaves out all the other details, wanting to keep Pru and the girls a secret until he knows more. "Hey, James, can I get you to look up a couple things for me? There's someone I want info on. Her name is Prudence Small. She runs the cafeteria over at the Catholic school."

"Oh, little brother—are you stalking some poor innocent lady?" James says with a chuckle.

"Can you look up relatives?" Fred says, ignoring the jab. "Like if she's got a niece? Also, an address and phone number maybe?"

"Sure, I can get all that, no problem. But you aren't gonna go all Peeping Tom on me, are you? 'Cause you can get arrested for that shit. And if you tell them I helped you find this poor lady, I'm implicated. Know what I'm saying?"

"No worries. No stalking, I promise. I'm just curious."

"Sure you are," James says, laughing unpleasantly. "I'll let you know what I find out about your new ladylove. In the meantime, you lemme know the second you have anything to report on our friend."

"Will do," Fred says, but James has already hung up.

No doubt about it. His brother's a prick. But he's paying Fred twenty-five bucks an hour to tail this kid around town. And Fred needs the money. He wants to move out of his one-bedroom apartment. Get a real place, a little house with a porch and a yard. He wants to build an outdoor aviary for the birds; give them more room, fresh air, sunshine. He imagines himself sitting out there every evening, watching the sun set with the birds. Maybe he could invite people over—someone besides his asshole brother, who comes over for chili, beer, and football once in a while and spends the whole time bitching about the birds, says they're noisy, that they stink. Maybe he'd invite Pru Small over. He imagines introducing her to the birds, taking them out, placing them gently on her shoulders. Wouldn't Pru love that? Hearing their talk, the soft flutter of wings. He smiles at the thought of it.

———

Fred follows his guy to an old-fashioned greasy spoon on Stark called the Koffee Kup. The sign in the window advertises BOTTOMLESS CUP OF COFFEE ONLY ONE DOLLAR! There's an old MG convertible parked in front with a glow-in-the-dark Virgin Mary statue on the dash. The kid goes into the diner, sits down at a booth with an older man. Fred stands behind the MG and has a good view of them through the window. This other guy is gaunt in the face, but he's well dressed in a pair of neatly pressed pants, a white polo shirt, and a navy-blue sport coat. The kid rummages in his messenger bag, pulls out an olive, military-surplus-looking satchel decorated with pins. The waitress comes over, takes their order, and when she walks away, they start talking. The older guy is looking through the satchel.

Fred takes a chance and goes in, heading straight for the counter to take a seat on a beaten-up black vinyl stool that is just close enough to hear their voices behind him. They're talking so low, it's hard to catch every word. It doesn't help that some guy in the next booth has just dumped quarters into the jukebox to hear some old Waylon Jennings song.

In front of him, the big grill sizzles as a cook in a white apron flips two burgers, puts squares of orange cheese on top, pops fries into a basket and lowers them into bubbling oil.

"She walked right in?" the older man asks.

The kid mumbles a response.

"You must have been a sight for sore eyes." He says something else that makes the kid chuckle nervously.

"Lucky I heard her coming," the kid says.

"But you didn't find anything? There was nothing else?"

"No. And I was thorough. The only thing hidden was this bag."

"So what's she doing with this stuff? It's got some other girl's ID in it . . . let's see, here it is . . . Theodora Sweeney. She's a senior over at the Catholic school. The place across the street from where Eva and her boyfriend were camped out."

The name pings in Fred's brain: **Theodora.** The girl Pru was with and a student at the school she works in. It has to be the same girl—how many teenage girls named freaking Theodora could there be?

And "Eva and her boyfriend"—that has to be the governor's son who got killed, and the homeless girl everyone, he and his brother included, is looking for.

He pulls out his phone, sends his brother a quick text as he listens to the conversation behind him: **Another person for you to look up: Theodora Sweeney. Student at the Catholic school.**

"I don't know," the kid says. "Maybe Eva stole it or something? Or maybe they're dealing drugs together?"

"Whatever it is, it doesn't help us, does it?"

The waitress brings them coffee and pie. "Cherry for you," she says. "And chocolate cream for you. Y'all let me know if you need anything else." They thank her and she walks away. Once she's gone, they start talking again.

"Hey, there, what I can get you?" the waitress asks Fred, popping up on the inside of the counter and smiling at him. SHARON, her name tag says.

"Just coffee, please," he tells her, even as his stomach rumbles. No time for a cheeseburger now.

"You sure, hon? We've got six kinds of fresh homemade pie. It's all over there on the board."

She points to a blackboard with white letters that has the lunch menu: CHICKEN AND STUFFING, MEAT LOAF, LIVER AND ONIONS, FRANKS AND BEANS, PATTY MELT. PIES: CHERRY, BLUEBERRY, PUMPKIN, LEMON MERINGUE, CHOCOLATE CREAM, RAISIN.

Fred's thinking that the very idea of raisin pie just seems wrong. He wishes he could order a patty melt, but if the kid bolts, he'll have to get up and follow. The waitress fills his coffee cup.

"Thanks," he tells her, "just the coffee's fine," and goes back to trying to listen to the men behind him.

". . . can't hurt to keep it. Could come in handy."

"Sure, whatever," the older guy says. "Are you going to eat that pie or what?"

"Not all that hungry," the kid says.

"Slide it over here, then. We can't let good food go to waste." There's the sound of a fork hitting a plate, scraping.

"So tomorrow, when she comes," the kid says, voice small and nervous sounding. "I mean . . . you're not gonna hurt her or anything, right?"

The older man laughs. "Not if you can get what I need from her first. I'll be right there listening. If you do your job, I won't even come out to say hello."

"But what if she doesn't have it? What if—"

"Of course she's got it! We've been over this a

thousand times. Miles didn't have it. Lily didn't have it. You don't have it. If she doesn't have it, no one does. And we've gotta do this fast. Gotta get her off the street and get what we need before the cops catch up with her."

There's the sound of the fork scraping the plate, a mug being picked up and set back down.

"I'm gonna go have a smoke," the kid says.

"Okay. I'll pay then meet you outside. I can give you a lift," the man says.

"That'd be good," the kid says. Thirty seconds later, the door opens and closes.

Fred glances to his right, where the older man is paying the check at the register. His gray hair is combed straight back, held in place with oil or pomade.

"Everything okay?" the waitress asks the man.

"Everything was just fine, sweetheart." He reaches for his change, and Fred notices an old, crudely done tattoo on his wrist: a pair of dice, each with one dot in the center.

Theo

〰

They're back at Pru's apartment and Theo is pacing, Pru's little dog, Emmett, making excited circles around her heels. "Shit," Theo says. "Shit, shit, shit."

It had been an awkward ride back to Pru's, after Necco told them she'd gone to where she'd stashed the stuff and the bag was gone.

"Gone?" Theo had asked. "What do you mean 'gone'?"

"Someone's trashed my place. They found my hiding spot . . ." Necco shook her head, as if she couldn't believe it herself.

"Who the hell is **they**?"

"I don't know," Necco said miserably. "Maybe whoever killed Hermes? Maybe someone followed me yesterday? I was so careful . . . but I guess I wasn't careful enough."

"No vitamins?" Pru asked.

Necco shook her head. "No vitamins. No bag. No money. Nothing."

"Oh my God," Theo groaned, clasping her hands behind her neck and gazing out the chipped windshield. "Do you have any idea how fucking fucked I am now?"

"Theodora, language, please!" Pru said. "It's hardly Necco's fault that her hideaway was ransacked, now is it? Necco, was there no sign at all of who it might have been?"

Necco shook her head. "Nothing. I got there, the whole place was completely wrecked, the bag was taken. I looked around for a minute, to see if there was anything I could salvage, but I had to get out of there—it wasn't safe."

Necco's voice was even enough, but something about the way she avoided eye contact made Theo feel like she was lying.

"But what took you so long, then?" Theo asked. "You were gone **forever.**"

"It just took a while to get in," Necco said, still not meeting Theo's eyes. "I had to take a certain route, be sure I wasn't being followed."

Theo had given up. There was no point grilling Necco; the bag was gone, she knew Necco wasn't lying about that much. Pru had suggested they return to her apartment to regroup, and neither Theo or Necco had a better idea, so here they were.

She has no way to pay Jeremy back. And now the cops are after her, waving around a photo of her and Necco. She's probably murder suspect number two.

"Shit, shit, shit," she continues, her own useless mantra.

"We'll figure something out, dear," Mrs. Small tells her.

"Bullshit!" Theo snarls, feeling both furious and helpless—not a winning combination. "There's nothing to figure out. It's gone. I'm screwed. Jeremy went to my house looking for me. What if he comes back? What if he does something to my mom?"

She imagines it: Jeremy showing up, forcing her mom to the ATM at knifepoint. Worse still, she imagines him telling her mom everything: about Theo and Hannah, about selling the drugs, all of it.

"That seems a bit drastic, Theodora," Pru says.

"Well, he seems like a drastic kind of guy. And he's pissed off."

"Maybe we can talk to him," Pru suggests. "Maybe we can go there and give him the little bit of money I have, and promise to pay him the rest later. And maybe he can get me more vitamins?"

This is the last straw. The absolute last freaking straw.

"Don't you get it?" Theo snaps. "Don't you get how totally fucked I am? I owe some scumbag drug dealer two thousand bucks. The one person I actually truly care about in this world was only pretending to give a shit about me so I could make some money for her and her boyfriend. And now, **now** the cops are after me because they think I had something to do with what happened to Necco's boyfriend, who just so happens to be the governor's son! And all you can think about is your fucking vitamins, which we all know aren't really vitamins, right? They're fucking speed! You're a fucking drug addict!"

She watches Pru's face go from cheerful optimism to devastation. The large woman's eyes tear up, and then she lets loose and starts to cry.

"I know," Pru says, through a large sob. "You think I don't know, but I do. I know how pathetic I am. The fat lady who needs her pills to get through the day. I know."

She's crying hard now, and it makes Theo's chest ache. Shit. She wants to tell Pru how sorry she is, but it all feels too late. The damage is done. How could she be such an insensitive fucking idiot?

"Pru," Necco says, shooting Theo a furious how-could-you glance before going to comfort the sobbing woman. "You're not pathetic. I think you're one of the most creative people I've ever met. I mean, look at what you've built here. Look at this circus!" She looks at it as if seeing it for the first time. "You've created a whole world in your living room."

"But it's not real," Pru says.

Necco walks over and picks up the ringmaster. "Sure it is. In some ways, it's probably more real than anything else because you've put your heart and soul into it. My dad, he was an inventor. He made windup animals and talking dolls, and sometimes, sometimes I swore they were real, they had souls, just because my father put so much of himself into each one. That's what your circus is like."

Pru rubs at her eyes, gives Necco a weak smile.

Necco smiles back, but before she can say anything more, her eye catches on something else.

"That elephant," Necco says, dropping the ringmaster to pick it up, and knocking the dancing bear over in the process. "Where did you get this?"

The elephant is different from the other animals in Pru's circus. It's not made of wire and papier-mâché. It's a brassy metal, and has a little loop on its back like it was once hung from a piece of jewelry.

"That's Priscilla," Pru says, wiping her runny nose with the sleeve of her dress. "The golden elephant. She's saving the circus."

"But where did she come from?" Necco asks, desperate, her eyes fixed on the tiny pachyderm.

"She was a gift. Just yesterday, Mr. Marcelle gave her to me."

"Mr. Marcelle? The little strongman in your circus?" Baffled, Necco looks down at the little doll in the center ring.

"Oh, he's more than a little man with a papier-mâché head, isn't he, Mrs. Small?" Theo says, smiling sheepishly at Pru. "The real, in-the-flesh Mr. Marcelle is a private detective. We actually ran into him this afternoon. He was out at the mill."

"There was a **private detective** at the mill?" Necco asks, voice raised.

"Well, actually, it's Mr. Marcelle's brother who's the private detective," Pru admits. "Mr. Marcelle just works for him from time to time."

"The strongman and Pru are a little sweet on each other," Theo explains.

"So what was he doing at the mill?" Necco asks.

"He said he'd followed a guy there but then lost him. A dangerous man who might be involved in what happened to your boyfriend."

"What? And you just decided to tell me all this now?" Necco says. "Did he say anything more about this guy? What he looked like? Why he thought the guy had anything to do with what happened to Hermes?"

Pru shakes her head. "No, dear. He didn't say too much. Just that he was following a bad guy. Someone dangerous."

A thought occurs to Theo: "Necco, you didn't see anyone else when you were in the mill, did you? You didn't meet anyone there or anything, right?"

"No! Of course not."

She's looking down at the brass elephant in her hand, turning it over and over, making it do tiny elephant somersaults. Now Theo is sure that she's lying.

"Really?" Theo asks.

"I was alone the whole time. I never saw anyone."

"Well, maybe the guy the strongman was following is the guy who took my bag! Maybe he went looking for you, found the hiding place, and grabbed the bag."

Necco is silent a minute, staring down at Priscilla the elephant, who is still now, laid out in the palm of her hand. Then she looks at Pru. "I need to know where your strongman friend got this."

"Why?" Theo asks.

"Because it's mine. It was my dad's. I'm sure of it—see this mark here at the bottom," she says, turning the elephant over, showing two tiny letters: **JK.** "I'd given it to Hermes a few days before he was killed. I always wore it around my neck, but the chain broke. He was going to have it fixed or get me another chain. The last I knew, it was in his bag."

"So how did Mr. Marcelle get it?" Theo asks.

"He said his brother gave it to him. It reminded him of me and the circus, so he brought it to the cafeteria yesterday."

"You need to call Mr. Marcelle," Necco says. "Ask him where he got the elephant."

"I think you should invite him over," Theo says. "You'll have better luck getting him to talk in person."

Pru hesitates, although there's a new light in her eyes. "I don't know, Theodora, having him here? Really, I don't think—"

"He's obviously really into you, Mrs. Small." She smiles encouragingly.

"Theodora, he's just being polite. He's a gentleman, Mr. Marcelle."

"He's more than polite. I've seen the way he looks at you—how he hangs on your every word. I know you can get him to talk, to really open up. If you ask him over, you can find out where he got that elephant. And more about this guy he was following today at the mill. I really think there's a good chance that if we find him, we find my bag, the money, more vitamins, and maybe even Hermes's killer."

Pru

〜〜〜

Pru carefully punches Mr. Marcelle's number into the phone, keeping her eye on the business card. She's committing it to memory; Mr. Marcelle's number will be the only number other than her own and the school's that she will be able to recite without looking up.

He answers on the fourth ring, sounding startled and out of breath. Like a man caught doing something he shouldn't. Maybe he's off chasing another criminal, getting his shirt even dirtier.

"Mr. Marcelle, it's Pru Small."

"Oh, Pru." She can feel him smiling into the phone. "I'm so happy you called. I was just thinking about you."

She gets that giddy rush she always gets talking to him. She takes a breath, reminds herself to stay focused. There's a reason she's called, and Theo and Necco are beside her, watching expectantly.

"I was hoping we could talk. That maybe you could come to my apartment, I mean, if it's not too much trouble."

"I can be there in fifteen minutes."

"Wonderful, Mr. Marcelle. That's wonderful." She gives him her address and they say their goodbyes. Then she starts fluttering around the apartment, tidying, setting the circus up just so, while Theo and Necco bombard her with details about the plan.

"Find out everything you can about the elephant," Necco says. "And about the guy Mr. Marcelle was looking for at the mill."

"Remember, we'll be right in your bedroom," Theo says. "You won't be alone with him."

"Mr. Marcelle is a total gentleman."

"But he's also working for a private detective," Theo says. "Which makes him dangerous. If he finds out you've got Necco here—"

"I know," Pru says. "I'm not a complete fool, Theodora. I know when to hold my tongue. I'll get what I can from him, then ask him, very politely, to leave." She turns, studies herself in the full-length mirror. She doesn't have time to change, but she goes into her bedroom to put on powder, a touch of silver eye shadow, and some lipstick. Her circus makeup.

"You look beautiful, Mrs. Small," Theodora tells her.

"Thank you, dear," Pru says. She puts donuts out on a plate at the table. Gets a full pot of coffee perking. She takes out the little cut-glass cream pitcher and sugar bowl that belonged to her grandmother.

There's a knock at the door. Two loud raps followed by three quiet ones. A secret message kind of knock.

"Coming!" Pru calls, gesturing with a sweeping, get-out-of-sight motion at the girls, who tiptoe into her bedroom, close the door most of the way. Emmett is barking.

"Easy, boy," she says, tidying her hair just before opening the door.

"So wonderful to see you, Pru," Mr. Marcelle says, giving her a little bow. "You look stunning."

"Thank you, Mr. Marcelle," she says, stepping aside. "Please come in."

"And this handsome fellow must be Emmett," he says, squatting down to give the little dog a scratch behind the ears, which quiets the dog instantly. "I've heard so much about you, little friend," he says to Emmett, who is wagging his tail, kissing Mr. Marcelle's hands.

"He likes you," Pru says.

"Dogs know who the good people are," Mr. Marcelle says. "They have a sense."

"Please, have a seat," Pru says, gesturing at the table. "I've made coffee."

"Wonderful," Mr. Marcelle says, settling into one of the ladder-back chairs.

Pru brings two mugs of coffee over and sits down opposite him. "Please help yourself to a donut," she says, her heart pounding. Her strongman is actually here, in her apartment.

"I'm so happy you called," he says, then suddenly seems a little unsure, a little shy. "Do you think . . . do you think before I leave you could show me the circus?"

She smiles. She was hoping he would ask. "Absolutely."

"You said on the phone that you wanted to talk? Did you see anything after I left the mill? Did anything unusual happen?" he asks, his face full of concern and worry. "You didn't have any trouble, did you?"

"Oh, no, that's not it at all. The truth is, I asked you here because I was hoping you could tell me about Priscilla," Pru says.

"Priscilla?"

"The little elephant you gave me." She pulls the elephant out of the pocket in her dress and sets it on the table. "I've been wondering where she came from. She's so unique, I figured there has to be a story behind her."

He seems surprised, and maybe a little disappointed, by her question. "My brother gave it to me."

"I see," Pru says, taking a sip of coffee. "And did your brother tell you where he got it?"

"Yeah, actually. And you're right—there is a story behind that little elephant." He sits up straighter now. "I'll tell you, but you have to keep it to yourself. It's business."

"I will," Pru said, crossing her fingers under the table like a superstitious schoolgirl.

"And if I tell you this, you have to answer some questions for me," he adds. "Tit for tat."

"Of course," she says, fingers still crossed.

"One of his clients gave it to him."

"Oh?"

"Not just any client, but the governor himself."

"The governor?"

"Yeah, apparently that little elephant was connected to some old crime. He asked my brother to look into it. It happened back in the 1970s, over in Braxton. The elephant was once on a bracelet worn by a woman who was murdered."

Pru starts to gasp but then hears a little creaking sound . . . the bedroom door opening a bit more. Mr. Marcelle hears it, too, looks toward the bedroom.

"Just Emmett," Pru says. "Please, go on, tell me about this murder."

"It's not the most pleasant story."

"You may not know this about me, Mr. Marcelle, but I like a good crime story."

He smiles, takes a bite of his donut, getting powdered sugar in his freshly curled mustache. "The victim was the wife of a local musician," Mr. Marcelle explains. "The musician was arrested; all the evidence pointed to him—bloody clothes and murder weapon found in his car—but he hanged himself before it went to trial. There was one witness—the couple's ten-year-old son. He saw his mother killed and swore up and down that the guy who did it wasn't his father."

"But they didn't listen to the boy?"

"Well, see, the killer wore a mask. A rubber chicken mask, of all things. They said there was no way the boy knew who was underneath."

"A chicken mask?"

"I know, strange, isn't it?"

"But I still don't understand," Pru said. "Why did the governor have this dead woman's elephant?"

"Well, here's the funny part of the story. The part where my brother comes in. The governor said his son gave it to him. You know, the poor kid who was murdered?"

Mr. Marcelle stops talking to help himself to another donut. Pru smiles approvingly. She likes a man with an appetite. She reaches for a donut herself.

"Well," Mr. Marcelle continues. "This kid, Matthew, and his dad didn't have a great relationship. Estranged, I guess you'd call them. The kid left college, dropped out of sight, wanted nothing to do with his parents or their money. The governor actually hired my brother to try to locate the kid, to follow him around, give him reports from time to time. So then this kid shows up at home to visit his dad just a few days ago with some wild story about this old murder. He wanted his dad to pull a few law enforcement strings and have the case reopened. He says he's discovered proof that the real killer is out there still. He won't say what this proof is—but he's got this little elephant that he says his dad can easily confirm is tied to the case. Kind of a token proving that this is all legit."

"And did the governor reopen the case?"

"No. He didn't want anything to do with it. He told my brother to get rid of the elephant and forget the whole thing. But maybe he should have pursued it."

"Why do you say that?"

"I was at my brother's office when you called me, going through all the notes, all the old newspaper articles and such. There were things that didn't add up."

He looks down at his donut, finishes it in one more big bite, wiping his hands on his jeans.

"What sorts of things?" Pru asks. "Is this all

somehow connected to the man you were following earlier?"

He gives her a sly smile. "I think I've answered enough questions for now. Your turn. Tell me about this girl, Theodora."

"My niece? What would you like to know? She's visiting. She lives down in Connecticut. She's out right now, but she should be back anytime."

"Pru," he says, leaning forward, elbows on the table. He reaches for her hand, takes it, giving it a gentle squeeze that makes her heart flutter like a small bird. "I know you don't have a niece."

"But I do—"

"You don't have any brothers or sisters. And you've never been married."

"How do you know?" She snatches her hand back. She's furious that he, of all people, knows just how alone in the world she is.

"Don't you remember what my brother does?" Mr. Marcelle asks, voice low and apologetic. "What I do after hours? I have access to information. And I didn't mean to pry or invade your privacy. I really didn't, Pru. It's just that when I saw you with those girls at the mill, at the very place where I'd chased a potentially dangerous criminal, I was worried that you might be involved in something you don't fully understand."

"You're assuming a great deal," Pru says.

Girls, she's thinking. He said **girls,** which

meant he'd been watching. He'd seen Necco join them. What else did he know? Did he have a clue who Necco truly was?

"Maybe," Mr. Marcelle says. "But it's only because I care."

Does he? Pru looks into his warm brown eyes and thinks that he looks like a man who would never lie to her. But she knows it's foolish to let herself believe in such fairy tales.

"And what I want to know . . . what I'm asking you to tell me, is who is Theodora, really? And who is the other girl I saw you pick up?"

Pru doesn't speak. She doesn't want to lie, but can't tell the truth: **Theodora isn't really my niece, she's a girl from school I buy drugs from.** What would he think of her then?

There's a scuffling sound from the bedroom; the door creaks open further.

"You have to go now," Pru says, standing up quickly enough that her leg bumps the table, spilling the cream in the cut-glass pitcher.

Mr. Marcelle stands, too. "Pru, please. I'm worried. If either of these girls is mixed up in any of the business I've been helping my brother with, it's very serious. They could put you in danger."

"I appreciate your concern. But I have to tell you, I don't appreciate being spied on."

"Do you know a girl named Eva?" Mr. Marcelle asks.

Pru doesn't answer.

"That's the girl who was living in the car," he continues. "The one everyone thinks killed the governor's son. If you know Eva, she's in danger. And I'm not talking about the police, Pru. If you know Eva, you've got to tell her not to—"

"I don't know anyone by that name," she tells him. "You really need to leave now."

"But I thought you were going to show me the circus," he says.

"Another time," she says, walking to the front door and holding it open.

He walks to the door and stands beside her.

"I hope so," he says, "I really do, Pru." He looks like he wants to say something more, but she doesn't let him.

"Goodbye, Mr. Marcelle," she says, eyes on the open door. He shuffles out, shoulders slumped in a defeated way. She shuts and latches the door before he has a chance to say anything else. She leans against it, listening to his heavy feet going down the stairs.

Has she just made a terrible mistake, throwing him out like this? But what choice did he give her, asking all those questions, ambushing her, really?

"How does your strongman know so damn much?" Theo asks, hurrying into the kitchen. "And what does he mean, Eva's in danger?"

"He's a clever man, Mr. Marcelle," Pru tells

her with a sigh, thinking, **a little too clever.** "If he says she's in danger, she must be."

"Me being in danger is kind of old news," Necco says.

"So is it true?" Theo asks, turning to Necco. "All that stuff about where the elephant came from? About the murder?"

Necco nods. "Yes. The woman who was murdered, she was my grandmother."

"Jesus," Theo says. "And your dad saw it?"

Necco nods. "Apparently. He always told me that his parents died in an accident. But there's a newspaper clipping about it in the envelope Hermes left. He saw this Chicken Man kill his mom and he knew that this guy wasn't his dad, but no one would listen. They arrested his dad and he hanged himself in jail."

"How horrible!" Pru gasps.

"It all makes sense now," Theo says. "I remember reading about this in your dad's book. How he saw his mom killed."

"He wrote about the murder in his book?" Necco asks.

"Wait, you never read your dad's book?" Theo says.

Necco shakes her head.

"Well, we need to get you a copy! He totally wrote about watching his mom being killed and how the police had the wrong man. He even wrote about the bracelet and the story that went with it. He ended up using it as a kind of metaphor about transformation and the things we carry inside us—how we all have the power to bring our true selves to life. But sometimes, it's a dark thing, you know? Sometimes there's something evil hiding there."

Pru bites her lip, thinking. "It sounds like maybe Hermes discovered something about the killer," she says. "That's why he brought the elephant to his dad."

"Oh my God," Theodora says. "Do you think that's what got him killed? He was on to whoever killed your grandmother?"

Pru rubs her head. "Wait a second," she says. "That was back in the seventies, right? When Necco's dad was a little kid."

"So?" Theo says.

"So, if the killer was a grown man, then he'd be what . . . maybe up in his seventies now?"

"A geezer killer?" Theo says.

"A killer is a killer no matter how old and what shape he might be in," Pru says.

"What do you think, Necco?" Theo asks.

Necco is still clutching the golden elephant, the showpiece of the circus.

"Hermes and my grandmother aren't the only murder victims," she says. "My mother was killed. And it was made to look like a suicide. Hermes was looking into it, trying to figure out what happened. And now, reading about my father throwing himself into the river, I'm thinking maybe that wasn't suicide either."

"You think both your parents were murdered?" Pru asks.

Theodora blows out a long breath. "This whole thing just gets crazier and crazier. What are we supposed to do now?"

"I think," Necco says, pausing, turning the elephant over in her hand to look at the mark on the bottom again. "I think that if I could only remember what really happened on the day of the flood, I'd have some clue about who the killer is. I think I need to go see Miss Abigail."

"Who on earth is Miss Abigail?" Pru asks.

"Yeah, and how's she gonna help?" Theodora asks.

"She can give me Devil's Snuff. The snuff shows you what you need to know."

Fred

~~~~

James was out. Fred wasn't sure where—James enjoyed being mysterious, often saying that he was "out on business" when, in actuality, he was probably at the gym. He never really exercised, just flirted with the girl who made smoothies with kale and whey powder and chia seeds, and occasionally floated around in the pool or went in the sauna. James got a lot of business from the sauna. There was something intimate about sitting around sweating together wrapped in a towel, something that made people share their problems: **I think my wife's cheating on me; I wonder if my son has a drug problem.** And there was James to smile his knight-in-shining-armor smile and say, "You know, I can help you find out."

Fred didn't care where his brother was this time. He was just glad he was gone.

He chewed on an antacid. The coffee and donuts Pru had given him sat in his belly like a cannonball. He'd blown it with Pru. He should have been more gentle with his questioning. He should have taken his time. Now she was furious; she'd practically thrown him out of her apartment. Any chances he had to get answers from her were officially blown. And it had been so nice, to be with her there in her apartment. To be sipping coffee and sharing donuts, knowing that at any minute she was going to show him her circus. He's imagined the circus for so long, tried to picture it from the stories she told, but he's always longed to see it. And he'd blown his chance at that, too. Idiot. He pops another antacid into his mouth.

Fred has the notes on that old murder out in front of him. One witness. A ten-year-old boy. Which would make the kid fifty now. He looks back through the notes and newspaper articles until he finds the boy's name: Miles Sandeski. He types it into the search engine on his brother's computer.

"Holy shit," he says when he follows the link to the first hit: **Professor Miles Sandeski sought for questioning in the disappearance of his wife and daughter. Foul play suspected.**

Fred reads on, one article and news story after another. Sandeski grew up to be a sociologist who'd written a popular book called **The Princess and the Elephant.** Then the poor professor turned up dead, remains found washed up on the riverbank, an apparent suicide, a couple of weeks after his wife and daughter disappeared.

But then, something truly interesting pops up, a small news story, hardly front-page material, from April 7, this year:

INDIGENT DROWNING VICTIM IDENTIFIED

The body of a woman authorities recovered from the Lacroix River last Wednesday has been identified as 49-year-old Lily Sandeski, who has been missing and presumed dead for the past four years. Investigators learned that Mrs. Sandeski had been living on the street, with a group of transient women known as the Fire Eaters. Her death has been ruled a suicide. A police spokesperson has confirmed that the whereabouts of Lily Sandeski's daughter, Eva, who also disappeared four years ago, are still unknown.

"Eva," Fred says out loud.

Eva was the name of the girl living in the parking lot, the girl wanted for the murder of the governor's son. The governor's son who had the brass elephant. And somehow or other, Eva is connected with Theodora, the girl Pru's been driving around with and calling her niece. Eva had Theodora's bag, according to the guy he'd followed to the Koffee Kup.

Fred types **Eva Sandeski** into the search engine and finds only news stories about the disappearance of Eva and her mother, how Miles was wanted for questioning. He rereads the quotes from Lily's sister-in-law, Judith Tanner, who showed up at the house after receiving a distressed call from Lily, and found Dr. Sandeski covered in blood and the house a wreck.

He does a search for **Judith Tanner;** there are hundreds of hits, but at last, he finds the right one. Fred's always amazed by the things you can learn online, even without all his brother's fancy connections. Within ten minutes, he's learned this much about Judith Tanner: her husband, Lloyd, had been killed in a fire at the garage he owned fourteen years ago; the fire was apparently set by the couple's son, Edward, who was six at the time. The son was sent to live in a facility for disturbed children, but eventually ran away.

Fred does the math. The son, Edward, would be twenty now. Fred can find no records of the right Edward Tanner online. It is as if the kid had truly disappeared.

He comes up with a current address for Judith Tanner. It's in a quiet suburban neighborhood about half an hour away. He looks at his watch: a little after 8:00. Not too late to pay her a visit.

Necco

~~~~~

The footpath that takes them down under the Blachly Bridge to the camp of the Fire Eaters is rough, and Pru is having a hard time; she's going slow, her breath loud and whistling. Necco is in the lead and keeps stopping to look back. Theo is trying to help Pru, but Pru won't have it. "I'm fine," she scolds.

"How do you know this Abigail will have Devil's Snuff?" Theo asks. "I wasn't even sure it was real."

"It's real," Necco says. "Miss Abigail and the other Fire Eaters are the ones who make it. It's how they do what they do. The snuff shows them things. Gives them the power to eat fire. To see the future."

"Have you ever taken it?" Theo asks.

Necco seems shocked at the idea. "No, never."

"But you've seen it? You've seen people take it?" Theo asks.

"Many times. My mother was a Fire Eater. We lived in their camp for a long time."

"No shit?" Theodora says.

"So it's a drug?" Pru wheezes.

"Yeah," Theodora says. "But not like anything else out there. Word is that once you do it, you're never the same. There are kids at school who would do anything for a taste. If I could get some, I could name my price. If I got enough, I could pay Jeremy back."

"Forget it," Necco says flatly. "The Fire Eaters don't sell it. It's a spiritual thing to them."

"Well, do they ever give it away?" Theo asks.

"They only give it to the people chosen by the snuff."

"Oh, **of course,**" Theo says, rolling her eyes. "The drug **chooses** who takes it. Makes sense."

Pebbles slide out from under their feet like marbles. They slip and slide down in the darkness, and Necco is starting to wonder if it was the best idea, bringing them here like this. The Fire Eaters are leery of outsiders, especially ones that don't respect the ways of the Devil's Snuff.

"It's late," Theo says. "Are you sure they'll be up?"

Necco hears the water now, can see the gentle glow of a campfire down under the bridge. "Moon's full. They'll be awake." These women live by the cycles of the moon, the turning of the seasons. There is a time for everything. For picking the berries, laying them on racks in the sun to dry, grinding them into powder, for inhaling the snuff and having visions. A time for eating fire. You do things in the wrong order, or when the time is not right, and it all falls apart. The snuff is no good. You get burned.

"Almost there," Necco calls back, her heart pounding hard, not from exertion, but from the idea of going back to the camp, to a place so full of memories. They pass the old shack where she and Mama used to live. The dented yellow road sign is still nailed to the left of the front door: SHARP CURVE AHEAD.

Necco's eyes are fixed on the sign, and she's thinking about all the curves life had in store for her and Mama, sharp curves with terrible drop-offs below.

Dead Man's Curve.

She takes her eyes off the sign, and there are the four Fire Eaters, hunched around the fire in a circle like points of the compass. Only something's missing. Miss Abigail always said the Fire Eaters were whole only when there were five, like the points of a star.

Mama. That's what's missing.

Necco's heart feels like a hollowed-out thing.

"Miss Abigail, Miss Stella, Miss Coral, Miss F," Necco calls. "It's me, Necco."

The women look their way. Their pupils are huge, and they have red stains from the snuff under their noses. This means it's a powerful night for visions if all four women have indulged.

"We've been waiting," Miss Abigail says. "And I'm so glad you've brought your friends. Come join us. Sit by the fire. I think we can help you with some of the questions you've come with."

Necco does as she's told, and Pru and Theo follow. Necco sits between Miss Abigail and Miss Stella, who smiles and gives Necco a bone-crushing hug. "Welcome home," Miss Stella whispers. "I've missed you."

Pru settles herself down on a large rock near the fire and tries to manage the hair that's stuck to her glistening face. Theo sits down between Necco and Miss Abigail, legs crossed, and studies the faces of the women. Miss Stella gives her a smile, her brown eyes warm. To the left of Stella is Miss Coral, who has her gaze focused on the fire and does not seem to notice when Pru leans forward, taps her on the shoulder, and says, "Nice to meet you, I'm Pru Small." Apparently undeterred, Pru turns to her right, where Miss F sits, with her short, dirty-blond hair and circles like bruises under her eyes.

"I'm Pru," Pru says, and Miss F turns away from her in disgust, spits into the dirt, then speaks harshly.

"I sense that there is one here who does not belong. One whose intentions are not pure." Her eyes stay locked on the fire in front of her. It spits and pops as if in agreement. Theo throws a worried glance to Necco.

"But I was just saying hello," Pru says defensively. "Being polite."

"The Great Mother welcomes all," Miss Abigail says. "She told us to expect you. We've learned other things, too. Things that will help you. It's important that you listen. That you all pay close attention."

"Once upon a time, the Great Mother laid an egg," calls out Miss Stella in her singsong storytalk voice.

"And that egg became our world," adds Miss Coral in a near whisper.

Miss Stella leans forward, picks up a fire stick: a fuel-soaked ball of gauze on the end of a metal wire. She dips it into the fire, and the tiny ball of gauze catches. "A bright and blazing orb, spinning through space." Miss Stella waves the flaming orb through the air in great arcs. Her face is lit up behind it, jewelry glinting and flashing, making her all the more beautiful.

Pru leans forward, makes a little "ohhh" sound.

Theo is mesmerized despite herself. No eye rolling now.

As she sits with these women, Necco misses her mother with the pressing weight of a building coming down on top of her, crushing everything else out.

"Fire is life," Miss Stella calls out, voice loud, untamed.

"Fire is life," the other three women chant back.

"Fire is breath," Miss Stella says.

"Fire is breath," the others echo.

"Fire, sustain me," Miss Stella says. "Fire, show me visions of what will come." She opens her mouth and puts the flaming torch inside, closing her lips, swallowing the flames down, letting the smoke curl out of her nostrils as her eyes roll back in her head.

Pru makes another astonished gasping sound, then claps like you would do for a fire eater at the circus. But this is no circus. And this is only the prelude of what's to come.

"Tell me, my Necco girl, what is it you need to know?" Miss Abigail says.

"I want to know about what really happened on the day of the flood. I want to know who Snake Eyes is; if I saw him that day. I want my memories back. I was hoping I could take the snuff, that it would show me what I need to know."

Miss Abigail looks at Necco, then closes her eyes. "The snuff is not for you, child. It never has been. Especially not now." She opens her eyes, gives Necco a meaningful look, her eyes moving from Necco's face to her belly, where the little baby grows. "You need to search your own memories."

"But I don't remember," Necco says, frustrated. "And whenever I asked Mama about it, she made up stories. Told me there was a flood that destroyed the house, killed Daddy and Errol. But that's not what happened."

Miss Abigail nods, closes her eyes. "Sometimes the people who love us most make huge sacrifices for us. They'll do anything to protect us."

"I know she thought she was protecting me," Necco says. "But now I need to know the truth."

"I can tell you what I know. It's not everything you need, but it's enough to get you started. You're sure you're ready? You're ready to hear it now?"

"Yes," Necco says. "I'm ready."

"Then let's begin," Miss Abigail says, and, perfectly on cue, all four women pick up their torches and light them, the fire illuminating their faces, making long, dancing shadows behind them as the women stand and begin to sway.

And just now, at this moment, Necco understands that her mother isn't gone. Not truly. She
feels her presence here with these women. She's
the ghost in the shadows. The popping shower
of sparks that jumps out of the fire and startles
them all.

Fred

~~~~~

Fred pulls up at a little blue bungalow with garden gnomes, gazing globes, and colorful whirligigs decorating the front yard. Though it's full dark, there are two lights above the front steps and a lamp on a post by the driveway blazing. Two cars are parked in the driveway—an old Corolla and, behind it, a car Fred recognizes from earlier this afternoon: the vintage black MG. Even from this distance, Fred can see the shadow of the Virgin Mary on the dashboard. The man with the dice tattoo from the diner must be inside. Maybe the kid's in there, too.

Now things are getting interesting.

He texts his brother again: **Can you look up this plate: VCS 314. Owner somehow involved with our kid.**

Fred looks around the neighborhood. The houses are fairly close together, and Judith Tanner's house, all lit up like a Christmas tree, is in full view of at least six of her neighbors'. The last thing Fred wants is to go sneaking around and have some neighborhood watch type call the cops on him. The backyard looks promising, though—fairly dark, at least what he can see of it. He's concocting a plan to circle around in the car and approach from the back when the front door opens, and the man with the dice tattoo steps out. He hesitates a moment on the steps before turning back to embrace a woman who has appeared in the door behind him. She's tall, wearing a blue dress. They hug, then kiss. It's a long, messy kiss that tells Fred they're lovers. Fred ducks his head down, pretends to be intently focused on his cell phone as the man goes down the steps, gets in his car, and backs out. He takes off down the street, his taillights fading like two dim red eyes in the distance.

Fred hops out of the car and darts up the walkway that cuts through the middle of her yard, passing the gnomes, which seem to glare at him like guards standing at attention. He knocks on the door. It opens quickly, the woman in the dress smiling, asking, "What'd you forget?" Then she sees him, and takes a step back.

"Judith?" Fred asks. He'd put her in her mid-fifties. Feathery, heavily highlighted hair. Her layers of makeup don't quite hide the fact that she's got one hell of a black eye.

"Who are you?" she demands.

"My name is James Marcelle," he says, simply because his brother's name pops into his head before anything else. He instantly regrets his choice.

She squints at him. "Do I know you?"

"No, you don't. But I think we might be able to help each other."

"How's that?"

"Can I come in?" he asks, thinking he is pushing his luck, but willing to risk it.

She seems to consider for a second, but keeps her hand on the door, ready to swing it closed in his face at any second. "No. What is it you want?"

"Your niece, Eva Sandeski," he says.

"What about her?"

"Do you know where she is?"

She shakes her head. "Probably dead. Poor thing. Never had a chance."

"What if I told you she wasn't? What if I told you I might know how to find her?"

"What did you say your name is?"

"James Marcelle. I'm a private investigator. And I think I can help you find your niece."

"Come in," she says, holding the door open. "Let's talk inside."

As he walks by her, he smells whiskey on her

breath. As if she is reading his mind, the first thing she says as she leads him into the living room is "Can I get you a drink?"

"Sure," he says, even though he's not much of a drinker, just the occasional beer on Sundays with his brother. He doesn't want to be rude. He wants to win her trust. His brother once told him, "I never trust a man who won't have a drink with me." He's also hoping that she'll refill her glass, lubricate the tongue. Though, as he watches her weave and sway across the living room, he wonders how much more lubrication she really needs.

"What's your poison?" she asks.

"I'll have whatever you're having."

There's a bar set up in the corner. She pours two glasses of Jim Beam, carries them back. When she hands him the drink, she stands a little too close. "A private investigator, huh?"

"Yeah. Do you mind me asking what happened to your eye? It looks pretty painful."

"I fell," she says.

Like hell, he thinks. "You know, if you didn't fall, if someone hurt you like that, there are—"

"So what do you know about Eva?" she interrupts.

"I know she and her mother disappeared four years ago. That you were the one who reported them missing."

"I was," she says. She takes a seat on the couch,

so he goes to sit in a chair across the glass coffee table.

"Can you tell me about that?"

"My sister-in-law, Lily, she called me that afternoon. Really upset. I could hardly understand her. She asked if I could take Eva for a while. There was some trouble with her and Miles."

"Did she say what kind of trouble?"

"No. She asked if I could come right away, and I said, 'Sure,' and told her I'd be there in an hour. Well, it took me nearly two hours. It was bad weather that day, the river had flooded, was up over the road in places, so I had to take a few detours. So I finally got there, and the door was wide open. The living room was trashed, furniture tipped over, lamps and vases broken. I knew something terrible had happened. I called out, but no one answered. I was scared. I drove home and called the police."

"What about Miles?" Fred asks.

"Miles?"

"Didn't you see him that day? Didn't he answer the door?"

She freezes a minute, then nods. "Yes, of course! He was there. That's what scared me off. Seeing him like that. He had blood on him. Looked half-crazy."

Fred does not need any of his brother's private investigator skills to know this woman is lying.

"He had blood on him?" Fred asks.

She nods. "All over his shirt, his pants. It was ghastly." She takes a long sip from her drink. More of a glug, really. He fakes a sip from his own glass.

"So you got back in your car and went home?"

"Yes. I called the police and told them what I'd seen. Told them I was worried Miles had done something terrible."

"But he wasn't there when the police arrived?" Fred asks.

"No. He'd run off. Gone without a trace. No sign of Lily and Eva either."

"Then a few weeks later, Miles shows up, drowned," he says.

She nods. "Suicide." She takes another sip from her glass—it's nearly finished. "Cowardly bastard."

"How, exactly, are you related?" he asks, though he knows the answer. "Was he your brother?"

She shakes her head vehemently. "No, thank God! My husband, Lloyd, he was Lily's brother."

"I see," Fred says, still not wanting to show her how much he knows. "He must have taken it hard—his sister and niece going missing like that? Foul play suspected."

She doesn't meet his eye. "My husband passed away years before this ever happened."

"I'm so sorry," he says.

"Don't be. In all honesty, it wasn't the most solid marriage. And his death, it was just shit luck. He was killed in a car accident." She keeps her eyes on the floor, takes the last sip of her drink. "Are you ready for a refill?"

"No," he tells her. "I'm still working on mine, but thank you."

A car accident? His research had told him that Lloyd Tanner died in a fire. Why would she lie? Because the fire was set by their son, maybe. Fred understood that some things were just too painful to discuss, and it was easier to make up another story, to tell it so many times that you yourself started to believe it.

Judith goes to pour herself another drink, staggering a little.

Good. Drink more.

"And of course, you know what became of Lily?" she asks.

"I know she drowned this past April."

"Poor thing."

"So you never heard from her? Not in all that time?"

She turns back with her drink. "No. I believed she and Eva were dead. That Miles had killed them and hid the bodies somewhere they'd never be found."

"Did Miles seem like the sort of person who might be capable of something like that?" Fred asks.

She plunks down hard on the couch, some of her drink spilling. "You never know what someone is capable of," she says. "You never know what they carry inside them."

"But it turns out he didn't kill them," Fred says.

"No. Apparently not. And poor Lily, living on the streets, panhandling, eating out of dumpsters, doing drugs . . . What did Miles do to her?"

Fred nods. "And Eva? You never heard from her either?"

"No. I was sure she was dead. Until you showed up here today. Now it's your turn. Tell me what you know."

"I don't have much to tell you, because most of what I've learned is part of a confidential ongoing investigation." He's doing his best to sound like his brother. "But I have good reason to believe that your niece is very much alive. Alive and in the city."

Judith leans forward, sloshing her drink. "I can't believe it! Where is she?"

"I can't say exactly, but I have a few leads."

"Will you call me? The second you find her?"

"Of course."

Judith gets up off the couch and comes toward him, staggering across the living room floor, banging her knee against the coffee table and losing her balance. He stands in time to catch her, and she throws her arms around him, hugs him hard. "Thank you," she says. "Thank you, James. You don't know what this means to me."

He gives her back a gentle pat, and she releases her grip. He guides her back to the couch.

"Easy now," he says. Standing there, he has a better view of the framed pictures on the mantel. Two show a much younger Judith, albeit one with dated hairstyles—in one she's in a rocking chair, cradling an infant; in the other, she's standing side by side in front of a Christmas tree with a little boy in striped footie pajamas, maybe three or four years old. And then there's one that's just of the boy, a little older. He's standing in front of a lake or pond, green mountains in the distance. It's a good photo—his face well lit and in perfect focus. He's grinning at the photographer, nose wrinkled a bit, wearing baggy red swim trunks, hands on his hips. He has brown hair, ruffled in the breeze, blue eyes. And a jagged scar over his left eye.

It's the kid he's been following. No question about it. The kid is a man now, but he'd recognize that face anywhere.

"You have an adorable son," he tells her, thinking this is just what all mothers love to hear.

She nods, reaches for her drink on the coffee table. "Edward. He's gone, too."

"Gone?" Fred echoes.

"He was killed in the car crash with his father. Not long after that last picture was taken."

Theo

〜〜〜

The three women are all eating fire now. Theo watches as they trip their faces off thinking this is nuts, and that they aren't going to be any help at all. The oldest woman, Miss Abigail, she takes a sip of something, whiskey maybe, holds a torch in front of her, and sprays a steady stream of fire out of her mouth like a dragon. She sets the torch down and begins to speak, still swaying, moving like her own flame.

"The day we found you and your mother by the riverbank, your mother told me you and she were in terrible danger. There was a man, a man she called Snake Eyes, who had tried to kill your whole family."

"Did she know who he was? Did she ever give you an actual name?" Necco asks.

The old woman shakes her head. "Nothing like that. But she did say he wanted revenge."

"Revenge for what?" Necco asks.

"Your father had tried to kill this man. In fact, he believed that Snake Eyes was dead."

"My father? Try to kill someone? No." Necco shakes her head.

Miss Abigail smiles. "As your father was famous for saying, every one of us is capable of doing something terrible."

"But my father—you don't understand. He never even yelled. He didn't have a violent bone in his body."

"This man your father tried to kill—he was the man who had murdered your father's own mother before his very eyes. A man he called the Chicken Man."

"Whoa!" Theo says, suddenly paying attention as she begins to grasp the relevance of what they're saying. "So this Chicken Man and Snake Eyes are the same dude? And he's the one who killed Necco's grandma, her parents, **and** Hermes?"

The old woman nods.

"And my mother knew?" Necco asked. "She knew that my father had found the Chicken Man and thought he'd killed him?"

"Not until the day of the flood. When the man came back. But there was another reason he came back, beyond revenge. The reason he's after you, still, I believe."

"He wants the machine," Necco says quietly.

"What machine?" Theo asks.

Necco closes her eyes. "Something my father built. It was a special sort of telephone. One that would let you speak to the dead."

Theo makes a little guffawing chuckle. She can't help it. It's absurd. She's gotta be hearing things. Maybe just being in the presence of the Devil's Snuff gives everyone a little contact high, she and Necco included. "A machine that can talk to the dead?" she says. "That's impossible."

"But it worked," Necco says.

"Oh, come on," Theo argues.

"I know it sounds crazy, but I swear I saw it work," Necco insists. "I heard the voices that came out of it. I spoke to my grandmother. She tried to tell me the truth. That she hadn't died in an accident, but I didn't understand. And that last day, the machine was on. My grandmother was warning us. I can't remember what she said, but I remember her voice, the word **danger.**"

Miss Abigail nods. "It was your father's greatest creation, put together from old plans stolen from one of the greatest inventors of all time—Thomas Edison."

"The lightbulb guy?" Theo says. "No way!"

"Shh," Pru tells her.

"But I still don't think it's possible—" Theo says, and Pru cuts her off.

"Let Miss Abigail finish," Pru snaps with a reprimanding look.

"Did my father steal the plans?" Necco asks.

"No. He was given them by his father. It is unknown how he acquired them. But Snake Eyes learned that your father had built the machine, that that's how Miles had found out he was the killer. Snake Eyes wanted the machine very badly. There is someone he wanted to talk to, someone who has passed. Someone he once loved very much."

"So who is this Snake Eyes guy?" Theo pipes in.

"A bad, bad man," Miss Coral says, looking frightened. "A man poisoned by the things he's done."

"And he's getting close," Miss Stella says, eyes full of concern. "Close to finding you."

"And he's not alone," Miss F says. "He has helpers."

"Great," Theo says. "So how do we stop him?"

Miss F shakes her head. "You don't. He won't stop until he gets what he wants. He's sure Necco has it."

"That's ridiculous—I don't have the machine! I don't even think it exists anymore!"

"But the plans still exist," Miss Abigail says. "Your father hid them. He understood their importance. Just as he understood that they mustn't fall into the wrong hands."

"What do you mean, **wrong hands**?" Theo says.

"Imagine it really is possible to speak to those who have passed. Imagine you could call up anyone you like, ask questions, get instructions."

"So what?" Theo says. "You're saying some lunatic could call up Hitler or Jack the Ripper and follow their orders? This just gets better and better." She can't keep the sarcasm out of her voice.

"What I'm saying," Miss Abigail tells her, "is that the world could easily be thrown out of balance. This device could do terrible harm."

Necco nods. "It's not just the people you call who can come through. I heard other voices, too."

Miss Abigail nods. "It's a powerful machine. We must not underestimate it."

"Well, it doesn't matter anyway, because my father didn't tell me where he hid any plans," Necco says.

"Perhaps not," Miss Abigail says. "But I believe he left you clues."

"Clues? What clues? Maybe he didn't leave them for me. Maybe it was Errol."

Miss Abigail shakes her head. "It was you."

"Miss Abigail," Necco says, her voice low. "My brother, Errol, is alive. He's been alive this whole time. And Mama knew."

"How do you know this?" Miss Abigail asks.

"I saw him."

"When?" Miss Abigail asks.

"Today. When I went to the Winter House to look for Theo's bag."

"Wait!" Theo interrupts. "Your brother was there?"

Necco nods.

"But you said you were alone." Theo tries to stifle the anger in her voice. "Jesus! Maybe he took the bag. Maybe he's the one who tore your place apart. And he's got to be the one Pru's strongman followed out there, right? The guy who is somehow connected to what happened to your boyfriend. Holy shit! What if he killed Hermes?"

Necco shakes her head. "It wasn't him."

"But how can you be sure? I mean, you haven't seen him for years, right? You thought he was dead. How well can you say you really know him now?"

"He's my brother!"

"That's another thing that's been bugging me," Theo says. "If he's really your brother, why isn't he mentioned in any of the articles about your family? Or your father's obituary. Didn't you notice that at all? It's like he doesn't exist. Like an imaginary friend. Or a ghost."

"He does exist," Necco says. "He's no ghost." She looks to Miss Abigail. "Tell her. Tell her Errol is real. That he's my brother."

Miss Abigail relights her torch, takes another sip of firewater, and breathes fire, spitting the flames out in a careful spray.

Pru is delighted. "Wonderful," she calls, clapping. Miss Abigail turns to her, and Theo is thinking that she's going to be scolded—this is like some kind of spiritual ceremony, not a sideshow. But Abigail smiles wide at Pru, showing teeth stained red. The old woman stands, takes a worn leather pouch from around her neck, holds it by the string, and walks over to the smiling cafeteria lady. She holds the pouch over Pru's head, and it spins in a slow, clockwise circle.

"You have been chosen," Miss Abigail says. "Chosen by the snuff."

"Her?" Theo says, incredulous. "Why her?" These women are supposed to be clairvoyant, so can't they see she's the one who needs it? The one who could actually have her ass saved by the stuff?

"Pru was brought here for a reason," Miss Abigail says.

"Yeah—and the reason is she was the one with the car," Theo snipes.

"What will happen if I take it?" Pru asks. "What will it do?"

"It will get inside you and change your life forever," Miss Abigail promises.

"Yes," Pru says, no trace of hesitation. "I'll take it."

Miss Abigail carefully opens the drawstring pouch, takes out a pinch of bright red powder, and places it in the palm of Pru's hand.

"Like this," Miss Abigail says, putting a second pinch into her own palm. She blocks one nostril with her thumb, brings the snuff to her face, and inhales it quickly, with one long sniff.

She watches now as Pru closes her left nostril with her thumb, brings her hand up to her nose, and inhales. "Ooh," she says, closing her eyes, smiling. "Oh, my."

Pru

〰️

The warmth hits her sinus passages first, then runs all the way through her, down her throat, into her chest, through her lungs and heart, then radiates its way out. It's a warm, glowing feeling, a strange tingling, like she can feel every molecule of air. She can taste the smoke, the breath of all these women, the river. Everything is alive, a woven-together tapestry of scents, sounds, color, and taste. And she is a part of it, oh, is she ever a part of it.

All the pain is gone from her body.

She has never felt more alive than she does right now, right here in this moment.

She stands, her legs two sure tree trunks beneath her, and begins to dance, staring into the fire in front of her, its flames leaping up in great colorful trails that connect with the stars above. She does her circus routine—a dainty pirouette, a dip, a leap. She's light on her feet. The river rushes behind her, within her, the fire blazes before her, inside her. She is nothing and she is everything. She is the Circus Fat Woman. She is the Great Mother. She has given birth to the world, big and round and beautiful, and now she dances.

The women are eating fire around her, cooing and humming a song with the most wonderful melody, breathing smoke out of their noses. Miss Abigail hands Pru a torch, and Pru dips it into the flame, waving it through the air: a burning marshmallow, a small comet streaking across the sky, her love for Mr. Marcelle, her circus dreams.

"Take the fire in quickly and close your mouth around it," Miss Abigail instructs. "Do not inhale. Just be one with the flames."

Pru does not hesitate. She is a woman who knows hunger, and she has never been truly satisfied. She knows what to do, how to open her mouth wide, invite the fire, in, close her mouth around it, and for once, for once in her life, she is full, she is satiated, she is so much more than herself.

She is a Fire Eater.

The smoke drifts from her nose and mouth, and she has a vision just then as she sways in front of the campfire flames. She watches the flames, sees a house inside them, a blue house, and Mr. Marcelle is inside, but he doesn't know the house is burning, doesn't understand the danger he is in. She's calling to him, trying to warn him.

"Stay where you are," he says to Pru.

Then, she sees Mr. Marcelle sitting on a couch with a woman with bleached hair. She has whiskey on her breath and she's telling him lies, but it doesn't matter because he sees through them. He's getting close, so close to finding out the truth. Then, he's the miniature version of himself—the little wire man in her circus, arms raised above his head, hoisting an impossibly large barbell.

Pru keeps her eye on the flames, and in them, she sees the circus, her own small circus, only, as she watches, it grows, expands. It's brought to life, made big and real and true, right here under the bridge. She sees a big ring, all the Fire Eaters dancing, twirling wands of flame. They are wearing colorful circus costumes of red and orange, fire colors, with sequins and beads that catch the light and flicker and burn. She sees a ticket seller with a line going all the way up the hill to the top of the bridge. And she sees an elephant. A great, golden elephant, all strung with lights, and she herself is riding on top, blowing kisses to the crowd because it's her they've come to see. And she opens her mouth to tell them all the secret, the secret they've traveled all this way to understand.

"Fire is life. And we are all fire. Each and every one of us has a flame burning inside. Rekindle your fire," she tells them.

And as she says these last words, golden butter-flies come out of her mouth, fluttering through the air, and the crowd claps, they clap as loud and hard as thunder. The ground shakes.

And it's all for her.

It's so beautiful, she starts to cry.

"You're the one," Miss Abigail says in her ear over the roar in her own head. "The one we've been waiting for. Welcome home, Miss Pru."

Necco

~~~~~

She and Theo are sitting on the bank of the river, which, in the darkness, is as black as newly poured tar. Theo is smoking a cigarette, and Necco is watching the way Theo's face is illuminated by the orange glow each time she takes a drag. She's still wearing the bowler hat; cocked to the side, it looks kind of perfect. Necco is wondering why Theo has stayed even though Necco knows she no longer has anything to offer her. No bag, no money, no drugs. Still, she's here, sitting beside Necco in her silly hat with their legs practically touching, the filthy river churning in front of them, and the occasional car crossing the bridge above them. Above them where the real city lies. Where the police and Good Samaritans are out searching the streets for Necco, the Fire Girl, Killer at Large.

While Necco would never admit this out loud, she's glad Theo is here. It's been a long time since she had a real friend. She had her mother and she had Hermes. There were other girls, in the time Before the Flood (there is no flood, stupid, let it go), that she played with from time to time, girls in pigtails she played Barbies with, or listened to music with, but there's been no one since she came to live on the street. None of the kids from the Catholic school were her friends—they just wanted to see the Fire Girl do her trick.

She recalls her mother's dire warning that she should trust no one, that anyone they befriended would be in danger. She wishes her mama was here, so that she could tell her sometimes it was worth the risk. Sometimes people surprised you, were more than they seemed. But Mama was right about one thing: knowing Necco had put Theo and Pru in terrible danger. Hermes, too. And look how that had turned out.

It's nearly one in the morning and Necco should be exhausted, but she's too pumped up, has too many thoughts flying through her brain like uncaged birds. Behind them, Pru is telling the other Fire Eaters about her snuff-induced visions: a circus, an elephant, how she believes the circus must be made real. "There were butterflies," she is saying. "And, oh, the costumes. You were all in such beautiful costumes." Pru is cooing, ecstatic. And the other women have embraced her, invited her to join them, to become a Fire Eater. To take Mama's place as the fifth woman. It all feels so unreal, yet meant to be at the same time. Necco often feels this way when she's with Miss Abigail and the other Fire Eaters. Like everything happens for a reason, the good and the bad.

"Tell us," Miss Coral says to Pru. "Tell us more. Tell us everything."

And Pru begins to tell them about her own small circus, how she sees now that this has just been preparing her for something larger. "Do you have paper?" she asks them. "And a pen? I can draw it all out—what I saw." Someone fetches her a notebook and she starts scribbling.

Necco picks up a small stone, throws it into the water. She hears the splash, thinks of all the things this river has swallowed. The blood from Hermes she washed off her clothes just yesterday morning.

Her mother.

Her father.

She wishes the river could speak. Maybe if she took the snuff, she'd be able to hear it. But the snuff has never chosen her. And now she's got the baby to think about. It was foolish to even consider. She probably shouldn't even be sitting here, breathing in Theo's smoke. She puts a hand over her belly, tries to imagine a tiny person inside. Half her, half Hermes.

Theo notices this small gesture. "How far along are you?"

Funny expression. Like pregnancy is a journey.

"I'm not sure," Necco admits.

"Have you been to a doctor or anything?"

"No."

Theo nods, doesn't hassle her or tell her what a crappy mother she's already being. But Necco almost wishes she would. Wishes for someone to take her by the shoulders, shake her, and say, "Do you have any idea what you're doing? This is not some game! This is another human being's life we're talking about here!"

She thinks about her own mama, the lengths she went to in order to protect Necco, building a cage of carefully woven-together stories and lies to keep her safe inside.

"Are you . . ." Theo hesitates. "Are you going to keep it? To go through with the pregnancy, I mean."

"Yes," Necco says before she's even had the chance to think about it. No hesitation whatsoever. Yes. She is going to have this baby. She is going to find a way. She will be a good mother. She will do her best. She will protect her child in whatever way she can. Just like her own mother did.

"Did he know?" Theo asks. "Hermes?"

The question, and just hearing his name, sends a jolt of sorrow through her. "Yes," she says in almost a whisper. "He was happy about it. He said he'd take care of us. That we'd be a real family."

She feels the hot burn of tears in her eyes and looks away, back down at the river. Then, she feels Theo's hand on her arm.

"I'm sorry," Theo says. She doesn't move her hand. She just leaves it there and they sit together like this for what feels like a very long time.

"I never thanked you," Necco says at last. "For helping me in the store today. I mean, I thanked you in my head, but not out loud."

"You're welcome."

"You didn't need to do that," Necco says. "And if you hadn't, if they hadn't taken that picture, you wouldn't be in this mess at all."

"Maybe not. But I'm plenty good at making my own messes." Theo turns and smiles at her. "And besides, I wanted to help you. It wasn't just about me hoping you still had the bag and the money and all that. It just seemed like . . . like the right thing. Like what I was supposed to do. Like destiny and fate and what all those women behind us are talking about while they snort their red berries and spit out fire."

"I'm sorry I couldn't get you your bag," Necco says. "What are you going to do?"

Theo stubs her cigarette out on the ground, puts the ruined filter in her pocket, not wanting to litter. "I don't know. If it was just Hannah, I could talk to her. Work something out."

"But it's not. This Jeremy guy sounds bad."

Theo shakes her head. "I think part of me knew Hannah was lying all along. Telling me what I wanted to believe. But I went along with it anyway. Doesn't that make me the dumbest fucking person on earth?"

"No," Necco says, thinking of Mama and her stories. How she'd listen with rapt attention when Mama spoke of the Great Flood, of the water that swept away their house, drowned Daddy and Errol. "It just means you put love first. Above truth, even."

Theo laughs. "Right. And now I'm gonna lose my left kidney or spleen or something to her psycho boyfriend. If I don't end up in jail first as an accessory to murder."

Necco flinches a little at the word **murder.** "You're not going to lose any body parts. And neither of us are going to jail. We'll figure something out."

"Right," Theo says. "You, me, the cafeteria lady, and the women tripping their brains out on snuff."

Necco smiles at her, then says, "You never know. My mama always said it's the people no one notices who are the most full of surprises."

Theo nods, eyes on the dark water of the river. "True enough. I just wish Jeremy and that cop weren't harassing my mom. My poor mom. She's worried sick."

"You should let her know you're okay," Necco says.

"And how am I gonna do that? I smashed my phone."

"Maybe the Fire Eaters can help," Necco says.

Theo laughs. "What are they gonna do, send her some kind of psychic message? Smoke signals, maybe?"

Necco stands. "Be right back." She leaves Theo by the riverbank and goes to find Miss Abigail. She is staring into the fire while Pru does sketches of large elephants and sequined dresses.

"Miss Abigail," Necco says. The old woman smiles up at her. "I need a favor. A big one."

"Tell me, child," the old woman says. And Necco tells her. She leans down and whispers it in her ear so the others can't hear. Miss Abigail sits and listens, stone-faced. She doesn't give an answer. She's considering. Maybe waiting for the snuff to tell her what to do.

"Whatever you decide will be the right thing," Necco says, kissing the old woman on the cheek. Miss Abigail nods, her eyes on the flames. Then Necco goes to Miss Stella, and asks her for a favor as well. Miss Stella nods. "Of course," she says.

When Necco gets back to the river, she sits down beside Theo and hands her a cell phone.

"Where'd you get this?" Theo asks.

"Miss Stella. She's kind of a tech geek."

"You're kidding, right? I thought they all lived down here surviving on nuts and berries, totally cut off from modern conveniences."

Necco smiles. "Stella says the cell's safe—it's a crappy burner phone and it's blocked so anyone you call won't be able to see the number or call back. You can text your mom. Let her know you're okay."

"I don't believe it," Theo says, taking the phone. She types in a quick text, then hands it back. "Thanks. Now at least my mom will know I'm alive and okay."

"I'm sorry," Necco says. "About not telling you about Errol. About lying when you asked me if I saw anyone while I was gone."

"It's okay. It must have been strange. Seeing him like that. And I don't get it, you haven't seen him in years, you think he's dead, then all of a sudden there he is and you only spend a few minutes with him? You just let him walk away?"

"I didn't want to. But he said it wasn't safe. Whoever had trashed the Winter House might come back. And we couldn't be seen together. Someone had been following him, and he knew the police were after me. He asked me to meet him tomorrow and said he'd explain everything then. He told me to be there at noon. To come alone and be sure to wear a disguise."

Theo frowns. "Where does he want you to meet him?"

Necco feels a hard lump growing in her throat. "Our old house."

"But you said it was destroyed! Not there anymore."

"I know, that's what my mother told me, but Errol, he said it's still there. I guess I'll see for myself soon enough."

"I don't like it," Theo says. "What if whoever is looking for you guys is watching the house?"

"I don't think Errol would have asked me to meet him there if it wasn't safe."

"I'll come with you," Theo says. "I'll stay out of sight, just keep an eye on things. Be your backup just in case."

"You don't have to do that."

"But I want to. Besides, at this point, with the cops waving a picture of the two of us around, you and I are in this together. Coconspirators."

Necco grimaces, but Theo touches her arm again.

"Hey, you want to know a secret? I always kind of wanted to know what it was like to be a bad guy. To be on the run."

Miss Abigail approaches slowly, shuffling her

way in the darkness. She squats down in front of them, puts her hand on Theo's shoulder, and looks into her eyes.

"Hi," Theo says, sounding nervous, unsure what the woman has up her sleeve.

"I understand you are in some trouble, girl." Before Theo can answer, Miss Abigail takes the younger girl's hand, opens it, and places a pouch of snuff in the palm. She wraps Theo's fingers around it. "You take this. But you take it under one condition."

Theo holds the bag up, realizes what she's just been given. "I—I never—"

"No more drugs. Selling the things you have been, making money on poison, it's bad for the soul. The Great Mother has a better path in mind for you."

"No more. I promise. I can't thank you enough." Theo stands up and hugs Miss Abigail.

Miss Abigail accepts the hug and gives Theo a gentle pat on the back. "You're a good person. I can see that. And most importantly, you're a good friend to Necco. You keep on being a good friend to her. She needs someone like you."

"Yes, ma'am," Theo says, letting go of Miss Abigail. "I promise."

Theo

〰️

They spent the night in the Fire Eaters' camp, sleeping on musty bedrolls in Necco's old shelter. Neither of them slept much, a few minutes here and there. Pru stayed up talking with the fire-eating women. Theo could hear them out there all night, speaking in hushed tones. Occasionally, Theo would catch a few words: **Great Mother, purpose, reason, believe.** And Pru's voice chortled out things like **circus** and **golden elephant.** Theo heard Pru sobbing, saying, "You have no idea what it's been like." Then, Miss Stella comforting her, saying, "You're not alone anymore."

Theo got up at dawn and found her knitting bag, pulled out the yellow angora yarn, and sat by the river knitting because that was the one thing she knew that might calm her thoughts.

"What are you making?" Necco asked when she came to find her later.

Theo held up the trapezoid shape that hung from her needle. "It's going to be a hat. For your baby."

And Necco's eyes got teary. "Wow. I don't . . . I don't know what to say."

"It's okay. You don't need to say anything," Theo told her. "Besides, the hat might not turn out too great. It might make the poor kid look like a sticky Lemonhead covered with lint."

Necco smiled. "It'll be perfect."

Now, it's nine a.m., and Theo is driving Pru's car around town. Theo had been nervous about asking for the keys, but this new, easygoing Pru with red stains under her nose had happily tossed them to her, asking only that Theo take good care of Mabel.

"They used to be all over the damn place," Theo says, desperately searching for a pay phone. "What happened to them all?"

She wishes now that she'd asked to use Miss Stella's cell before they left. It hadn't occurred to her how hard it would be to find a pay phone.

"I guess people decided they didn't need them anymore," Necco says. She's put her wig and sunglasses back on, along with the blue fringed jacket. "Maybe you should just show up at Hannah's place, talk to her there."

"Jeremy's probably there. And he's so pissed off that he'd probably rip both my fucking arms off just for fun, even if I came with all his money."

"Right. Getting her alone would be better."

"Oh my God, I think I see a phone! An actual phone!" Theo pulls into a convenience store parking lot, the tires of Pru's huge car squealing a little as they bump over the curb. "Land ho," she says, putting the car into park and hopping out. She goes to the pay phone mounted on the brick wall on the side of the store, dumps in change, and dials Hannah's number.

"Hello?"

Hannah's voice is like an ice pick in Theo's chest. She almost can't speak, can't breathe from the sound of it.

"Anyone there?" Hannah asks. Then, "Theo?"

"It's me," Theo says.

"Theo, my God, where are you? What's happening?" She sounds like she cares. Like she's worried. But it's all a ruse. She wants her money. She wants to keep her boyfriend happy.

"What if I could get you guys Devil's Snuff?" Theo says. "About half an ounce of it."

"Devil's Snuff? You're kidding, right?"

"Would the slate be wiped clean? Would that make us even?"

"Shit, Theo, you know what that stuff is worth. It's like powdered gold. Ground unicorn horn."

"Well, I've got some. Meet me at the diner we went to that first day. Come alone. No Jeremy. I'll give it to you and then we'll be done."

"Theo, I—"

"Half an hour," Theo says and hangs up. She can't listen to Hannah's voice another second.

She goes back to the car, and her hands are shaking a little as she puts them on the wheel.

"You okay?" Necco asks.

"Yup," Theo says. "Fine. I told her to meet me in half an hour."

"And we'll do it just like you said," Necco says. "Watch from across the street. Wait for her to go in first, make sure she's alone. And I'll be watching the whole time to make sure there's no surprise visits from Jeremy. If he shows, I'll be in there in a flash."

Theo smiles at Necco. "A no-fail plan," she says. She thinks of Necco coming blazing into the restaurant, of her showing Jeremy her knife, telling him she's a wanted killer so he better back the fuck off now. Theo takes in a breath. Tries to channel her inner Necco. When she goes into that diner, she needs to be just as badass (or at least fake it). Theo's mom used to have a really dull boyfriend named Mr. Candles, who was into AA and full of those cheesy slogans. One of them was **Fake it till you make it.** That's just what Theo has to do right now.

It's breakfast rush time and the Koffee Kup is crowded.

"My mom and I used to come here," Necco says.

"They have good milk shakes," Theo tells her.

"We always just got coffee," Necco says, nodding at the sign in the window that says BOTTOMLESS CUP OF COFFEE ONLY ONE DOLLAR!

They're in Pru's car across the street, watching the front door and waiting. So far no Jeremy, no Hannah. Theo is smoking a cigarette, blowing the smoke out the open window so Necco won't breathe it in. She's got Pru's bowler hat on and a pair of sunglasses. She's touched up her lipstick. Put on extra-dark eyeliner. She's ready for battle.

"Is that her?" Necco asks, pointing.

Sure enough, there's Hannah, making her way down the street. She's alone, wearing jeans and her old fisherman's sweater. Her hair is pulled back in a loose ponytail, and she's got huge sunglasses on.

Seeing her, Theo feels less sure about the plan, about her ability to face Hannah.

"It's her," Theo says, watching her walk into the diner. Hannah looks around inside, then gets a booth at the end by the window.

"Looks good," Necco says. "No sign of the boyfriend. You go in and I'll be watching."

"Back in ten minutes," Theo says, tossing her still-burning cigarette to the ground.

Fake it till you make it.

She gets out of the car and crosses the street, enters the diner, and takes a deep breath of bacon- and coffee-scented air.

She remembers that first day with Hannah: **You don't look like a girl with a single bad habit.**

She approaches the booth, and Hannah jumps up when she sees her, throws her arms around Theo. Theo fights with everything she's got to remain rigid, to not hug her back or melt into her embrace. She remembers being in the closet, listening to Hannah and Jeremy kiss and roll around on the bed, the unmistakable sound of the zipper on Jeremy's jeans being pulled down. She pulls back until Hannah lets go, and takes a seat on the vinyl bench opposite.

"I've been so worried," Hannah says, sitting down, pushing hair out of her eyes.

Like hell you have, Theo thinks. She looks out the window with its kitschy curtains printed with salt and pepper shakers, finds Necco in the driver's seat of Pru's car.

"Coffee, ladies?" the waitress asks, holding a pot.

"I think we're fine with **just** coffee," Hannah

says, and then gestures to Pru's old bowler after the woman leaves. "Cute hat. It suits you."

Theo ignores the compliment, reaches into her bag, and pulls out the brown paper lunch sack that has the pouch of snuff inside.

"Under the table," Theo orders, and when Hannah takes it, their hands touch.

"This is it for real?" Hannah says, peering down.

"For real."

"Jeremy's going shit himself." She smiles wide, excited.

"So no harassing me about the missing money? This makes us even?"

"Absolutely," Hannah says. "I promise."

Theo looks away; Hannah doesn't realize how little her promises mean.

"You and I both know that this is worth more than two grand," Hannah says.

"Yup. We're good, then," Theo says, and stands up to leave, but Hannah grabs her wrist.

"Wait," she says. "Please."

Her hand is warm, and the warmth radiates up Theo's arm, all the way to her chest. Theo sits back down, knowing she shouldn't, that she should pull away.

"I just wanted to say . . ." Hannah says before pausing. "I wanted to say how sorry I am. For how things turned out."

Theo feels rage ripple through her. "How they

turned out?" she snaps. "You're sorry I found out about Jeremy. Sorry I lost the fucking money. But what about all the rest of it? How you set me up, pretended to give a shit, let me believe that what we had was the real deal. What about all of that, Hannah? Are you fucking sorry for any of that?"

Some of the other diners, hearing Theo's raised voice, have turned to look. Theo feels a flash of shame. For a person of interest in a murder investigation, a person who's supposed to be lying low, she's doing a real shitty job.

Hannah presses her back into the seat, eyes teary. What a fucking great actress you are, Theo thinks. Academy Award material.

"No," Hannah says, voice low. "I'm not sorry. Because everything between us, Theo, all that was real."

"Bullshit," Theo hisses, voice low now. "Tell me. Did you have the whole thing planned all along? You and Jeremy? Were you out hunting for some girl to use? Some idiot high schooler who didn't know any better?"

"Theo, it wasn't like that."

"Right," Theo says, shoving her untouched coffee away.

"Theo, once I give Jeremy this, I'm leaving him."

It's what a part of Theo longs to hear, but it's too little, too late. It's too late for any of this.

She's got to go. Got to get the fuck out of here before Hannah says any more.

"Whatever," Theo says, standing again. "I don't care what you do."

Hannah takes her wrist again. "I love you," she says. Theo tries to pull away, but she stops, looks Hannah in the eye. And in that one second, everything goes to hell. All her plans to stay strong, to be cold and tough and play it like she doesn't give a shit. Hannah's hand is on her wrist, her index finger gently caresses Theo's pulse point, and Theo is about to say, **Yes. Leave Jeremy. Take me back. Run away with me. We'll take the snuff and sell it. We'll go start over somewhere. That's how it's meant to be.**

"Everything okay here?" Necco has come in, is standing over them, right next to Hannah.

"Fine," Theo says, shaking herself back to reality enough to pull away from Hannah's grip. "I was just leaving."

"Who's this?" Hannah asks.

Theo looks at Necco. She's wearing her blond wig, the suede jacket, fresh makeup. She looks a good ten years older than she is, and everything about her face says, **Don't fuck with me.** Theo knows that under her right pant leg, she's got a knife strapped to her boot.

"A friend," Theo says, right before she links arms with Necco and walks away, not looking back.

"That explains a lot!" Hannah calls. She's crying now, and everyone in the diner is looking at her, at them. But Theo keeps her eyes on the ground until they are in the car.

Later, when she's two blocks away, Theo pulls into the parking lot in front of Express Dry Cleaners.

"Fuck!" she howls, punching the wheel, letting herself cry. She cries and swears, and hits the wheel.

Necco sits beside her, silent, watching.

At last, Theo pulls her shit together. "Sorry," she says, taking out a cigarette.

"Nothing to be sorry about."

"It's all so fucking hard, you know?" Theo says. "Loving people, trusting them, then having it all fall to shit."

Necco nods. "I know."

Theo looks at Necco, holding her unlit cigarette. The Fire Girl looks so calm, so pulled together. Two days ago she woke up with her boyfriend dead beside her. Theo has no fucking right to be sitting in this car, next to this girl, feeling sorry for herself. "God, I totally suck. You're the one who's lost everything, the one with a killer after you. I've just been screwed over by my stupid girlfriend. And now I'm sitting here about to breathe my secondhand smoke all over you and your baby again. I am such a selfish idiot." She throws her cigarette out the window.

"No, you're not," Necco says. "You're very brave. Facing Hannah like that, doing what you needed to do."

"But I'm not brave at all. If you hadn't been with me I'd never have done it."

Necco considers this for a minute, says, "Maybe that's what friends do, right? Make each other brave when we need it most. Me, I'm scared out of my mind to go back to my old house. But somehow knowing you'll be with me makes it a little easier. A little less scary."

Theo smiles, throws the rest of her pack of cigarettes out the window. She's been meaning to quit forever and it seems like there's no better time than right this second. "Let's go see this house, then. You and me," she says and starts the car.

Fred

~~~~

Fred doesn't know much about the women who live under the bridge. Just a few rumors he's picked up over the years. They live in makeshift huts by the river. They're all addicted to some sort of drug called the Devil's Snuff. He doesn't know much about the snuff either, just that it's rarer than rare, but these women seem to be able to get it anytime they need. Maybe they're the source. Fred doesn't think much of drug addicts. He understands that addiction is an illness, but try as he might, he can't help but see it as being weak willed. And he doesn't get what would make someone try something like that to begin with, when they know it's illegal and addictive. People make dumb-ass choices. That's what it comes down to.

People go to the Devil's Snuff women to learn their future. Give them some coins and they'll tell you whether you should take that new job or if the boyfriend is going to ask you to marry him one day soon. Foolish stuff. Witches and fortune-tellers and a bunch of superstitious nonsense. But he's hoping that there will be someone there who will talk to him about Lily Sandeski. Surely she didn't just show up out of the blue and ask to become a Fire Eater? She must have had a story. Maybe one of the women could help him solve the mystery of how Lily, wife of a college professor and a mother, ended up living under a bridge. He's brought cash with him. If these women will tell your future for coins, maybe they'll also tell about someone else's past. And maybe, just maybe, if he's lucky, they might know where he can find Eva. He's got to get to her before the kid and the man with the tattoo do.

He gets to the Blachly Bridge and stands on the edge, looking down. He can't see anything—too much heavy vegetation, a thick curtain of leaves camouflaging whatever's below. But he smells woodsmoke, and he thinks, if he holds still and listens hard, he hears the faint sound of talking and laughter down there. It's eerie, the way the sound travels up, like voices from another world.

He walks to the end of the bridge and starts to search for a way down. Eventually, he finds a narrow, cleared path. It's steep and the trees and saplings are right against its ragged edge. Thick stands of a tall plant—bamboo?—reach high over his head. Growing up along the trunks of these, as well as the trunks of other small trees, are bittersweet vines with yellow pods that have popped open, showing the bright red berries inside. There are bugs in here, and the air feels wet and murky. It's like a goddamn jungle. He should have brought a machete.

His brother wants him to bring in information on the mystery kid. But what his brother wants most is the girl, the suspect in the murder of the governor's son. There's big money in it if they find her and bring her in. But Fred hasn't told his brother about these new leads. He hasn't told his brother because he thinks the girl is innocent, that maybe she was set up.

As if they've got some kind of psychic link and James knows his brother was just thinking about him, he calls.

"Hey," Fred says, pausing under a bush, waving mosquitoes away.

"Want to tell me who the fuck Judith Tanner is?"

Fred pauses, thinking, **Oh, shit.**

"'Cause I just got a call from her wanting to follow up on our apparent conversation last night where I told her I knew how to find her niece. What the fuck is going on, Bro?"

"I can explain," Fred says. "Not now, though.

Give me a couple hours. In the meantime, see what you can find on a guy named Edward Tanner—I think—"

"Bullshit!" James cuts him off. "I don't appreciate you running around town impersonating me. Get back to the office. I want a debriefing—now! If you're not here in half an hour, you're officially off the payroll."

"Prick," Fred says when James hangs up. He tucks the phone back into his pocket, continues down the path.

Last night, after he'd left Judith, he'd circled around to the back of the house, watched her through the kitchen window for a few minutes. She was on her phone, talking, voice raised, arms gesturing. The window was open a crack, and he was able to catch a few words: **Private detective, questions, Eva, Miles, trouble,** and **I promise.**

The ground levels out now and the path takes him along the edge of the river. Above him, the bridge looms like a big green cage, a hand waiting to grab him. He shakes the foolish thoughts from his head. The voices are clearer now, a group of women talking, laughing. He can make out the shapes of wooden shacks, and as he gets closer he sees they're covered in roofing paper, cardboard, trash bags, and blue tarps.

There is an old woman dressed in colorful layers, scraggly white hair tied up in rags. She's tending the fire. She looks up as he approaches. He sees three other women down by the river, gathering water in buckets, doing washing. They're singing something, but stop when they hear him.

"Hello," he calls. "I was hoping you could help me."

The old woman stares at him, but says nothing. He's almost to her now, so close he can feel the heat of the fire. She stirs at the coals with a long stick, sends sparks shooting up.

"Are you lost?" she asks him.

"No, I—"

"Mr. Marcelle?"

He turns.

Pru Small is coming out of one of the rickety wooden shacks. She has dirt smudged on her face and clothes. Her hair is in tangles. She looks like a woman who's been lost in the wilderness for weeks.

"Pru?" he stammers, unable to hide his shock at finding her here, in this place. Just like he hadn't expected her out at the old mill yesterday. Pru is full of surprises. "What the hell— Are you okay?"

"You know this man?" the old woman says to Pru.

"Yes. He's a friend." She turns to him. "Mr. Marcelle." She smiles, her dirty face lighting up. "What brings you down here?"

He's not sure just where to begin, but decides to cut to the chase.

"Eva Sandeski," he says. "That's what brings me here. Do either of you know where she is?"

"I don't know anyone by that name," the old woman says, and turns away from him, continues to poke at the fire. The other three women have approached now. They move in unison, silent, and form a rough circle around Fred, watching, waiting. One is young with a crazy punk hair-cut and tattoos; there's an older, frumpy-looking woman with her hair in a bun, and a tiny, blond, wild-eyed woman with gritted, red-stained teeth. Despite his size and strength, he knows he's outnumbered, that they have the upper hand here.

"But you knew her mother, Lily. She came to you about four years ago. Her husband, Miles Sandeski, was a professor at the college. For some reason, Lily took her daughter, Eva, and ran. And she ended up here. I want to know why. Please."

"I don't know anyone by those names," the old woman says, still poking the fire, sending a stream of sparks flying up. The woman with the blond hair and wild eyes takes a step closer; the other two women do the same.

"Please," he begs. "I'm just trying to help. I'm not sure about this, but I think that Miles Sandeski and Lily were murdered. And Matthew Stanton, the governor's son; two days before he was killed, he asked his dad to reopen an old murder case."

"What old case?" the old woman asks. He has her attention now.

"When Miles was ten, he watched his mother have her throat slit by a man in a mask. Somehow Matthew discovered something, some new information about who the killer was. And I think this got him killed. And I also think that now whoever murdered Matthew is looking for Eva. She's in terrible danger. Please."

"Miss Abigail?" Pru says to the old woman. "What do you think?"

Miss Abigail looks long and hard at Fred but says nothing.

"Please, Pru, where is Eva?" he asks. "She is supposed to meet a young man this afternoon, a man with a scar above his eye, but it's a trap. There's another man, a man with a tattoo, who will be waiting. They think she has something they want. Something they won't leave without, whatever the cost."

"Tattoo?" The old woman turns, looks worried. "What kind of tattoo?"

"A pair of dice on his wrist."

"Snake Eyes," the old woman hisses. She looks down into the flames, then turns to face Pru, eyes like glowing coals. "Pru, tell him what you know. Our Necco is in serious danger. Theo, too."

Pru frowns. "Necco—Eva, I mean—she's gone off with Theodora. They took my car. They went to meet Necco's brother. He must be the boy with the scar."

"Her brother?" Mr. Marcelle asks. "Are you sure?" He remembers the photo of the little boy on Judith Tanner's mantel. Her son, Edward, who supposedly died years ago.

"Where are they meeting him?"

"At Eva's old house. He's supposed to be there at noon."

Fred looks down at his watch. "It's five of now."

"Then we better hurry," Pru says.

"We? Pru, it could be dangerous, I don't think—"

"I'm coming with you," she says, not a question but a loud and clear statement.

He nods. "I've got the address in my papers in the car. Let's go."

Necco

〰️

Necco holds her breath as they cross the Blachly Bridge. They're heading southeast, into what Necco has come to think of as the Forbidden Zone. It's all still here. Still the same as she remembers it: the market, the little cafés, the brightly colored bungalow houses.

Theo turns right on Old Route 3. As they move farther away from the heart of the city, the houses get farther apart. There are fields. A barn with horses, even.

"Pretty out here," Theo says.

"Yeah," Necco agrees. There's so much green. Houses with swimming pools, big gardens. Theo makes two more turns and they're on Birchwood Lane.

Now, Necco blinks her eyes helplessly, looks

out the car window and knows just where she is. She's bumping along the little lane they used to live on, the river running at her left side, just through the woods. She can see it sparkle like diamonds through the trees, like a treasure waiting to be discovered.

But she knows better. She knows that sometimes a thing masks its danger with beauty just to lure you closer, to lull you into believing you are safe. She reaches down, feels the outline of her blade strapped to her boot, which offers some comfort.

And just then, they come around the bend and the house comes into view and it takes the air right out of her chest. She can't believe she's seeing it: that it's still there, that it looks just the same. There is her little house, complete with the swing set in the yard. Errol used to push her on it, give her underdogs and sing a silly little song while he did it. She'd forgotten that until just now—that there were things called underdogs and silly songs her brother sang.

The blue paint on the house is peeling, the yard is overgrown, and her mother's garden is all choked out by weeds. (She'd forgotten this, too—how her mother loved to garden.) Off to the left, between the house and river, her father's workshop—the old metal-sided shack—looks a little more rusted now, the windows cracked, but it's still standing. Not swept away by the river.

"It's all still here," she says, the words breathy and light, more of a gasp than a sentence. "Just like Errol said. There was no **Great Flood,**" she says out loud, because she needs to hear the words, to repeat them again and again in the hope that, one day, they'll sink in. For years now, her life has been divided by this marker: Before the Flood and After the Flood. Every story her mother told was based on this story, this mythology.

Sometimes the people who love us most make huge sacrifices for us, Miss Abigail said. **They'll do anything to protect us.**

Necco yanks open the door before the car even rolls to a stop and jumps out, stumbling.

"Hey, wait a sec," Theo calls behind her, shutting the car off.

Necco runs straight for the old workshop, remembering its familiar smell: pipe tobacco, grease, burning coal and hot metal if the forge was going. An aluminum ladder is hung on a rack on the building's side. A rusted shovel and hoe lean against the side of the building. Necco bites her tongue to keep from calling his name—**Daddy!**—as she yanks the thin metal door open and steps inside. There's no trace of Daddy left here—it's as if she'd imagined the whole thing. No rows of tools, boxes of gears; no mechanical bat circling on a wire overhead, no windup raccoon watching her from a shelf. The place has been completely stripped, the heavy iron forge gone, even the workbench torn away and carted off. She stands for a minute, breathing deeply, hoping to catch a hint of the smell she'd remembered, but this place smells damp and abandoned.

She touches the wall at the far end, remembers the invention her father kept there covered by a tarp on his workbench.

She sees it then, what happened in here that last day.

She'd come into the workshop first, heard a crackling hum. The machine was on. Then the hum turned into a voice. The machine spoke.

Daddy went over to the workbench, pulled back the tarp in one quick movement, like a magician about to reveal his best trick.

There was his machine, his own terrifying version of the Edison invention. The machine itself was housed in a wooden cabinet—about two feet long and a foot wide. It was electric, and had knobs and wires and small glass tubes, which were glowing then, because the machine was on. There was a large, funnel-like piece attached to a thick cord. It reminded her of an old-fashioned record player, like the kind you see in history books in school.

And from the speaker came a soft buzz, like bees leaving a hive, and the buzz built into a sound, a moan almost, then the buzz turned into a word, a word she knew to be spoken by the voice of her grandmother: her grandmother who looked out at them from the old photograph Daddy kept above his workbench. In the photo, she's looking up at the camera with an expression of surprise, almost alarm, her mouth slightly open, as if she's about to scream.

Danger, she said through the crackling of the speaker. **You're in danger.** Then, **He's here!**

And Daddy had sent Necco back to the house, told her to go and lock all the doors, but not to frighten Mama. On her way across the yard, she'd passed Errol. He was hurrying to the shed, his face panic-stricken.

"What is that?" she'd said, because he had something in his hand, something brightly colored, and he didn't answer, just jogged past her, but she saw what it was: a rubber chicken mask. And she wanted to laugh, because it was so absurd, but she was too scared.

"Everything okay?" Theo is sticking her head into the empty shed.

"Fine," Necco tells her, the long ago warning echoing in her ears: **Danger. You're in danger.**

"What is this place? Like a garden shed or something?"

"It was my father's workshop. But everything's gone."

"Is this where he made the invention I keep hearing about?"

Necco nods. "He made other things, too. One time, he built this windup raccoon out of scrap metal and old clock parts and gears. He used to make all kinds of mechanical creatures; things that walked and talked and had little secret compartments he'd put candy inside. It was a game, to see if I could figure out how to open them."

"Wow," Theo says. "Sounds like your dad was a man of many talents."

Necco's head begins to pound. She feels lightheaded, hears a buzzing in her ears **(danger, you're in danger)**. She stumbles, leans against the back wall of the shed.

"Necco?" Theo hurries into the shed. "You okay?"

The light pours in behind Theo, turning her into a dark shadow, a silhouette, and Necco remembers her father standing over her when she was very little and giving her the doll he'd just made.

"She's very special," he'd said. "Promise you'll take good care of her?"

And she had promised and clutched the doll tight against her chest.

"She even sings," he'd told her. "Do you want to hear?"

She'd nodded, and he'd shown her how to pull the cord on the doll's back to start the tiny recorded voice.

"Daddy," she whispers now, but he doesn't appear. No man, no ghost, only Theo, who is right beside Necco asking if she's okay.

"I'm fine," Necco says, pushing off from the wall, but her legs feel rubbery and nothing is fine.

She steps out of the shed, crosses the weed-scape of a yard, to the front door of the house, sees a No Trespassing sign. She puts her hand on the knob, hesitates, then tries to turn it. Locked. Necco steps to the left, puts her face against the cool, dusty glass of the living room window, cups her hands to block out the light. There is the couch, her father's chair, the old TV. Everything is wrecked, stuffing yanked out, cushions and pillows sliced open, walls kicked through.

What happened here?

Vandals who came to see what damage they could cause to an abandoned building, or was it something more?

Theo comes up behind her, peers in, whistles. "Pretty wrecked. Guess no one's living here now."

"Let's go in," Necco says. If being in her father's workshop triggered memories, she's sure going into the house will unlock even more.

"Door's locked," Theo says.

"I'll find a way," Necco says. After all, she's the Fire Girl. She knows how to get in and out of a place. To look for entrances and exits no one else can find. Hermes taught her how to pick a lock, to break a window safely without making much noise.

She walks around the side of the house, check-ing the windows, all shut up tight. The back door, the one that leads into the kitchen, is ajar; the edge of the doorframe that held the lock plate has been pried off.

"I'm not sure about this," Theo says, as Necco pushes the door open; it lets out a long squeak.

"It's my house," Necco says, the words feeling like a lie. Like something borrowed from another girl's life. **My name was Eva. I lived in this house. I lived here with my mother and father and brother, Errol. I had a purple room, a closet full of clothes, shelves full of books, and a canopy bed.**

Necco reaches down, takes out her blade.

"Stay there and keep lookout," she orders and steps into the kitchen. The cabinets are open, their contents scattered across the counters and floors. The sink is full of dirty dishes. When Necco turns on the faucet, no water comes. When she flicks on a light switch, no electricity. She goes to the stove, fiddles with the burners. No hiss of propane, no spark of flame.

The floor is filthy with mud, sticky with goo from broken glass jars that litter the floor: maraschino cherries, artichoke hearts, butterscotch sauce. These were things from her kitchen. Things her mother had bought for them at the market in the time Before the Flood. Back when they sat around the table with ice cream sundaes. Errol's favorite flavor was chocolate. Hers was strawberry. She hasn't tasted strawberry ice

cream in years. Suddenly she finds herself wanting it so bad her mouth waters.

She walks through the kitchen kicking the
broken glass away, and into the dining room.
The table is covered with books and papers,
empty bottles of beer and wine. Candles have
been stuck into the necks of bottles, and burned
down to stubs. Cigarettes have left burn marks
and sad piles of gray ash on the table. Her family did not leave this mess. Must have been years
of squatters, kids looking for a place to party.
Amid the mess, she recognizes some of the books
stacked there: her father's sociology and science
books, her mother's art books. The papers strewn
all over the table are a mixture of things pulled
from file cabinets and drawers: old electric bills,
appliance manuals, letterhead from the univer-
sity. Here and there, a scribbled list or note in
her father's writing: columns of numbers added
together, a reminder to buy butter at the store.
Nothing unusual, but all of it heartbreakingly
normal—the detritus of their lives Before.

She remembers standing in the kitchen that
last day. She'd gone back to the house, just like
Daddy asked her to, and locked all the doors.
Told Mama that they were to meet Daddy and
Errol at the boat in fifteen minutes. She didn't
tell Mama about the voice on Daddy's machine
or the strange rubber mask in Errol's hands.

The rain pounded on the roof. Mama was worried. Frantic. She was busying herself stuffing things into an old duffel bag she'd pulled from the closet: warm sweaters, the wedding photo from the mantel, the doll Daddy had made Eva when she was little.

Then, there was the sound of breaking glass. One of the living room windows being shattered. Mama screamed.

"Run," Mama told Necco. "Go find your father and Errol!" Mama grabbed a big carving knife from the rack by the stove.

Necco didn't even stop to get her coat or her shoes. She ran out the kitchen door and went to the workshop to find Daddy. But Daddy wasn't there. Errol was. And he was busting the place apart. He had a sledgehammer and was smashing the machine. The wooden cabinet was shattered, the tubes smashed. Wires had been ripped out, thrown onto the floor. The speaker they'd talked into swung like a pendulum in front of the bench, still attached by its cord to the ruined remains of the machine.

Necco jumped on Errol's back, grabbed at the hammer. "Stop!" she screamed. "What are you doing?"

But he was bigger, stronger. He shook her off like an ant. She fell to the floor and he stood over her with his huge hammer.

"Daddy told me to," he said.

"No! He wouldn't do that! You're lying!"

Necco goes up the stairs now, hand on the familiar worn railing. She pads down the carpeted hallway to her room, remembering the purple walls, canopy bed, the string of dragonflies her father had made that fluttered over her at night. She imagines throwing herself down on the bed, burying her face in the pillows. But when she yanks open the white painted bedroom door, the bed is gone. The room has been stripped clean. No clothes in the closet, no books, nothing with her name. Nothing to say she was ever here. Only the peeling purple walls, now covered with graffiti:

Lenore was here.

Eddie Sucks Dick.

Don't Fear the Reaper.

Necco's head is pounding now, her breath coming faster. She goes across the hall to Errol's room and stops in her tracks. There's a sleeping bag on the bed (why did they take her bed and not his?), a flashlight and camping lantern beside it. Candy wrappers everywhere. Comic books. Newspapers. A neat pile of clothes, a pair of worn boots.

Theo comes in behind her, takes a look around. "Someone's been staying here," she says.

Necco should scold her, tell her she should have stayed outside like she'd told her to, but she's actually relieved to have company.

"It's my brother's room," she says. "Errol."

"Shit. You think he's been staying here?"

"Maybe," Necco says. She looks at the candy wrappers, sees the cellophane from root beer barrels—they always were Errol's favorites.

"Well, where is he now?" She looks at her watch. "It's after noon."

"I don't know."

"Necco, don't you think it's strange that . . . well, in all the papers Hermes left you—the newspaper articles and stuff about your family— that they never mentioned a brother? Not even in your dad's obituary. Just you and your mom and dad."

"But he's my brother," Necco says, blinking at Theo, who now stands in front of the window in her bowler hat and round glasses, her silhouette dark and wavering.

"Are you sure you **had** a brother? Could it be a story your mother told you?"

"No. I'm sure."

Necco's head is swimming. She starts to feel faint again and sits down on the bed hard. She puts the knife back into the sheath on her boot, her fingers trembling. Mama lied about so many things—that Errol was killed, that the house was gone, that the whole thing washed away. But her memories of Errol are from before that.

She remembers Errol's hands on her back as he pushed her on the swing in the yard.

You wanna go straight up to the moon? he asked. **You want an underdog?**

There's a banging sound from downstairs, then footsteps.

"Eva?" Errol calls.

Necco jumps up off the bed, throws Theo a glance that says:

See, he's real after all.

And she knows this is her brother, and that she should be happy, excited that he's here. But what she really is is scared. Suddenly, she doesn't want to be here.

Danger, a voice calls from way back in her memory. **You're in danger.**

She looks around frantically for a way out, but there's only the window and they're on the second story.

"Where are you?" he calls now.

She remembers yesterday, how he'd told her to come alone.

"Theo," Necco whispers. "He's here! Quick, hide!" She gestures at the closet.

"Oh, great," Theo whispers. "Another freaking closet." She quickly tiptoes into the closet and shuts the door almost all the way.

"I'm up here," Necco calls, and suddenly, there he is, standing in the doorway.

But something's not right. He's got a black eye; half his face is swollen.

"Oh, Errol, what happened?" she asks, going toward him.

But then she freezes when she sees he's holding a gun.

"What are you doing with that?" Necco feels all the air leave her lungs. She takes a step back.

"Go sit on the bed," he tells her, more like an order than a kind, brotherly request.

Necco obeys. She thinks of what Theo said: **Are you sure you** had **a brother?**

But she is sure. Once upon a time, they lived here, in this house. He was Big E and she was Little E. They played cribbage. He gave her underdogs.

"Take your knife out slowly and lay it on the floor," Errol says.

Necco leans down, unclips the blade from its sheath, and sets it on the floor.

"Now slide it over toward me," Errol says.

Necco gives the knife a shove, and it slides across the floor so that it's out of her range, but close to the closet.

Errol comes forward and begins to pace back and forth at the foot of the bed. "Eva, we don't have much time." His voice is desperate, pleading. "I need to know what Daddy did with the plans."

"Plans? What plans? I don't know—"

"He told me they were safe and that you would know how to find them."

"When? When did he tell you this, Errol, because I have no idea what you're even talking about."

"He told me that last day. The day of the flood."

Errol stops pacing. He holds the gun in his right hand, rubs his face with his left. This bad-guy-with-the-gun thing seems all wrong for him. Not a role he's comfortable with.

"I tried to warn him," Errol says, voice whimpering, little-boyish. "But I was too late. And now, now I'm trying to warn you."

Shit, Necco is thinking. This is bad. Very bad.

"So you brought a gun? Subtle warning, Errol."

"Eva, the man who's coming, he'll do worse. Much worse."

"Snake Eyes, you mean?"

"That's what Mama called him."

"What's his real name?"

Errol shakes his head. "It's not important. All you've gotta know is that he's a bad man, Eva. You've gotta trust me when I tell you this. If you don't tell me where the plans are, I don't know what he'll do to you. To both of us. You saw what happened to your boyfriend. This guy doesn't fuck around. He's good at what he does. He tricks people. Manipulates them. He puts you in positions where you have no choice but to do what he says. He'll fuck you up, Eva."

She's sure her head is going to explode. How many times does she have to say it? "I don't have any plans!"

"But Daddy told you how to find them. Think, Eva. He must have told you that last day."

Necco is shaking her head. "I don't remember."

"What **do** you remember about that day?"

More than I did just a few hours ago, she thinks.

Being here in the house is helping to bring it all back. The gates are opening.

Necco falls onto the bed, closes her eyes. "It was raining," she says.

"Yes," Errol says. "Good. And the river was rising."

"And Mama was worried about a flood. She said we had to be ready to go. To evacuate. And you, you were excited because the road had washed away. You said we were living on an island, cut off from the rest of the world. You always wanted to live on your own island, remember, Errol?"

Errol nods, gives her a sad smile, lowers the gun. "I remember, Little E. Go on."

Necco continues, "Daddy and I went to check the workshop. You went down the road to see how high the water was. Then Daddy sent me back into the house and Mama was in there packing things up. There was a crash. A window breaking. Mama told me to run. To go find you and Daddy. I went out the back door and found you in Daddy's workshop."

"Yes," he said.

"And you were smashing everything. I tried to stop you, but you threw me off. You sent me away."

Errol nods encouragingly, shows Necco she's got the story right so far. "I told you to go back to the house, but you never made it."

"What?"

"He got you first. He got you and brought you down to the river. Do you remember?" Errol asks.

"No," Necco says, frustrated. "Who got me? What happened? I don't remember anything after being in the shed with you, seeing you holding the hammer."

"Try," Errol tells her. "You left the shed. Started running back to the house. And Mama was outside. Calling your name."

Necco closes her eyes, and she's back there just leaving the shed, afraid of Errol, sure that he lied, Daddy never would have told him to do such a thing. Her mama is on the front steps, calling, calling her name, her voice barely audible amid the pounding rain and roaring thunder. She can hear it so clearly now, Mama calling, "Eva!" and it's like Mama is calling her back through time, back to that day four years ago. She can feel the raindrops pounding against her yellow slicker. The way her rubber boots slip on the soaked grass.

She's crossing the yard, running toward her mother. Mama is screaming now, frantic, saying, "Look out! Run!" Suddenly, the wave hits her from behind, and at first, she thinks it's Errol with his sledgehammer: a big hard thump right in the back that knocks her to the ground, takes the breath out of her. The wave lifts her in its arms, carries her to deeper, bone-chillingly cold water. It speaks, the wave, has a deep voice that says horrible things, calls her a little bitch. Tells her it's time to die and won't her daddy be sorry then.

"He tried to burn me alive," the man said. "But you can't kill me. See what happens when you try, Miles? See what you get?"

Mama is somewhere behind her, far off now, screaming, screeching.

The next thing she knows, she's underwater, thrashing, swept away by the waves. The water has hands, fingers, arms that push her down. An arm reaches around her, grabs for her throat. But this is not water, she realizes, this is a human arm, with thick black hair.

And there, on the wrist, is a crudely done tattoo: a pair of dice, the two dots looking up at her like eyes.

She's struggling. Fighting for breath, but water fills her mouth and nose and she's choking, can't get any air. She bobs to the surface for a second, gulps at the air, is pulled down again.

Die, a hoarse voice shouts in her ear.

Then there is only water, cold and black. She feels it flow into her mouth, fill her lungs. It tastes like rot and ruin, and fish and dirt. Iron and rust and the way the sidewalk smells after a summer rain. A child's rain slicker. The skin of a frog. The bottom of a wishing well.

Down she goes.

Down.

Down.

Down.

The hands holding her release their grip, and she bobs to the surface to hear shouting; two men fighting.

"Eva!" her father screams.

"You did this to her," the other man says. "You did this to her the moment you lit that match. It didn't have to be this way."

Her father reaches for her, but the man hits him hard, sends him under. Daddy's in the water, too, sinking.

And now she's released, being carried downstream, a bit of flotsam, bumping against rocks and logs, her own boat bobbing, and sinking, being churned like the laundry in Mama's big machine.

"Eva!" her daddy screams, as he rises to the surface, but the other man has his hands around Dad's throat, choking him, pulling him back underwater. They thrash and struggle before they both go under. The river is carrying her so fast that they're soon out of sight. She's on her side, then on her back, unable to see where she's going, unable to right herself as the water churns. She is slammed into a big rock headfirst, the back of her skull hitting it and making a cracking sound that travels all the way through her body. She thinks of Humpty Dumpty, of his big old egghead. She thinks heads are fragile things.

A hand reaches for her, pulls her out.

She turns, and she's not in the churning black water of the river, but here, in her old house four years later and Errol is touching her arm, wrapping his fingers around it.

"Do you remember how you got out of the water?" Errol asks, tightening his grip, as if he could squeeze the truth from her. In his other hand, he still holds the gun.

"No," she admits. "The next thing I knew, Mama was standing over me in the woods. She'd bandaged my head with a sheet, wrapped it round and round to stop the bleeding. She told me you and Daddy were dead. 'It destroyed everything,' she said. 'The house, everything we had. It's all gone. And now, we've got to go, too.'"

Necco thinks hard, tries to remember how

she got out of the water. Maybe she washed up downstream, caught on a logjam, tangled up a beaver dam.

"It was just dumb luck that I survived," Necco continues. "Mama always said the Great Mother saved me."

Errol shakes his head. "It was me, Little E. I pulled you out. You'd hit your head hard, there was a lot of blood, but your eyes were open and you looked right at me. Don't you remember at all?"

"You?" She blinks up at him. He's shifting from foot to foot, swaying slightly, like he's being rocked by waves, pulled along by some invisible current. The gun is still in his hand, but it's pointed at the floor now.

"I saved you then just like I'm trying to save you now. I pulled you out of that river. Don't you remember?"

"I'm sorry," she says. She doesn't remember. Isn't sure what to believe.

"I couldn't save Daddy. He was swept away. Once I pulled you out, and brought you into the woods, I waited until I heard Mama coming toward us. Then I ran."

"Why? Why leave us like that?"

"Because everything that happened that day . . . to you, to Daddy, it was all my fault." He looks away.

"How?" Necco asks. "How was it your fault?"

He doesn't answer.

"And why is it that you were never mentioned in any of the articles about our family?" Necco asks. "Or in Daddy's obituary. It's like you don't exist at all. How can that be?"

He looks at her a long time. Sets the gun on the dresser, rubs his face. "Shit, Eva. There isn't time for all this."

And there really isn't, because just then, the closet door bursts open and Theo comes barreling out, scooping up Necco's blade and heading straight for Errol, knocking him to the floor and pushing the knife against his throat.

"Get the gun!" Theo shouts, and Necco moves. Necco grabs the gun, aims it at Errol, who is under Theo, the blade pushed so hard against his neck that she's nicked the surface of his skin, a little trickle of blood running down.

"The gun isn't loaded," he says. "Jesus. Did you really think I was planning to shoot my own sister? Let me up, please. There's still time. He's not here yet."

"He?" Theo says. "He who?"

Just then, there are footsteps in the hall. A man steps into the room. He's dressed in a suit jacket, has slicked-back silver hair. And he's carrying a gas can in one hand, a handgun in the other, the smell of fuel wafting in with him like a pungent and deadly cologne. And behind it, as though following him through the door, the smell of smoke, faint at first, but growing stronger by the second.

Necco recognizes the man immediately, though it's impossible.

"Eva," he says, his voice a low purr. "How lovely to see you again."

Pru

〰

"Hurry," Pru urges, as if Fred needs encouragement. As if he wasn't already breaking the speed limit.

She's riding shotgun in his tidy little Honda—a strangely small car for such a large man—and they're following the GPS directions to Necco's house. It's an area Pru doesn't know well, out in the country, where the houses are far apart, and people have real yards. There are even a few farms here and there.

They've crossed the river and are racing down Elsworth Avenue. Mr. Marcelle takes a left on Willoughby Drive, says he knows a shortcut. Pru is thinking how clever he is. To know a shortcut way out here.

The voice on the GPS unit scolds him, says, "Recalculating."

Pru's picking at her cuticles. She's got red stains on her fingers from the snuff. She pulls down the visor in Mr. Marcelle's car and sees what a mess she is: her hair in tangles, dirt on her face, red stains under her nose. She is ashamed, embarrassed that Mr. Marcelle is seeing her this way. But honestly, her worries over Necco and Theodora overshadow her own insecurities. They've got to find the girls. Fast. "Maybe we should call the police, have them meet us there."

"No," he tells her. "They'd just grab Eva and arrest her."

"At least then she'd be safe," Pru says, wiping at her face with the sleeve of her shirt. "There are worse places than jail, I suppose." The cage would keep her in, but would also keep those trying to do her harm out.

"Yes, but there are better places, too. And Eva doesn't belong there. You and I both know that. Her only crime is being caught up in something much bigger than she is. She is the victim here."

They turn in to the center of a small village and pass a butcher shop, a library, a little café where people are sitting at outdoor tables sipping lattes and eating pastries. Pru imagines herself and Mr. Marcelle there, having Saturday morning coffee together, sharing the newspaper, telling each other about their weeks.

They drive in silence for a few moments.

"Pru," Mr. Marcelle says, twirling one end of his mustache. "I'm sorry about yesterday. How badly our conversation went. And most of all, I'm sorry I didn't get to see your circus."

She smiles. "When all this is over and the girls are safe, I'd love to show you the circus."

He clears his throat. "Do you mind me asking what you were doing down there under the bridge with those women?"

There goes her happy vision of the two of them having coffee, sharing a little pitcher of cream, hands touching as they pass each other the butter for scones.

"They're friends," she says.

"They're drug addicts."

"It's not like that," Pru tells him.

"Well, please tell me then, what is it like? I want to understand."

And how can she tell him? How can she begin to explain that for the first time in her entire life she feels she belongs somewhere, she feels she is part of something bigger than herself? How can she tell him about her vision, how the snuff showed her her true purpose? She is going to build a circus, an actual circus—not just a silly model hidden away in her living room, but a real spectacle that people will line up to see.

"Necco—Eva—introduced us to them last night. She said they would be able to see things we couldn't, they'd know what we should do next."

"And did they? Did they tell your future, Pru? Tell you what you wanted to hear?"

She shakes her head. "No. I saw my own future."

He turns from the road, looks right at her for a second, his eyes questioning, concerned. She knows how she must seem now, disheveled, telltale red stains on her hands and face. The fat lady who's gone round the bend.

"Mr. Marcelle," she says. "Do you have a dream? A big dream?"

He thinks for a minute, twirling his mustache as he drives.

"Come on," she encourages. "There must be something. Something deep in your heart. Something you might not have told anybody, maybe you haven't even admitted it to yourself."

He sighs, bites his lip. "I'd like a house. A real house with a yard. I want to build a big aviary. Someplace where the birds can really have space. I'd like to try raising cockatoos. Get a breeding pair." He smiles, suddenly far away.

Pru smiles back at him. "That sounds really nice. And I believe you'll find a way to make it happen."

"I hope so," he says.

"See, Mr. Marcelle, that's the thing right there. We have to do more than hope. When we have a vision, we have to take steps. We have to make that vision real. Bring our dreams to life. I think that later today, you should go home and draw out plans for that aviary. Look at the real estate listings and see what sort of place would work best. Make an appointment at the bank to see what kind of mortgage you can get."

"I don't know, Pru. I—"

"You **do** know. And I do, too. You know what I learned from the Fire Eaters last night? That there is no someday. We spend so much of our lives waiting for someday, don't we? There is only right now. Right here. **This is our someday,** Mr. Marcelle. We don't want to wake up years down the road and see we missed our chance."

"Okay," he says, turning left on a narrow road that runs along the river. According to the GPS, they are only a minute away. "So what's your dream?"

You, she thinks. **My dream is you and me together.**

This is not what she tells him with words, but for half an instant, when their eyes meet as they bump along the dirt road in Mr. Marcelle's little Matchbox car, she's thinking it so hard that she is sure he can read her thoughts.

"I'm going to make a circus. Not just a little toy circus like the one in my living room, but an actual, life-size circus with clowns, and fire eaters, and a big golden elephant. And I think, Mr.

Marcelle, that there might just be room in my circus for a strongman. Are you interested?"

He turns, looks at her, smiling his dazzling smile. "Can the strongman do a show with trained birds?"

"Can he? He needs to! It'll be a one-of-a-kind act. It'll be perfect!"

She can see it now: her strongman in his striped outfit, mustache waxed and curled, bald head polished to a shine, and a flock of birds around him. She thinks of a stained-glass image she saw in a church once: St. Francis and the birds.

"This is it," Mr. Marcelle says. The road up ahead dead-ends in a driveway. They can see two cars in the drive: Pru's own dented, rusty Impala and an old black MG with the Virgin Mary on the dashboard.

"Whose car is that?" Pru asks. Mr. Marcelle stops his own car, puts it in reverse, and pulls back down the road, where they're out of sight.

"The man with the dice tattoo," he says.

Pru is out of the car before he can even turn it off.

"Pru," Mr. Marcelle whisper-yells. "Wait! I have a plan."

She stops, and he hands her his cell phone.

"I'm going to go in," Mr. Marcelle says. "You're going to stay here and watch and wait. If I'm not out in ten minutes, you use my phone to call 911 and get them out here. Okay?"

"No. I go with you," she says.

"And if it's a bad scene in there, what good does it do your friends? If you're out here, you can help them. I'll try first, and if I fail, you're my backup. Got it?" He looks at her, his brown eyes huge and pleading. "Will you do that for me, Pru? Will you be my backup?"

Yes, she nods. Yes. She will be his backup. The fat lady and the strongman, an unbeatable team.

"Wait here," he tells her. "Stay out of sight."

He jogs down the road and driveway, past the two cars, toward the house. At the side of the house, he crouches, pushing his body against the wooden clapboards as he peeks in a window. Then he moves to the next, going window to window as he tries to get a sense of what's going on before he walks inside. A clever man, Mr. Marcelle. At last, he disappears through a side door.

She tries to stick to the plan. She paces around his tiny car, clutching his phone and turning it on, even though doing so feels like a breach of his privacy. It opens right to a text message screen. James Marcelle asking, **Where the fuck are U, Bro? I'm waiting.** Then, in a minute, the phone chirps and Pru looks down to see another text from James: **Looked up Edward Tanner. Holy shit! Guy apparently torched his father alive. Got sent to a home for f-ed up boys, then escaped. Never heard from again, no records of him as an adult. Is he our kid?**

Then, a few seconds later, a new text. **If he's our guy, stay away from him. The dude is Dangerous! Stand down, Bro. Call me. Now! And remember, with all the BS you pulled, you're off the payroll!**

Is it just the thought of a kid burning his father alive that brings the smell of smoke to mind? Pru sniffs at the air. No, that's smoke. She definitely smells it. She turns and looks at the house, sees a curl of black come from a cracked window, the orange glow of flames flickering inside.

She looks down at the phone in her hand, quickly dials 911.

"What's your emergency?" the dispatcher asks in a calm monotone.

"I need the police! And the fire department! Ambulances! I'm at the end of Birchwood Lane. Fire! Murderers! Hurry!" she says frantically. Then she clicks off and begins to run.

Theo

~~~~~

Theo stays where she is, straddling Necco's supposed brother with the knife held against his
throat. She's relieved to finally be out of the
stupid closet. She'd gone her whole life without
being rushed to hide in a bedroom closet; now
it's been twice in one freaking week. Was this the
universe's idea of some Theo's-in-the-closet joke?
She is not amused.

The man holding a gun and a gas can smiles
at her before looking at Errol.

"Looks like you're in a world of hurt, son," he
says.

"Come any closer and I slit his throat," Theo
warns.

"Easy there, little lady," he says. "If everyone
cooperates, we can all walk out of here in one

piece. And trust me, you don't want to have any-one's death on your conscience. It's a real shitty way to go through life."

The boy beneath her (and he is more of a boy than a man, really, Theo sees that now) flinches, all his muscles tighten. Suddenly, he looks like he might cry. Theo actually feels bad, takes the knife up so that it's just hovering above his Adam's apple.

"You know who I am?" the man with the gun asks Necco.

She nods. "I remember you from the photo on the mantel. You're Uncle Lloyd."

"Good girl," he says.

"But . . . but you're dead. You died in the fire at the garage."

Jesus, Theo thinks. What's next with these people? Floods that didn't happen, grandparents and parents who turned out to have been mur-dered, a brother who doesn't exist on paper, and now Uncle Lloyd has come back from the grave.

He shakes his head, clucks his tongue. "A ter-rible thing, that fire. Halloween night, it was. Hell of a trick, having Miles show up and douse the place in the gasoline."

Necco speaks slowly, as if trying to put the pieces together. "My father set the fire?"

"Now you're catching on," he says.

Theo looks at the gas can in the man's hand. When he first came in, she thought she smelled smoke, but there's no doubt about it now. It's getting stronger. She looks up at the ceiling, spots some smoke crawling through the top of the doorframe.

Shit. She thinks. She tries to remember the layout of the house, the doors in and out of the first floor. But if there's only the one set of stairs, and if the fire blocks that, there's no way out. Theo tries to reassure herself that the man with the gas can would have planned for this. He may want to scare, or even kill, everyone here, but he must have an exit plan for himself. The very fact that he's standing here, looking perfectly calm and determined, gives Theo a strange sense of comfort. Maybe it's all an act. Maybe he fired up a smoke bomb of some sort and came waltzing in with the gas can just to terrorize Necco, and make her tell him whatever he wants to know.

But then again, maybe the guy is just nuts and intends to turn this whole fucked-up family reunion into a murder-suicide marshmallow roast.

"Jesus, is that smoke?" Errol asks, turning his head and craning his neck to look at the doorway. "What have you done?"

"Fitting, isn't it?" the man says. "Symbolic, even. For Miles's house to go up in flames."

"You'll kill us all!" Errol says.

"Maybe," the man says, glancing out the door at the smoke. "But maybe not."

Theo turns her attention back to Errol, but it's too late—Necco's brother grabs her right wrist, pushes the knife away, and bucks up, causing Theo to topple off of him. He scrambles to his feet, but Uncle Lloyd already has the gun on him. Theo stays on her knees on the floor, still clutching the knife, eyes darting between Lloyd and Errol.

"Easy there, son. I'll shoot if I have to. Go stand in the corner. Bring your new girlfriend with you. Oh, and no need for the knife. Let's just leave it on the ground, right?"

He gestures to Theo with the gun, then back to Errol, who is backing up into the corner near the closet. There's no question in Theo's mind now that this psycho will shoot her. She drops the knife and goes to Errol.

"Take a seat, kids," he orders. "Make yourselves comfortable."

They sit side by side on the floor, almost touching.

"Lloyd," Necco says. "I don't understand. Everyone thought you died in that fire."

"It wasn't my body they pulled out of the torched garage. It was a poor old bum that had no one, nowhere to go. I let him sleep in the garage when it was cold out. He was passed out drunk in the back, and your father didn't know he was there. Just like he didn't know my little boy, Eddy, was in the office that night playing

Nintendo, stuffing himself full of Halloween candy."

"Eddy?" Necco says.

Lloyd gestures to Errol. Errol looks up at Necco, watching for her reaction.

"You?" Necco says, looking down at him. He nods.

"Wait a sec," Theo says. "So how'd you go from being Cousin Eddy to Brother Errol?"

"Miles felt horrible about what happened. I almost didn't make it out. The roof came down. That's how I got my scar. I was blamed for the fire, sent away to a special school, but Miles and Lily got me out of there, brought me home, gave me a new name, raised me as their son."

"But what about your mother?" Necco asks.

"She was fine with the arrangement," Errol says. "She didn't want to see me—was happy to get the occasional photo from Uncle Miles and notes saying how well I was doing. She couldn't look me in the eye after what happened. She blamed me for the fire. Thought I was a killer."

"She didn't know it was my dad who set the fire?" Necco looks at Lloyd. "And she thought you were dead?"

Lloyd nods. "She didn't know the truth until later, when I came back looking for my son, only to find out he was being raised by Miles, of all people."

"So you're the Chicken Man," Necco says,

looking at her uncle. "That's why my father tried to kill you. Because you killed his mother. But why?"

"Ancient history," Lloyd says.

"Tell her," Errol says. "Don't you think she deserves to hear the whole story?" He waits a beat, sees Lloyd isn't going to start talking, so he begins. "He was eighteen," Errol says. "Working at Chance's garage. Elizabeth would bring her car in all the time."

"She had an old car," Necco says. "A convertible. I've seen pictures."

"It was an MG," Errol says. "Pretty much an exact replica of the car Lloyd has now. How's that for twisted?"

"Shut your mouth," Lloyd says, turning the gun on Errol. "You don't know a damn thing."

"I know you killed Miles's mother. You had an affair with a beautiful older woman, she dumped you, and you were pissed off, so you slit her throat while her son watched."

"I **loved** her!" Lloyd roars.

"But you couldn't have her. Then, as an extra twist in the gut, little Miles grows up and marries your sister."

"Maybe I wanted it that way," Lloyd says. "Maybe I'm the one who kept sending Lily over to check on the poor new kid in the neighborhood, the one whose parents had died. I kept

Miles close. He was the only piece of Elizabeth I had left."

"Right," Errol says. "You loved him in your own fucked-up way. And you were all one big happy family until Miles found out the truth."

"How'd he find out?" Necco asks.

"Elizabeth told him," Lloyd says. "He'd built the machine, from Edison's plans, and she spoke to him through it. Told him who'd killed her."

"I was there, in the office on that old ripped couch playing Nintendo," Errol explains. "I heard the whole thing. I'd been out trick-or-treating, was still in my Batman costume. Uncle Miles came in, furious, crying, yelling, 'It's you. You're the Chicken Man.' I heard him order my dad to lift up his shirt so he could see his back. I always wondered about that, but now I understand. I read what happened in Uncle Miles's book: how he shot the Chicken Man with an arrow. And that night in the garage, he was looking for the scar, final proof that the voice on the machine had told him the truth."

"Seriously?" Theo says. "The machine really worked. Dead people could talk through it?"

"Yeah, it worked," Necco says. "But the machine is gone. Errol destroyed it the day of the flood. Daddy told him to because he knew Lloyd was coming."

Lloyd nods. "I'd been out of the country for

years, playing dead, and when I came back, I went looking for my son. That stupid cow Judith told me Miles and Lily were raising him. My son. How fucked up is that? I watched the house and waited. At last, one day, that spring, he was walking down the road, along the river. I talked to him. He told me about the invention in the workshop, that the box Miles had heard Elizabeth through was still there under a tarp."

Necco looks at Errol. "You're the reason he came back. The reason he came to the house that day."

Errol is crying now, his body trembling. He's crouched into a tiny ball like he's trying to make himself disappear. "I'm sorry," he says. "It's all my fault. Everything that happened that day. Daddy drowning. Lloyd came back for revenge. And because he wanted that damn machine."

"What for?" Necco asks, turning to Lloyd. "Why do you want it so badly?"

"So I can talk to her," Lloyd says, voice soft and low. "Elizabeth. So I can tell her I'm sorry."

Necco's eyes are filled with a fiery rage. "And are you going to tell her you're sorry for killing Miles, Lily, and Hermes, too? I'm sure she'll be real forgiving." She glares at him. "Why Hermes? Why kill him and leave me there, alive?"

"I didn't need your fucking knight in shining armor getting in my way."

Necco snorts disgustedly. "A lot of good it did you. You've got me now and I don't have what you need."

"Yes, you do. This is your last chance. Don't you see, it's my last chance, too." He looks desperate, pleading. A man out of options. "It's all or nothing. You've left me no choice."

Theo sees a shadow on the hall floor through the open doorway. Is it a trick of light? Caused somehow by the flames moving ever closer? No. There is someone out there.

The room is starting to fill with smoke. Theo looks around. If the hallway becomes impassable, the only way out is the window behind her. She's thinking about a jump from the second story; it's dangerous, but a few possible broken bones beats being burned alive.

"Like I told Errol, I don't have any plans," Necco says.

"Your father said you did. He told Errol they were safe with you."

"Well, he lied. Or maybe he got bumped on the head, too, and his memory was gone. I've got nothing."

He starts to approach, swinging the gas can as he stops in front of the old twin bed. His gun is trained on Necco. Slowly, he holds the gas can over her head.

"Are you sure about that?" he asks.

"I don't have the plans. I don't know where the plans are. Nothing you do will change that, Lloyd." Necco's voice is calm, rhythmic, almost a chant. "You will never get that damn machine."

He tips the can, she closes her eyes and mouth as the gasoline pours down over her head, soaking her wig, the blue suede jacket. She doesn't flinch. Doesn't scream. When the can empties, she keeps her eyes closed and says, in a low voice, "In the beginning, the Great Mother laid an egg and that egg became our world."

Errol jumps up from his spot against the wall on the other side of the bed, and Lloyd trains the gun on him. "Sit down!" he bellows. Errol backs against the wall, drops to a crouch.

Lloyd tosses the empty gas can on the floor.

"You can't do this!" Theo screams. "She's pregnant!"

Lloyd pauses, looking at Necco, clearly thrown by this news. Then, he takes in a deep breath, pushes on. "One last time, Eva," he says, voice a little less sure of itself now. "And remember you're answering to save not just your own life, but the life of that little baby inside you. **Where are the plans?**"

She doesn't answer. Just continues her strange chanting. "Imagine it, a bright and blazing orb, spinning through space."

Lloyd reaches into his pocket for a lighter.

"Fire is life," Necco says.

That's when the strongman bursts into the room with a terrific roar, throwing his full weight on Lloyd, pushing him over sideways. The silver Zippo lighter falls from Lloyd's hand, skitters across the floor. The two men struggle, wrestling, fighting for the gun, all four hands wrapped around it.

When it looks like Mr. Marcelle is winning, pinning Lloyd to the floor, Errol charges into the fray. Lloyd thrashes his left leg out, tripping him. As Errol collapses into the two of them, knocking Mr. Marcelle off balance, Lloyd takes control, flipping Mr. Marcelle over. Someone is screaming, a high-pitched, incoherent scream, until Theo realizes it's her and slaps a hand over her mouth.

Errol is flat on his back on the floor at Necco's feet, but he rights himself quickly and starts to scramble across the room on all fours, away from the fight. Theo almost shouts "Get the knife!" but manages to stop herself, because she sees that's where he's headed, to the spot where Theo dropped Necco's big, beautiful knife. Lloyd finally wrests the gun out of Mr. Marcelle's grip, brings it up over his head, and swings it down in a short, swift arc, bashing the strongman right in the temple with it. There's a dull thunking noise. Mr. Marcelle's eyelids flutter.

Lloyd stands, breathing heavily. Scooping up his Zippo, he steps toward Necco, flicks the lighter, the flame glowing in his hand.

"Last chance, kid," he says. "Don't make me do this."

She closes her eyes, face calm and peaceful. "Fire redeem me."

Lloyd holds the burning lighter a few inches from Necco's face. Theo thinks: **The fumes oh shit the fumes are gonna blow, I've got to—**

Leaping forward, Errol plunges the knife into the center of Lloyd's back, forcing all six inches of blade in. The lighter and gun fall from his hands. Lloyd turns, looks at Errol, Edward, his son, then drops to his knees, falls forward. Says one word in a raspy whisper: "Elizabeth."

Then all is silent.

"Oh, Jesus," Theo says. "Is he dead?"

Errol feels Lloyd's neck, searching for a pulse for a moment. In that moment the bloodstain on Lloyd's back seems to double in size. "Yeah, I think so," he says. Then he turns to Necco. "You okay, Little E?"

Her eyes are bright red, burning from the gasoline, and maybe those are tears, too? She nods. Theo runs to her, yanks off her wig and suede jacket, mindful to throw them well away from the door, away from the fire. She grabs the bedspread and uses it to try to clean the gas off Necco's face and skin.

Mr. Marcelle is groaning, heaving himself to his feet. Blood runs freely from his temple, dripping onto his collar. He staggers into the hall, comes back coughing. "The fire's reached the stairway," he says. "There's no getting out that way."

There's a banging sound from downstairs, someone knocking, pounding on the front door. Pru Small's voice pierces through the wooden door, travels up the stairs to reach them, muffled, but frantic.

"Theodora! Necco! Mr. Marcelle! Fire!"

Pru

~~~~~

Pru is pounding on the door.

"Mr. Marcelle!" she screams again. She can see the flames cover the wall behind the couch, and back in the hallway. The whole kitchen is engulfed.

She knows about fires. How quickly they spread. How deadly they can be. Fire is death to the circus. She has read about what happened down in Hartford before she was born—how the whole tent was engulfed. There is a famous picture of Emmett Kelly carrying a bucket of water to throw on the flames in full clown makeup.

Pru slams her shoulder into the front door, putting the full force of her weight behind it, feels the rotting frame give a little. She wishes for more strength. For one of the circus elephants; Priscilla the golden queen of the elephants could knock this door down with one nudge.

Then, she thinks of her strongman, Mr. Marcelle. If only he were out here. Mr. Marcelle, with his carefully curled mustache, his shirts straining at the shoulders from the muscles beneath. She wishes for his strength, then tries to channel her own, to concentrate on how it must feel to be so strong as she throws herself into the door once more. She thinks of her vision last night—Mr. Marcelle in a burning house. The snuff was trying to warn her.

"Pru! Up here!" comes a cry from just above and behind her. Pru turns to see Mr. Marcelle leaning out of a second-story window.

"Are you hurt?" she cries.

"I'm okay, Pru. We're all okay."

"You've got to get out!" Pru shouts up, breathless, shoulder and side aching intensely. "The fire's spreading fast."

Smoke is pouring out the open window. She hears the girls coughing inside.

"The stairs are gone!" Mr. Marcelle calls. "The window's the only way!"

He's looking down at the ground, too far below to safely jump. Size and strength can't protect anyone in a fall.

"There's a ladder!" Necco shouts, her head

coming out the window beside Mr. Marcelle's. "On the side of the workshop. The little shed in the yard."

And Pru is running, running faster than she thought she could, and she's thinking, absurdly, of the circus. Of the comical act the clowns do with the burning building, the slapstick comedy of knocking each other down with ladders, spraying each other in the face with water, the audience roaring with laughter, but still worried for the girl clown who is trapped at the top of the burning tower. But they need not worry, because, at the end, she'll jump and they'll catch her with the net and everyone will applaud.

No net here and no team of clowns to hold it, but Pru's found the ladder and lifts it off the hooks. She expects it to be heavier than it is. She's thinking of the clown act again, of working herself into it: the fat lady coming in at the end and surprising everyone with her daring rescue, with her grace amid the clowns' klutzy antics. It's up to the fat lady to save the day. This is what she's thinking as she pulls on the rope to extend the ladder (she's never done this before, but she understands how a pulley works) and gently places the ladder against the wall of the house, just below the window Necco and Theo are leaning out of, red faced and choking.

"Come on, now," Pru says. "I've got the ladder. I won't let you fall." She holds on firmly, has her own feet braced against the feet of the ladder, using her great weight to stabilize it.

She thinks of her father again, swooping her up and carrying her on his shoulders, how frightened she'd get. The way he'd promise, "I've got you. I'll never let you fall."

Necco comes first, Pru talking to her the whole way, saying, "That's it, you're doing great. A few more steps to go." But really, Necco needs no reassurance: she scurries down the ladder effortlessly. The girl climbs like a monkey, like an acrobat, fearless, speedy. Theo is next, Mr. Marcelle helping her climb out the window. She moves more slowly and carefully than Necco. "Hurry now," Pru says, "I've got you." Behind her, she hears sirens in the distance. It'll be too late by the time they get here. The whole place will be engulfed soon.

Mr. Marcelle helps a young man through next: black jeans and shirt, blond hair, arms circled with tattoos. Is this Necco's brother? He practically skids down the length of the ladder, leaps off gracefully.

Last comes Fred Marcelle. Pru tightens her grip, feels the thrum of vibration he makes climbing down, so much more **substantial** than the smaller ones before him, feeling connected to him. "Almost there, Mr. Marcelle," she says. When he gets to the bottom, she steps away as he finishes his descent. Then, once on solid ground, he turns to her and embraces her, kisses her on the cheek, his soft mustache brushing her damp skin.

"You saved us," he says.

He keeps his arms wrapped around her. He smells like smoke and soap and something spicy.

She kisses him back.

Necco

~~~~~~

She's sitting in the backseat of Pru's car, riding back to her apartment. Promise the doll is on her lap. It's early the next morning. They've spent the entire night at the police station, answering questions, being videotaped, signing statements. Necco is no longer the prime suspect in Hermes's murder. The police found a coat with blood on it in Lloyd's car. They are waiting for lab results, but believe the blood is Hermes's. They also searched Lloyd's house and found evidence linking him to Elizabeth Sandeski's murder all those years ago. Errol has told the police that Lloyd killed Miles and Lily, and Hermes, too. Errol is being held at the police station as a possible accessory. Necco, Theo, and Mr. Marcelle told the police how Errol had saved them; it was because of him that they were all still alive.

Necco has pulled the doll from Hermes's backpack and runs her fingers over her old toy. The only thing her father made that she has left.

Promise's pink gingham dress is stained, tattered at the edges. Her hair is tangled, her face splotchy with dirt and oil and years of grime from living on the street. Life has been hard on Promise.

"What's her name?" Theo asks.

"Mina," she says. "Her name was Mina. My father suggested it. It was the name of Thomas Edison's wife. But I called her Promise."

She's very special. Promise you'll take good care of her?

She thinks of her father's other inventions: of the way he'd sometimes build secret compartments into them that she had to find and figure out how to open to reach the treasures inside: gumdrops, tiny wrapped chocolate bars.

She picks Promise up, turns her over. She tries gently tugging and twisting on different body parts: her ears, feet, hands, nose.

She recalls her recent dream: her father with his left eye gone, a telescoping monocle stitched in place, a needle in his hand. "A way to keep an eye on you."

An eye on you.

Eye.

She touches the eyes of her doll, gently at first. She fits her fingernails into the little grooves around each eye, gives them a tug. Nothing happens. She gets a firmer grip, tries wiggling, twisting. The left eye budges, turns slightly counterclockwise. She turns it again, and the eye unscrews.

"What are you doing?" Pru asks. They're at a stoplight and Pru is peering into the backseat. "Don't hurt her."

The glass eye comes off in her hand, revealing a tiny key, like on a windup toy.

"What is that?" Theo says, leaning in to get a closer look.

Necco turns the key slowly, carefully, until she feels it click. She thinks of her father's workshop, the cogs and gears, the tiny clockworks, the smell of oil, coal, leather, and pipe tobacco. How when she was in there, anything seemed possible: the inanimate were brought to life, the dead could speak once more.

Under her dress, the doll's torso swings open. Necco lifts up the folds of dirty fabric to reveal the hollow body under the door of Promise's belly. There's a bag made of thick translucent plastic. Inside the bag is a stubby brass tube, about four inches long. And inside the tube, she knows, even before she unscrews the cap, is a sheaf of papers folded carefully and rolled up tight.

Here it is: the secret her parents and Hermes had been killed for.

Crazy to think of.

Killing anyone for a few pieces of paper stuck inside a doll.

But it wasn't just any paper, was it?

She had seen the invention. She knew what it could do.

I'm whoever you want me to be.

How wonderful it would be, to talk with her parents again. To tell her mother how sorry she is for not believing her; to tell her father that she'd kept the plans safe, that the Chicken Man and Snake Eyes are really dead this time. That she'll go on keeping them safe.

But she understands that if you open a door, anything might come through. And she isn't going to risk it. Not with a child of her own to protect.

She tucks the plans back inside, clicks the doll's belly closed, and hugs her to her chest.

ONE YEAR LATER

Necco

〜〜

Necco has a difficult time traversing the path; the sleeping baby in the sling on her chest pulls her off balance and makes it impossible to see where she's putting her feet as they go down the embankment. Theo is beside her, holding a flashlight to illuminate the way. Necco clings to Theo's arm, knowing her friend will not let her and the baby fall.

Necco smells the fire, fried food, something sweet and sugary that makes her mouth water. Circus smells. And from down below, they hear voices, laughter, applause. They pass a hand-painted sign: THIS WAY TO THE CIRCUS. Another says: COME SEE PRISCILLA, THE GOLDEN ELEPHANT. MARVEL AT THE FIRE EATERS; ASK THEM TO TELL YOUR FUTURE IF YOU DARE.

At last, they reach level ground, and Theo takes Necco's hand, leading her along the path. When they get to the clearing under the bridge, they have to push their way through a small crowd. There are college kids, young couples, families with little kids who are clinging to their parents' hands and watching, wide-eyed.

"Make way," Theo says, tapping people's shoulders. "VIP with a baby coming through."

Some people turn to look at them, but their gazes don't linger long—they don't want to miss what's happening up front, by the river.

The center ring is there, all lit up with oil lamps and candle lanterns that hang from the trees. But the lights are nothing compared with what's happening in the ring itself.

There, in the center, stands an enormous elephant: Pru's greatest creation. A life-size model of Priscilla, made of wood and wire and papiermâché. She is painted metallic gold, and because this wasn't enough, Pru covered her in a mosaic of tiny pieces of broken mirror. She shines, she glitters and flickers in the firelight, and sends pinpricks of light out into the crowd like a giant disco ball. On top of this huge elephant is Pru, dressed from head to toe in purple and black: tights and a ruffled dress covered with little mirrors just like the elephant she rides upon. She is waving to the crowd. And just when people think they understand, think the elephant is a simple statue, the great beast turns her head. Pru controls it with the golden cord she clings to, fastened to a pulley system rigged up in the elephant's neck.

The crowd goes wild. A little girl squeals, "Mommy! It moved! The elephant moved!"

Pru is glowing, smiling, her face sparkling with a gold powder, her lips a perfect painted red bow, her eyelids purple to match her dress, her hair in curls, woven with purple ribbons. She is stunning, and she and Priscilla have the crowd's total focus.

"Imagine, ladies and gentlemen, boys and girls," Pru commands. "Imagine that you have the power to bring your dreams to life. To have your greatest wish come true. What would it be? Where would your dreams take you? That's what tonight is all about. To help you remember. To help you believe."

As she says these last words, the Fire Eaters come out and encircle the elephant, swinging burning wands through the air, playing with the fire, stretching it with their fingers, making it jump from one torch to another. They are spectacular in flame-colored dresses Pru has made them—orange, yellow, and red—and as they move and sway, the flames of the fabric flicker and bend, mimicking the flames in the torches they hold.

"Fire is life," says Miss Coral, and swallows her

ball of fire. Her hair is back in its usual bun, but it's surrounded by a spray of bright red, yellow, and orange feathers. Her lips are painted red, her eyelids covered with sparkling gold eye shadow.

"Fire is breath," says Miss Stella, taking the flaming tip of her own torch into her mouth. She has orange and yellow ribbons braided into the dark hair on the left side of her head; her right side has its usual buzz cut.

"Fire redeems us," says Miss F, gulping hers down.

"Fire, show us the way," says Miss Abigail, eating hers.

"The things that scare us most, the things we think might hurt us," Pru says, waving a torch Miss Abigail has passed her through the air, "they're the things that make us whole." And with this, she opens her mouth and chomps down on the fire, putting it out, releasing the smoke through her nostrils.

There is music now; some woman Necco doesn't recognize comes out playing the accordion. Another woman joins her with a violin. It sounds like Gypsy music, sad and happy at the same time. Pru is on the elephant, swaying, turning Priscilla's head this way, then that, bobbing in time with the tune.

Behind her, Mr. Marcelle, Pru's strongman, comes out, wheeling a large box covered in a red velvet cloth. He's dressed in red pants and boots,

a red-and-white-striped shirt. His head is polished to a shine, and his mustache is waxed and
curled.

"In the circus," Pru is saying, "just like in
your life, anything is possible. You just have to
believe."

Mr. Marcelle pulls off the red cloth, revealing
a golden cage full of white birds with crests. He
opens the cage, and the birds flutter out, landing
on his shoulders and arms. It's an absurd sight:
this muscle-bound man covered with delicate
white birds. Then he reaches up to Pru, and she
takes his hand. Their arms form a bridge and
the birds walk along it, climbing from him to
her, flapping their wings—one bird, two, three,
then all six birds are on Pru, on her shoulders
and arms; she even has one on her head. The
one perched on top of her head takes flight, but
it doesn't go far. It circles her head once, twice,
three times, a living halo, and Pru is smiling,
smiling like she's never been happier.

Theo takes Necco's hand, leans over, whispers
in her ear, "Isn't it amazing?"

Yes, Necco nods. Yes. Amazing. The circus.
Pru and her elephant. The strongman and his
birds.

Little Lily Elizabeth is awake now, eyes wide
open. She's watching the circus, the birds and
giant sparkling elephant. Necco strokes her soft
hair, kisses the top of her head. Her feet stick

out from the bottom of the carrier, clad in the striped rainbow booties Theo knit her.

The police, after hearing Errol's story and Mr. Marcelle's backup of Lloyd's confession, did their own investigation. They found the arrow Miles shot at the Chicken Man all those years ago, and information Lloyd had been gathering on Necco and Hermes. Necco was no longer a suspect. Errol confessed to helping Lloyd, saying Lloyd had left him no choice, that Lloyd would have killed Necco, then Errol himself, if he didn't assist him. Errol cooperated fully with the investigation and was sentenced to ten years in prison. His lawyer thinks he'll get out in much less time.

Necco will tell little Lily Elizabeth about Hermes. She's already started. She tells her all about her daddy, how clever he was. How once, when he was a boy, he was thrown from a horse and it gave him a scar down the lip so that he looked like a rabbit. Her Bunny Boy. Her Hermes. Her God of Thieves, bringer of dreams, most cunning trickster.

She loves telling stories to Lily Elizabeth, stories that often begin with the beginning of it all: "Once upon a time, the Great Mother laid an egg and that egg became our world." She tells Lily all about her grandmother the Fire Eater; how they lived together under the bridge in a city called Burntown. How her grandmother saw visions, told stories about a Great Flood.

"You're named for her," she says. "And for your great-grandmother, who was the most beautiful woman in the world."

She tells Lily about her grandfather the inventor, who populated his workshop with mechanical animals and talking dolls. How very clever he was. And how once, he built a machine so special, so magical, that it could reach through the veil between the living and the dead.

Necco has locked the plans away for now. Put them someplace safe where no one will ever find them. One day, she'll show Lily.

The audience applauds as the circus act concludes. Pru waves and blows kisses right to Necco and Lily from the top of her large golden elephant, which turns its great head to look at them. Little Lily squirms in the pouch, reaches up with her tiny starfish hand. Necco knows what she's going for: the little brass elephant, now on a sturdy leather cord Necco wears around her neck. The baby wraps her fingers around it, makes a contented cooing sound, and drifts back to sleep.

Acknowledgments

Many thanks to . . .

Leslie Roth, knitter extraordinaire, for talking knitting with me, and for remaining calm when I asked what sort of knitting needle would make the best murder weapon.

Dan Lazar, the best agent in the world, who always finds a way to push me to be a better writer.

Anne Messitte, Andrea Robinson, and the whole team at Doubleday for the thousands of things they do expertly that make it possible for me to get my stories out into the world.

Drea and Zella, for accompanying me on research trips to old mill towns and being very patient while I spent hours in museums, took endless photographs of old buildings, scrambled around under bridges and in vacant lots, and nearly fell into rivers and canals.

And also . . .

Pru's tiny circus was based on the amazing work of Alexander Calder—there's a film out there of him performing it and you just can't watch it without smiling.

Many years ago, I worked at a homeless shelter in Portland, Oregon. I owe a huge debt of gratitude to each and every person I met there who shattered my stereotypes of homelessness and shared their stories with me.

ABOUT THE AUTHOR

Jennifer McMahon is the **New York Times** bestselling author of eight suspense novels, including **Promise Not to Tell, The Winter People,** and **The Night Sister.** She lives in Vermont with her partner, Drea, and their daughter, Zella.